Landed

by
Rita Donovan

BUSCHEKBOOKS

Canadian Cataloguing in Publication Data

Donovan, Rita, 1995-
    Landed

ISBN 0-9699904-2-1

    I. Title.

PS8557.O58L35 1997   C813'.54   C97-900115-3
PR9199.3.D5554L35 1997

Other books by Rita Donovan:
    Dark Jewels (1990) Ragweed Press (now distributed by BuschekBooks)
    Daisy Circus (1991) Cormorant Books

Landed
ISBN 0-9699904-2-1

Design: Marie Tappin
Printed and bound in Canada by Gilmore Printing Services Inc.

Cover design: detail of an oil painting entitled *Paddler Floating In Time* by David
George Taylor; private collection of the artist.

BuschekBooks
PO Box 74053
35 Beechwood Ave.
Ottawa, ON K1M 2H9
Editor: John Buschek

Note: While some of the names in this novel are of historical persons, this is a work of
fiction and the characterizations and some of the events are fictional.

To my parents, John and Anne,
for the years you've given freely

and

To my daughter, Eleanor Anne,
for the years I will give freely

Acknowledgements

The author would like to thank the Canada Council, the Ontario Arts Council and the Regional Municipality of Ottawa-Carleton for grants that aided in the completion of this book. The author also made use of information provided by the Warroad Historical Society, acknowledged here with gratitude.

Thanks also go to Frances Itani and to Greg Gilbert for their astute readings of the manuscript. And to John for his care of, and dedication to, this project.

Snowing, bending deciduous trees, willow waving, birch bowed, snows of sub-lunar heaven; silence of snow rounding oval-crowned red pine, smoldering jackpine's jagged spike. Snows of another time, snows of no time at all, everfall of silence over trees, and after trees, and before.

Glacial movement over dance-waxed granite, smooth as staring monuments. Look! I can see my face!

In the wall of ice called Wisconsin. Solid, it is Wisconsin, liquid it is Agassiz, a raindrop dividing into three directions, one part to northern Canada, one to the St. Lawrence, one part to the Mississippi. Treading on magma that rises underfoot as Agassiz II gives birth to the Lake of the Woods.

After, deep green waters and black lakebed clay, meltwater washing silt and soil as the walls and reflections recede. Stepping into peat bogs, or onto hardpan of another time, old rocks from the earliest mountains, secrets under shields.

PART 1

New World: Rose: 1961

Their father had always lived in the north. The men in the family were fishermen and loggers, the women healthy mothers with constitutions that would have made the ladies of Minneapolis jealous, which is exactly what happened when Rose Ellis married into this family, and the upset ones were Rose's own sisters who could not understand how or why Rose had insinuated herself into a tribe of northerners only to go up there and not die, after all, in the Land of God Forsake. They never visited, of course; they could barely find Warroad on the map. But by then Rose had settled into life on the edge of the world, the border of America, with the wilderness and Canada beyond.

She stood at the window sometimes, gazing out toward Muskeg Bay, sometimes watching her boy, Luke, atop his regular lookout rock. She had never seen two boys so different; her sons, Ray and Luke, hardly two years apart yet as different as night and day, Rose thought, snapping the dish towel flat and folding.

Ray was older and still a little taller although Rose could see that this would soon change. He was built like his father, strong legs and a sturdy torso. Not short, mind you, just squared off; complete, at age eleven, perfectly proportioned.

Luke, only nine, had not yet begun his growth spurt, but Rose had known since his birth that the boys would not mature identically. Luke was, or would be, tall and angular like the men in her family. He was already blessed with a curious grace of movement that one just didn't associate with nine-year-old boys. Which didn't prevent him from coming home with his knees completely bloody, with ripped sleeves and the behind out of his pants and all the 'evidence of play' as Rose tended to put it.

The boys got on well together, and this was important to Rose. There were only the two of them, and after the miscarriage the doctor had told her categorically that there would be only two. So it was important, especially up here, that the brothers got along.

Eric had been glad of sons anyway. He told Rose that a daughter would have been fine, but, if it was one or the other, he preferred sons.

"Sons go away," Rose said, somehow hurt.

"But they take your name and your history with them."

Not like daughters? Rose finished the thought. Not like her. Rose's family had not liked Eric, and he, in turn, thought they were excessive. He wasn't in favour of the attention they lavished on Rose. He was a simple man, and if she wanted him she would have to get used to that, he said, and to life without a record player and tickets to the movies.

She did. With the exception of the record player, which she missed terribly, a pain that was only alleviated when Eric finally caved in and bought her a radio, reminding her almost daily what house improvements it had cost him.

"Did you fix that stoop yet?" she'd smile when he came in.

"Could have put in a whole new porch if we hadn't spent it on that radio."

A ritual that never really subsided but was converted, somehow, as the boys grew and began to join in.

"Eat those beans. Folks in the poor countries are hungry for them."

"Could have sent them over if it wasn't for the radio."

Rose sighed. That would be Ray's voice. Luke was much more reticent. He was the one who appreciated the jokes; Ray was the one who told them. This is what she meant. Luke was a solemn boy, complicated in ways that Ray was not. Rose had never had a moment's concern about Ray. If she saw him standing stock-still with his eyes to the ground or the water, it was because he was looking for something, or he'd dropped something, or he was just about to sneeze. But Luke—right now, standing over on that rock—there was no way on God's green earth she knew what he was doing.

She remembered one mid-summer evening; Luke must have been about seven at the time. Rose was strolling with Eric, a thin sweater light on her shoulders. It was one of the rare perfect evenings with sun and warmth and yet very few mosquitoes. She and Eric were walking past the sunflowers, unspeaking, when they spotted him. Laying out long boards from his father's pile next to the shed, huge slabs—she didn't know how he'd managed to move them.

"What are you up to?"

And no response.

And the one thing Eric Anderson hated was no response.

"Answer your mother when she's talking to you!"

But he appeared not to have heard either of them, so intently was he crouched, straining at the end of a board, hoisting it over to the left, grunting it a bit more to the right.

"Luke!"

He looked up.

"What are you doing?"

And some fanciful story about the Red Lake Indians, about David Thompson and Canada, ancient steamboats and forgotten portages.

"It's for a boat."

"A boat?" Eric Anderson laughed.

"It's a Red River cart," the boy said quietly.

That was when Rose first noticed the combination of faraway look and frowning brow. Well, he had frowned in his cradle, that was true. But now the two were linked, the furrowed forehead and the slightly-squinting, faraway eyes.

She no longer pried into his thoughts, hoping he would volunteer them on occasion. He never did. He remained unfailingly polite when she did ask, but he was for the most part mute and mysterious, sentinel on a rock, looking out at Muskeg Bay.

—⁓—

Rose's radio was important to her. It connected her with cities.

"It has short waves," Ray told Luke, and demonstrated a quick vibrating movement, a spasm shaken through a bowl of turkey drippings. "And long ones," he undulated, turning into a snake.

And nobody remembered afterward whether this was where the nickname originated, that deplorable "Snake" called out from a car on a Saturday night, and her christened son Raymond responding from the house.

Rose's memories got mixed up when the years wouldn't sit straight. The boys had been boys as the saying went. They listened to baseball on the short waves. They attended the Warroad Lakers' hockey games with their father, Ray even going so far as to predict he would one day play for them, a notion which pleased his father greatly.

But for all that, the boys were just boys, and for all that Rose hoped they would have Eric's approval, things didn't seem to be working out that way. Oh, Eric talked to the boys—he talked hockey with Ray and canoeing with Luke; he talked wilderness survival with both of them and even made Rose sit in on those sessions. But this great bond between father and son that Rose had hoped would occur was simply missing, or was buried under fish in the clear waters of Lake of the Woods.

She could see that their lives were going off course, yet she felt powerless to alter the evening meal. She imagined this was how Columbus must have felt, getting ever nearer to land but with a voice inside beginning to wonder, to form small subtle "uh-ohs" on barely-moving lips.

It was all right, she thought.

Columbus discovered America.

Look at Columbus, she nodded her head firmly. Three little boats and they all got to shore.

At least she hoped there had only been three.

Because she needed this reference; it fit her own family: Eric, Ray, Luke—the Niña, the Pinta, the Santa Maria, and Rose the principal navigator-cum-explorer, guiding them safely and comfortably to the New World.

She heard a symphony on the radio once. Mr. Dvorak's *New World*, it was called. It had, frankly, disappointed her since she couldn't hear herself in any of the music and—worse still—couldn't hear her noisy young family resonating through it. That it might somehow be inappropriate to think of oneself as the inspiration for the *New World Symphony* entered her mind only briefly. She was an inland Columbus, after all, charting the waters from the edge of her country, and the *New World Symphony* (which Rose wasn't sure was about Columbus) had just better shape up and include a few more catchy musical themes if it wanted to be designated the Theme Song of the Anderson Family.

Which, she supposed, didn't make her much different than Luke, building a Red River cart over by the woodshed. Perhaps she understood him better than she thought, with his serious eyes and explorer's zeal. But she sometimes wished he was more like Ray. Raymond Anderson, later to be known as Snake, was named, Rose swore, for an uncle of hers in Philadelphia but was, in fact, named for a shaft of sunlight that entered the room just as Rose was giving birth. She pushed her son out into the world and looked first at the stream of light, then at the wet and quivering infant and knew, absolutely, that his name would be Ray.

Everything in Rose's life was connected like this. Which, she understood, was part of the problem. When Rick and Lon called for Snake from out on the road, it was Rose, too, they were referring to. When Luke declared that his history teacher was 'spreading stories' about the Civil War, it was she who went in to untangle the accusations, to confirm—yes, confirm—that her son would not lie. And during all the exhilarating episodes, Rose would hear the small voice beginning to whisper and would drown it in the less difficult sections of Mr. Dvorak's symphony.

One afternoon in late fall, seven or eight years later, while Rose was cleaning kitchen cupboards, her husband walked in through the side door and did not wipe his feet on the mat and told Rose that he and Eddie had had a good idea. Rose was by now used to the sporadic warnings coursing through her system and scarcely acknowledged Eric's impending revelation. Her head did not even emerge from the cupboard.

"I said, me and Eddie have an idea."

As opposed to any of the other ideas her husband and his fishing buddy had come up with? Rose thought about this a moment and added a "that's nice".

"Come out here, will you? We have to talk it over!"

Rose's posterior protruded from the bottom centre cupboard. Her body contorted, and a door opened next to the swaying buttocks, and Rose's face peered out.

"Dear?"

Rose would later remind herself never again to be in such a position when her husband was threatening her with a new idea.

Because this was the Big One. Eric rhapsodized. He talked of the spirits of fish (and their commercial value); he spoke in awe of the northern woods (although, Rose admitted, he had always done this); he gave her good reasons for counting the lakes on one's fingers and then pocketing their treasures like so much loose change.

She was confused. She was uncomfortable. She was stuck in the cupboard, a captive audience.

"Dear...wait...I can't...."

It was in this position that Rose learned of their destiny. Eric's eyes were split silver with light off the lake. His mouth watered describing fish cooked over regulation stoves. He might get Ray to help with the maintenance, and Luke could canoe in supplies and take the vacationers back, and Rose, maybe, could....

"Uh-oh."

She said it. And so it began, The Adventure, the natural world out there for the picking, and who better to act as guide than Eric T. Anderson, and who better than Eddie Griffin to book tourists from New York and Chicago?

"State's opening up to it," Eric said, laying the facecloth across Rose's bruised knee. "I tell you, everybody approves. It'll be as big as Land o' Lakes."

G. and A. Wild Wilderness Tours as big as the Land o' Lakes Dairy? As big as the Land o' Lakes motto on the license plates? And all those little slabs of butter?

"I'm the perfect guide; who else knows The Woods and the Lake from here all the way up Angle Inlet?"

Rose was about to say—almost anybody in town.

"What about...couldn't we think about it for a while?"

"Time's a'wastin', Rose. And there's a wilderness out there."

The boys were recruited to be partners in the heroic endeavour.

"I need your life's blood, men," their father said, and switched stations on Rose's radio until he came to a rousing, brassy march.

"Probably West Point," Eric Anderson said. "Probably Washington, DC."

—⁓—

G. and A. Wild Wilderness Tours.

"Don't you think the name is...a little on the long side?"

"Yeah, but we can't leave Eddie out."

And Rose knew that she would be required to sacrifice jars of already-setting preserves. She would have to sew sheets and curtains and mend camp blankets before long.

"Some people like cabins better. Me? I'd just as soon be out in a tent."

She would have to beat the dust and twigs from canvas.

But it was going to be Eric's chance with the boys, and, who knew, it might even be profitable. Hadn't she heard that the area was being touted as a tourist's paradise? Hadn't she wanted her boys to have special moments with their father? Well?

"Well?" Rose wrote on the unfinished letter to a cousin in St. Paul.

—m—

When you get a lemon, make lemonade, Rose silently preached.

Ray liberated a cinnamon bun from the perfect symmetry on the plate and turned to look earnestly into his mother's eyes.

"He's crazy," the boy said, of his own father, and flaked out in front of the fireplace.

This was three months into the adventure, and money had been spent; advertising had been placed. There had been a forced optimism in the house during this period, and Ray's comment hit Rose like a tomahawk. She watched him drop pieces of the bun into his mouth, too tired it seemed to chew them properly. He studied his fingers a good long time before licking the syrup from them.

And Luke? Well, she had not actually seen Luke in a while. Ever since the ice broke on the lake, he had been canoeing his father and his father's supplies here and there: picks and shovels, brawny men with hooks in their heads who would sometimes take the stern.

"What are you doing to my boy?" Rose joked nervously.

"Leave him alone. He's a soldier for the cause."

Rose put one of the cinnamon buns under an inverted bowl for Luke.

G. and A. Wild Wilderness Tours, which was shortened to *G. and A. Wilderness Tours* and finally to *Warroad Wilderness Tours,* was not exactly taking off on paper. There were a few amazing commitments from sport fishermen across the state, a handful of enquiries from church groups and retirement clubs, and a letter from a mother of four from Baraboo, Wisconsin. But for the most part it appeared as though the wilderness would hold its own against the influx of seasonal Appreciators of Nature.

Birch and oak and red pine shook cautiously, sumacs reluctantly parted their fringes as two men and two boys cleared and cleaned, stocked and painted. Wood violets, mints appeared on cue, and the clouds shifted in furrowed patterns overhead.

Rose would listen to the radio, waiting for her men to come home. The counter top was loaded with dusty jars of preserves, pickles she'd put up the autumn before, and sometimes she felt like taking her bean jar, the deep one, and bowling it clear down the counter until it smashed the green tomato headpin into a dozen separate condiments.

Strike!

I have discovered the condiment America, she sighed, wiping the ten-pin lids of jars.

Mrs. Harding was first to arrive. She pulled her station-wagon up beside the house, and three small children scrambled out, two of them clutching their crotches and dancing.

"Halloo...Halloooo! Anybody home?"

Uh-oh, Rose thought and opened the door.

"Little Robbie couldn't make it; he's contagious," the woman explained and held out a hand made of sponge curlers. The lady from Baraboo! Rose returned the handshake just as one of the boys urinated on her sunflowers.

"Jason! Not there, wait 'til you get inside!"

Inside?

"Betty Harding. Call me Betty...please. We're so glad we got he...Warren!"

Warren Harding?

Rose withdrew her hand from the folds of her apron as Betty Harding set about arranging the children in order of emergency.

"Jason's okay...you okay now, Jason? Well, put it back in, for goodness sake! Boys!" Mrs. Harding shook her head at Rose.

Boys.

Where were her own? Where were Ray and Luke, and where was one half of the management team of *Warroad Wilderness Tours*?

"My husband...that is, the partners of...."

"Oh, I know. He said to show up whenever we could, anytime on the fifteenth, and there'd be somebody here to meet us."

Meet them? He said?

"But...I live here."

"Sure...nice...LINDA! Gerlinda Harding, come down off that...thing. Just what is that, Rose? Do you train all your flowers to grow like that?"

Rose thought she heard the lonely cry of a loon wafting back across the lake.

"Wow! Look at all this neat junk!"
Or perhaps only a timber wolf dying in the woods.

—⁓—

It was the summer of Mina Jacobs and Lee Ann Corrigan. It started with Mina, who was fifteen going on twenty-one as far as Rose was concerned, who had been dragged up north by her father for two weeks of watching Dad fish. Rose admitted she had felt sorry for the girl, as out of place as a person could be, as Rose herself had been, although Rose had been older and married by then with no one to blame but herself.

The girl hated the outdoors it seemed. Upon her arrival she threw what Rose could only assume was a tantrum and reminded her father that he only had custody of her for the four weeks and that this was supposed to be her vacation and wasn't it an unfair way to spend virtually half her time? And the father, the wrinkled young Ernest Jacobs, replying that in case she hadn't caught on it was also *his* vacation—and then promising to spend the following two weeks doing what she wanted to do.

This truce lasted until Mina discovered an innate fear of garter snakes. She awoke one morning in the cool cabin air to find a sleepy garter snake braceleted around her ankle.

She screamed.

"Scared the fish right out of the water!" Eric exclaimed.

"Doesn't that make it easier for you?" Rose asked, yet knew even then, that Mina Jacobs would be moving up to the house.

Uh-oh.

Mina surveyed the family home and fixed upon Rose's radio.

"You pick up anything decent?" she asked.

Mina knew all about radios. Her father said Mina had been born with one and had had to have it surgically removed.

Rose began to come in from the yard only to find Mina perched on the edge of a kitchen chair, balancing as she manipulated the dials on the radio, swinging the aerial this way and that until it fixed like a trained pointer on the path of a fallen duck.

"Dear?"

Mina made no quick moves; there were no disguised motives. By now she was comfortably settled into the house having taken over the alcove room and having strewn the path to it with old movie magazines.

"Tryin' to get a damn...uh...something on this dumb radio," she muttered.

Rose glared at the nail-polished toes and stormed out of the room. Down in the cellar she arranged the jelly jars. Annoying tears stung the edges of her eyes. Someone else had marched into Rose's very kitchen and had turned *off* the station that carried Mr. Dvorak's symphony and turned on some Elvis Presley-Bobby Darin creature! And Mina, swaying and jiggling on the chair, her costume jewelry flying! This little five-foot thing in a pony-tail, this...!

Rose.

Now, Rose. Calm down, she told herself.

Rose was getting used to The Adventure taking a few odd turns. Eric himself admitted he couldn't keep it going without her.

"Without Eddie, gladly. But you?"

Rose paused. Eric didn't talk like this much, never had. Perhaps this was why she was so upset about the radio; it was the only thing, the only gesture he had ever....

But Rose knew that wasn't the reason.

It was Mina—simply—fifteen years old, a city girl as Rose had been. It was Mina and Ray the few times they were together, Ray straightening to his full height, Mina giggling softly. And all of it, as far as Rose could tell, completely unconscious.

Rose had made a pact then and there to keep those two apart. It was only a couple of weeks, and Ray was busy with his chores.

But Mina had to throw those tantrums. Any time things weren't going her way, Mina's head flown back, her bosom heaving....

This was bad enough without the addition of Lee Ann Corrigan. They didn't need Canadians on top of everything else. The Corrigan girl arrived with an aunt to visit the Normans down the river. Rose hadn't remembered the Corrigans. She asked Loretta Norman how she could have missed them. Sister? Cousin?

"Step-sister," Loretta told her. "Haven't seen her in years. Living up in Canada; can you believe it?"

Rose could believe it. People lived in Canada.

"Well, Winnipeg," Loretta reminded her.

Winnipeg wasn't far at all. Canadians lived in Winnipeg. But, Rose wondered, truly puzzled over, why Canadians would be coming to Warroad to see the wilderness.

Lee Ann was twelve. She was a tomboy with thick brown hair tied back in a single braid. She took an immediate liking to Luke which Rose thought was harmless enough although she wished Lee Ann wouldn't follow him around when he was trying to do his work. He canoed for hours every day, his tall figure now a light bronze. He was in good condition for a boy, strong and muscular on top like a gymnast which made him look older than his fourteen years, as Nancy Sheridan mentioned to Rose. "You watch him," Nancy said, and then she said, "Boys."

Everyone was always saying this: Boys.

When it was *girls, other peoples' girls* who were causing the problem!

Lee Ann bashed a message on the screen door.

"Luke back yet, Missus A.?"

How long would the Canadians be in town?

"He's still out at the cabins."

"Okay. I'll just wait here."

With that, Lee Ann plunked herself down on the stoop appearing to have every intention of waiting hours, or until doomsday, for Luke to return.

Rose handed her a bowl of peas to shell for the evening meal.

This was happening so fast. Her children quotient had doubled with the arrival of these girls only they didn't seem like girls to Rose, and she didn't know how to treat them.

Lee Ann was more of a boy; even her body was thin and flat like a boy's, and this was somehow comforting to Rose. Mina, on the other hand, paraded around in cotton top and shorts and sat most unladylike in the living room waiting for Ray, although Rose was still convinced that Mina didn't realize it.

Girls.

Is this what it would have been like if Rose had...if the doctor hadn't told her, and that little one she hadn't been able to carry...? Is this what she...?

Rose looked through the screen at Lee Ann Corrigan, her dungarees rolled to the knee, splaying open and eating the contents of a pod. Rose watched for a full minute before hearing her radio go on in the kitchen.

—▨—

Of course the girls were not to get along. That would have been too much to ask. Mina would hang out the wash when Rose was too busy, and Lee Ann would volunteer for any outdoor work, although Rose felt a little guilty putting Lee Ann to work since she wasn't even staying at the house; but it was clear that the girls would not stand one another.

They had that fatal three years between them which five years from then would mean very little, and ten years from then would not even be remembered, but which had to occur during the summer of 1961. It just had to, Rose thought.

Rose was checking the clothes on the line. Mina had made a great show of putting them out earlier: reaching, bending, tattooing lipstick patterns on the billowing white sheets, utterly disgusted with manual labour. Now Rose fanned out the sheets that had blown together when the wind had been up and had played the line like an accordion. There, she said, double-pegging a sheet on the end.

Deciding to leave them out overnight, she turned.

And saw.

Her son Ray—and Mina Jacobs—heading for a path at the very back of the property, Mina still in shorts but with a light jacket across her shoulders, Ray...Ray with an arm holding Mina's jacket in place. It was the strangest sensation, as if Rose was in the movie house in Minneapolis, and the male lead was a young actor who looked something like someone she knew. It was a queer helpless feeling. Sure, she could call him back. She could probably embarrass him into not seeing the girl for the rest of her stay, although Rose was beginning to doubt even this. But she couldn't stop it. Rose saw the clothes bunch along the line once more and felt the sleeve of her boy's shirt flap through her fingers.

Warroad Wilderness Tours was counting its blessings. Eric Anderson sat at the kitchen table counting money. He had hunted for his father's old briar pipe, something Rose had not seen or smelled since their wedding, and he proudly packed it and lit it and sat in a cloud of smoke and victory.

Door bashing was never something he approved of. And poking one's head against the screen so that it bulged on the other side like a large compound eye was never on his list of things that children of decent parents did.

"Hey...hey, Luke! LUKE!"

Bash, bang. Hook, doorknob rattling.

"Anybody in there? MISSUS A.?"

From the living room Rose watched Eric get up and walk slowly toward the door.

The noises stopped.

The bulge retreated from the screen.

"Uh...Mister...is Luke there?"

"My son? You want to see my son?"

"Mr...Luke, you know...is...uh...Missus A.?"

"My wife. You want to talk to my wife?"

Rose thought the girl would be halfway down the steps by then, but to her surprise the door opened and in marched Lee Ann Corrigan, right past an astonished Eric Anderson, straight up to Rose in the living room.

"I gotta know. I'm leaving soon and I hardly seen him this week."

"*I've* hardly seen him."

"You too, Missus A.? What's going on with your boy, Mister Anderson?"

Eric's jaw was making motions, but Rose didn't hear him talking.

"Now, dear, you know I talked to you about how busy Luke is."

"I'm busy, too!"

"Yes, well, we're all busy, Lee Ann."

"He's my friend...I gotta see him, you know? He's...." She whirled around to face Eric who had followed her into the living room. "Well, don't you think you're working him kinda hard?"

"Who are you, girl?"

Lee Ann Corrigan exhaled frustration until it lifted the bangs on her forehead.

"Talk to him, will you, Missus A.? I gotta go find Luke."

And she was gone.

There were fireflies that night. Rose and Eric sat out on the porch, Rose noticing again how the dew made everything smell. As a child she thought it was the dew itself that was scented, although this had never explained the different odours the dew would have as she moved on past the houses along the avenue with the trees. It was wonderful on the dark, dark nights when there was just the smell. Mornings it was always the sights that caught her, her other senses pulling back, folding in, before the beads of light.

At times like that, she guessed she understood Christopher Columbus. He must have gotten bowled over, just as Rose had. He must have been blown off course; then there was nothing to do but ride it out. He must have, maybe, prayed or hoped. And when he got there he was bowled over.

"Eric?"

"Hmmm?"

"Is it nice...in the woods? Out on the lake while you're fishing?"

Eric tapped his father's pipe against the porch railing.

"Rose, there's nothing like it in the world."

Even the post was damp against her cheek. She felt like she'd been sleeping, although she remembered Eric getting up and warning her not to stay out too long.

Had she?

Rose's eyes tried to see to the edge of the property, but she was squinting, so she reached her hand back over her head and turned off the porch light.

Dark. And damp. And Rose invisible in this yard, like how many natives in the brush along the river? How many people had the settlers passed by, unknowing, so sure of their direction?

She saw Mina first. The white shorts.

And Ray's dark shape and what seemed a silent embrace. Then low laughter and a run around the perimeter of the property to enter the house, no doubt, from the front.

A few more days, Rose told herself, and raised one leg, then the other, up to the railing. She crossed them and stretched back, closing her eyes and breathing in deeply.

This time she must have been sleeping for the words came muffled to her ear.

"I can't, Lee Ann."

"Come on, Luke, you gotta."

Rose opened her eyes uselessly in the dark and then closed them to listen more carefully.

"You're the only one. Please, Luke."

No response from the voice that was Rose's son.

"I'm going tomorrow!"

Was Lee Ann crying? Rose sat up straight and opened her eyes in spite of herself. She could vaguely make out two figures in the yard.

"I know...hey, Lee Ann."

"No, you don't. You *don't*!"

The figures pulled together in...the two of them were hugging!

No, sir! Rose decided and brought her chair forward with a slam.

"What was that?" Lee Ann sniffled loudly.

"No, sir!" Rose called out from the porch and bounded toward the silhouettes.

"Mom?"

"Mom, indeed!"

Rose could not believe it! She stood before the children with her arms crossed and her heart thumping.

"So?"

They were both wordless now.

"Luke? Luke Anderson, I want an explanation! Do you know how old this girl is? Answer me! Do you want me to call your father out here?"

Luke held Lee Ann, who was shivering or crying, and made no attempt to release her from the embrace.

"Mom, you don't understand."

"You're darn right I don't! But I wasn't born yesterday! Have you taken leave...and you!" Rose shouted at Lee Ann Corrigan who wailed and hid her face against Luke's chest.

"Mom, you're making it worse!"

"Well, maybe you should have thought about that before you...."

"Leave her alone, will you?"

"Don't talk to me like that!" Rose started. "I'm your mother, for God's sake! Oh, if your father heard that! I can't believe...no respect...."

"Respect is *earned*, Mother, just like everything else around here!"

Luke brushed past Rose's shoulder and took Lee Ann up to the porch.

Rose stood in the yard as tears came, knowing that natives were passing her property in the dark, knowing that Indian wars were still being fought in the woods, and there were fur traders out on the lake. Mr. Columbus was discovering someplace else, and these tears were real, they were right down her face, and these ones were cried in silence.

What was happening?

She could still hear Lee Ann and Luke on the porch, although she didn't want to listen any longer.

"Your aunt's probably nice, isn't she? You'll like it there, Lee Ann. It's just a vacation."

"Okay. I gotta go."

"I'll walk you back," Rose heard her son say, and she was torn by the simplicity of the gesture and the mature, alien creature that voiced it.

Next morning, Rose paced the length of the kitchen waiting for her sons. She would have to talk to both of them. Eric would only make things worse. This bothered Rose because at the back of her mind was the reminder that the whole enterprise had been designed to bring the boys and Eric close. Well, not designed, but it had been the opportunity. And instead, what? Ray gets close, too close, to Mina Jacobs. And Luke gets...?

Ray was first in, his hair still messed from sleep but his eyes bright as he bounced up to give his mother a kiss on the cheek.

"Morning, lady of the house," he said and headed for the refrigerator. His shorts were ragged at the edges. She would have to get rid of them.

"You seem full of energy today."

"Day off, Mom. Going into Baudette with Mina."

"Going...with Mina? Wait a minute. I haven't heard anything about it...your father will...."

"Dad knows. He said he'd drive us in after breakfast."

Rose felt a tomahawk hit the side of her head. There was blood, she was sure of it; her temple ached. She bobbled the milk pitcher and a couple of useless eggs and placed them awkwardly on the counter top. She gazed around the room and focussed on the radio.

"Something wrong, Mom?"

She was flicking the dial left and right. "I can't seem to get it," she murmured in a voice that must have puzzled even Ray because he came over and reached a hand out to the radio.

"Which one you want? The one with the long boring music?"

"No," Rose said, "leave it alone; just leave it alone, okay?"

Mina and Ray sat along the bench discussing their plans for the day. Eric came in with a loud yawn that turned into a lion's roar as he walked by Rose. He looked over at Ray and Mina and glanced back at Rose and winked.

"Where's Luke?" he asked. "LUKE! COMING DOWN FOR BREAK-FAST?"

"He's gone," Ray said. "Was out before I got up."

Rose whirled around to the window over the sink. There he was in the distance on his ancient lookout rock. She couldn't remember the last time he'd been there. She left the kitchen without a word and let the screen door slam shut.

Luke, facing out, did not see her approaching. He stood like someone measuring something with his eye, not moving a muscle lest he alter the calculation. He looked like a man about to spread his arms and dive. She didn't know who or what he looked like.

"Luke?"

Black curls. The only thing moving.

"Yes?"

Santa Maria.

"Did Lee Ann leave?"

"I guess so."

"About what happened...."

Luke shifted his footing on the rock.

"You're fond of her, aren't you?"

"She's a kid."

"*I know!*" Rose exclaimed. "*That's* why I was so...."

"Worried? Because Lee Ann is a kid? She was upset. You don't know."

"Luke? I *know* I don't."

The Red River cart across the unmapped years, rich deep furrows in a forehead much too young. All the years, Rose thought.

Just then something streaked a pattern across the water. A pea-green frog surfaced once and skimmed and then dove deep, to the bottom of the lake, and the surface became smooth once again.

"You want to know, Mom? You want to know? That's Cynthia."

Rose smiled at her son. "Dear?"

"It's Lee Ann's little sister, okay?"

Luke stuffed his hands in his pockets and stared straight up at the morning sun until Rose had to take his arm to warn him.

"Lee Ann. Her sister was born like that. She has a frog's arms and legs. That's why Lee Ann caught Cynthia; that's why she was in Warroad."

Rose looked back at the surface, but nothing broke across it. A few small insects walked along the shimmer with ease. Rose remembered hearing about those babies; the report said their mothers had been given some drug. Rose remembered thinking that it could have happened to any woman. It could have happened to her.

"There she is!" Luke pointed, and the frog appeared further down along the water's edge.

"You're not keeping her? Isn't that what Lee Ann would have wanted?"

"I can't. It'd be too cruel."

Rose walked back behind her son, not knowing what to say. She was wrong about everything these days. She seemed to be losing her grip on things. She thought about Lee Ann Corrigan, a frog with her sister's name, in her pocket; Lee Ann and Luke and everyone, Rose most of all, not able to understand. Not able to do anything more than....

"Mom?"

She looked up.

"Having pancakes?"

He held out a hand, and they walked arm in arm back to the house where yesterday's sheets slapped the breeze. They walked as they would probably walk the day they would bury Eric Anderson, as they would walk the day Luke Anderson would leave Warroad forever.

Inside the house Eric had the coffee brewing; the smell was especially strong. Luke took his place down the table opposite Mina.

"When we're in town," Mina chattered, "I *have* to get a souvenir for Cheryl. She's my best friend and she *hates hates hates* postcards! It's a present or nothing, so I have to find her something really good."

"Don't go spending all your money," Rose instructed. "Your father will be back this evening, and you'll be wanting some for the rest of your trip."

"He'll give me more; he's like that," Mina bubbled, excited it seemed, at the prospect of leaving.

Ray's face was a mess of confused emotions, but his lips were smiling at Mina. Then he turned to Luke and hit him with the fly-swatter, and Luke kicked at him under the table.

"Where's Lee Ann, Luke? She's usually breaking the door down by now."

"Shut up."

"Oh...what's wrong? Hey everybody, what's the matter with Luke?"

"Shut up, Snake!"

"Lee Ann left early this morning," Rose said placing the plate of pancakes in front of Ray.

"Well, it's about time!" Mina jeered. "I tell you, I couldn't stand that kid!"

"So who asked you?"

"Ssshhh...quiet down, will you?" Eric was up at the refrigerator, playing with the aerial on the radio.

"Listen! Well, I'll be...."

"What, dear?" Rose wiped her hands on a dishcloth and joined her husband by the radio.

"The news. Follow-up to that promise the President made. You know, about putting a man on the moon. You kids listen to this; this is educational.

Imagine it, Rose, a man on the moon! What do you think of that?" Eric strutted. "That's ingenuity. That's the American Way calling out to you, that's what it is. The moon, Rose! Can you believe it?"

Rose stood beside her radio. Her eye caught Luke's, and it was nothing she understood, and they all kept quiet in the kitchen, listening hard, and thinking about the moon.

MIRACLES: LUKE: 1964-1965

"

W)hat are you watching, Luke?"

Ray in the dusty reeds. He rarely asked Luke this, and Luke was aware of the quiet balance they kept, and how it, too, was unspoken, as if to speak it would have been to throw the words into the water and watch their whirling halos funnel deeper and deeper.

Luke was also becoming aware of the difference between looking and watching. His mother would have asked him, "What are you looking at?" Only Ray would have asked the other.

Luke jumped off the rock, stuck his hands in his pockets and wordlessly they both turned back toward the house.

Sunday afternoons, sometimes, they would play with Ray's hockey game on the floor of the work shed. Ray sat captivated and was always Detroit while Luke was Chicago or Toronto.

"Leafs," they laughed.

"Let's pack up our wifes."

"Our better halfs."

"And go to see the Leafs!"

And they would play until supper, or until Luke's attention would drift allowing Gordie Howe to zip past a stationary piece of tin and score for the Wings yet again. Then they would forget the game and jostle one another into the kitchen where they would sit through meatloaf surprise and their father's latest home improvement plans.

Barney Noble's name would come up and Ray would blush for just a moment, but Luke would catch it and know that Ray was thinking about Sally Noble and how he'd almost managed to get her dungarees all the way down except for the Sorensen's dog and for Luke, who happened along at exactly the wrong moment. Luke, not saying a word to Ray but calling out instead to Punches the dog, allowing himself to be chased down the street until the schoolyard was over two blocks away, until his brother was two blocks away. Maybe Ray was thinking about what happened after that and blushing for some other reason.

Luke wondered, in turn, what Ray might have thought of him when he caught Luke canoeing alone at night, or when years before Luke looked for miracles in the church. Their mother had left her religious fervour with her sisters in Minneapolis, and while she still attended church, it was a quiet display of organized faith. Luke's father was less inclined even than this, and there were no miracles coming home on Sunday mornings with his parents.

So, he had begun sneaking into Father Aluneau's Memorial Church to watch Rick Henderson up at the altar, suddenly silent, suddenly pure in white vestments over what Luke was sure were running shoes. Rick holding cruets and clacking incense, Rick having blessings passed over him.

Blest.

Rick Henderson who threw up in the playground the week before, whose older sister had teeth like a beaver's. Rick Henderson, blest.

Luke had always wanted. He didn't know. Church smelled nice, smelled holy. Even Rick Henderson smelled holy afterward and this, truly, was a miracle.

He had. Always. That is.

His father would have none of it.

"So that's it!"

Ripping pictures of saints from the inside of his son's closet.

"Where'd you get this idolatry?"

Ten-year-old Ray standing between his father and the man's eight-year-old son.

"Leave him alone, okay, Dad? He's a kid!"

"Kid nothing! Which one is it? As if I didn't know."

And Luke was banished from the quiet flickers, the good wood of the pews, the sanctuary lamp and his favourite suffering saints. And Rick Henderson was on the corner by the school, as always, but waiting for Newell Rogers now.

Miracles. Or quiet.

"You can't watch quiet," Ray said trudging along beside Luke.

But he could. It almost trilled it touched the ears so profoundly, and then to the left and right it was visible. Silence made the animals come down from the woods, right to the back of the property—a lone deer, or rabbits in and out of burrows. Silence brought flies to hover fixed above water, brought insects to flit like skaters across the surface. Silence, before the seaplane motor started up, brought the fish in close to the jetty, brought the old men out to the porches and, Luke believed, the old medicine man out of the rest home, rubbed the ill-fitting pants and shirt from his body and dressed him again in the buckskin of the trapper who wandered the November brush, ancient Chippewa chanting in silence.

How could Luke explain that watching silence exhorted miracles, pulled them right out of the air?

The church would disappear, the medicine man taking medicine in the Warroad Senior Citizens Home, but—Luke listened—and still heard the dull echo of a perfect blessed silence.

"Your brother...your brother's a freak, a voodoo curse," they taunted.

Ray arose from the bench and dropped his glove in the dirt.

"Say that again," he threatened.

Luke remembered afterward that he was never sure of the tone of that remark. Had it been a threat? Or a command?

Luke, on the sidelines, carting water from the neighbour's house, retrieving the occasional impressive home run.

Ray knew his brother Luke would have made a good player with his long legs and quick reflexes. He had the best reflexes of any canoer his age, but Ray knew it was Luke's choice and therefore unspoken.

Still, Luke noticed that there was a kind of respect that came with being the strange one, the voodoo curse. He was never tortured in school like poor Billy Friedl. Kids like Billy Friedl were born to be abused, and there was nothing anyone could do about it. Luke felt sorry for Billy, sensing their common affliction, the kinship of the dispossessed. But Billy ran after his oppressors trying to ingratiate himself. Luke wandered back to look for a lost foul ball, forgetting and just wandering away.

They were both athletic, but one was with the boys, always, always on the team, driving through town in a car full of uniforms. One canoeing alone on the Lake of the Woods, hiking into the bush, swimming, tracking. Their mother had even jokingly, perhaps jokingly, noted that her two sons were dancers: Ray had the broad-limbed ability of Gene Kelly, Luke the polished finesse of Fred Astaire.

Both liked girls, and both were awkward around them, a similarity either would have been glad to have done without. Ray's ideal girl would tend to smile a lot and would have a dimple or two.

"Like Shirley Temple?" Luke teased. "Merry Christmas, Love, Snake and Shirley."

Ray thought about it. "No, no not Shirley Temple," he agreed, and they both laughed.

Luke's ideal girl? He would never say, perhaps because he had no name for her. Or perhaps it was....

Katherine Sorensen. He liked her well enough. She was good at math and history; she sat by herself under an oak tree after school; and she had once walked past Luke, stopped, and looked at him like she was about to cry, and hurried on. She was slender, with no breasts to speak of, no shape at all, in fact, and she looked the right balance in a canoe, and Luke had heard that she planned to be a painter.

"You should ask her for a date," Ray said, out of the blue, and startled Luke yet again.

"Who?"

"That Sorensen girl."

"What about her?"

"What about her—what about her—I can tell the way you look at her. Well, she's the only one you do look at, anyway."

"Doesn't mean...."

"Forget it. I was just wondering why you're in on another Saturday night."

"Could ask you the same thing," Luke replied.

"Yeah, but that's different. You're home 'cause you didn't even try to get a date. I'm home 'cause I couldn't get one. So it's better to be me!"

"Terrific."

Sitting out on the porch late at night, Ray rocking back on a straight-backed chair, and Luke sitting on the top step reaching his feet down into the blackness.

"Snake?"

"Yeah?"

"You ever gonna leave this place?"

"What, home? Nah, I figure after marriage and five or six kids I'll just build an addition back here."

"Warroad. You ever gonna leave?"

"What for?"

Luke stretched his arms back so that he was actually lying on the porch steps.

"See the world. Ever want to see the world?"

Ray stopped in his chair; the creaking halted.

"Luke, this is the world."

And again Luke heard strange, absolute silence.

Ray Anderson's high school graduation was the major event in their parents' lives in 1964, or so it seemed to Luke, watching from the living room as his mother ran back and forth across the kitchen in her curlers, racing to the radio as soon as a quiet sombre tune came on, playing with the dial until something loud and 'perky' blared out.

Their father had taken Ray down to the hardware, or so he had said. In reality, he was going to present his son with Ray's grandfather's watch and have a beer with the boy on the steps of Ruddy Hardigan's. "No one'll be the wiser," he told Rose Anderson and gave Luke a nod as if to say: one day your turn will come, just you wait.

Graduation. Listening to Ray's classmates spouting their dreams.

"Hairdresser," Ginny Fredericks breathed.

"Professional wrestler or welder," Nat Rogers shuffled away.

And Ray?

"I'd like to play for the Warroad Lakers and work for Marvin Windows. That is, if they'll have me."

Their father beamed; he couldn't stifle his pride, was mussing Ray's hair every chance he got, giving him pantomime rabbit punches.

"You've got a good boy there," Mrs. Clyde told Eric Anderson.

"Two!" Luke's mother replied, pushing Luke over beside Ray. Luke glanced sideways, then they both posed for the last obligatory picture before Ray was allowed to take off the tie.

"Luke's will be next year," Rose reminded everyone. Luke who was right on time, Ray who had been kept back a grade.

"Mother," Luke muttered. And then saw Katherine Sorensen. Her brother Chris was in Ray's class. Of course! And here she was in a beige doe-coloured dress with her hair in a ponytail. She looked over and gave him a smile, and Luke nodded her way and decided then and there that if he and Katherine did have to go through this same ordeal the following year, then he would ask Katherine Sorensen to go through it with him.

"You got your whole future ahead of you!" their father called from the kitchen.

Luke heard the cap go on another bottle of beer.

"What's it look like?"

"Hmmm?" For by now Ray was succumbing to the quiet of the evening, interrupted only by their father's punctuations.

"The future. What's it look like?"

"How the hell do I know?"

"I just thought...."

"What?"

The moment was fading.

Luke tried. "I just thought that you, a high school graduate and all...."

"Oh, shut up, will you? I saw you there, with Kathy Sorensen."

"Katherine."

"Yeah. I've heard what they're saying."

"What?"

"You and her. How it isn't just nature hiking you two are doing in the bush. How there's a little skirt hiking you and Kathy are...."

"Katherine!"

"Sorry, Katherine."

"Yeah, well, maybe she's not your ideal girl, but to me...."

And it was gone. The moment, control over the ten or twenty seconds.

It was just like the year before and those few seconds in November, Kennedy being shot over and over again on T.V. until everyone watching was sure he, too, would have fixed the shot from that same angle. Move, Luke mouthed, after the third or fourth time the pink wife bent over. "Move, damn it!" As if to replay were to correct.

This is the world, Luke nodded.

And a finite place with only promises beyond. Even the window factory burned down and had to be rebuilt. Even the President couldn't get out of Dallas. Even his brother would smell of glue and shavings when he came off shift, like Warroad smelled through all the men.

"Have you sent in those forms yet, Luke?"

"What forms?"

"You know, dear, those ones to the universe-city."

His mother spoke the word so that 'universe' stood alone, coupled at the last moment with her version of 'city'. The universe-city. Where was it? Not here. No city lights that were on all night to advertise arty films from Europe. No civil rights marches, unless they marched right through the marshland, through brush land, and on past the timber wolves.

This was the paradise, the one with the gates. This was the paradise where seventeen-year-old almost-graduates of the local high school prowled the dark roads searching for other forms of life, largely non-human, largely cross-bred from the dreams and nightmares that crept up the chimneys of the sleeping town. This was the paradise of the Medicine Man, except it wasn't. For his paradise was The Lost Forgotten, the traplines running along the trail, medicine bag bumping against him gently as he moved through the apple-eaten Eden, not the Paleface Father's Paradise, the missionary martyrs' paradise, the crossbeams of the church like some strange inbred teepee, the paradise of the fixed time and place, the paradise with gates.

VILLAGE OF WARROAD
PROCLAMATION

"Whereas, KaKaGeeSick, the senior citizen of Warroad and possibly the oldest living resident of the United States of America, does not have a registered birthdate, and Whereas, KaKaGeeSick is a resident of the Warroad Senior Citizens Home, where it is customary to celebrate the annual birthday of every resident, the Paleface Village Fathers in this Village of Warroad feel it fitting and proper that a birthdate be set by proclamation.

Now Whereas, it is reported that KaKaGeeSick was born approximately one hundred and twenty years ago and Whereas, it was known that the time of his birth was after the return of the geese and also shortly after the ice left the Lake of the

Woods, we, the Warroad Village Fathers hereby do proclaim that the 14th day of May be established as the official birthdate for KaKaGeeSick, Medicine Man of the War Road Chippewas.

Signed this 6th day of May, 1964."

Happy Birthday, KaKaGeeSick.

Do you think of cake? And understand paper hats?

Luke hears the ancient *anishinabe* chanting quietly to himself somewhere under the sounds of HAPPY BIRTHDAY, sees the old man try to verbalize, to remember back to his own birth, the wind, the breeze creasing the water, the first smell of his mother, of earth, of blood next to him on a blanket.

May 14, 1844.

Okay, Luke thinks. Now it has a beginning. Now there is control over the dead woman's labouring breaths.

Luke, this is the world.

And then Luke is standing having his picture taken in his shirt and tie, with his mother so excited that she cannot hold the camera. Katherine Sorensen is on the arm of Rod Morgan, her hair cut and curled, her lips bright with a colour from the drugstore. Katherine Sorensen the painter, Katherine feeling the exposed roots of an oak tree, walking along with the taunts and the silence.

And Luke, trying to talk to Barbara Crowel, who has attached herself to his sleeve these several weeks, his brother Ray smiling from over with the guys, the older brothers who now work in the factory together.

"I make windows," Ray would sing. "I make windows. I make lots and lots of windows!" And didn't mind the shifts; they worked right into his training schedule, and this was fortunate for both Ray and the Warroad Lakers.

"We'll have a star in the family, you mark my words," Eric Anderson crowed.

"Two stars, won't we, dear? Luke will go to the universe-city, and then, heaven knows, maybe we'll have a doctor in the house!"

"He could fix Ray up when he got banged up in a game."

"Oh...," Rose paused. "Do you suppose he could get hurt?"

"Get hurt? Come on, Rose, he'll be playing defence! Besides...Luke hasn't said what he's gonna be yet. Have you, boy? What is it? Doctor? Lawyer?"

Indian Chief, Luke finished. The words thundered past the sound of ducks and geese, the thumping of grouse tails on a carpeted forest floor.

"You know," he faced his father. "I thought I already WAS."

That night, the canoe slips so silently into the water that it hardly disturbs the sleeping fish. Luke cannot imagine ever being on the water any other way, even the groans from the rowboat oars would have been too loud. Just this, the plash of the paddle cutting, dividing the surface, dropping into the ancient world beneath and emerging with stars, pointed light on the edge of the paddle.

Some time later, Luke is packing a duffel bag and a suitcase. Everything is on schedule; he will get his lift and then his train and will arrive in time to be shown to the dorm.

His mother has been baking; there are pies along the sideboard, a platter of cupcakes on top of the refrigerator. She has wedged crumbling cookies down the sides of his suitcase.

"You might get hungry on the trip."

Luke smiles. There is no point in fighting it. He knows his mother's necessary kindnesses. His father is out back, trying to mend a trailer hitch for somebody, and the clanging and the cursing come as regular as breathing.

But where is his brother on this last day of Luke's Warroad Time? He realizes that this is how he has thought of it all along: Warroad Time. Post-Pleistocene hiccup.

His brother? He is on shift at the window factory, of course. He will have sawdust or shavings all over him by now. Or not. Maybe just a thin layer of nameless dust. Luke didn't know and confessed to himself that he never actually determined what it was his brother did over there. As Ray often said, there was more than one step in making a quality window. Where was Ray in the queue? Woodworking? Framing? Finishing? Did he work with glass at all?

For Luke, the factory was something to ride past on his bicycle, to drive past when his father sent him somewhere in the car.

Did Ray have—and the thought struck Luke as funny—a window where he worked? Could he look outside?

"I make 'em, I don't use 'em," Ray would have said.

"And he certainly doesn't clean them!" their mother would have quipped.

Luke walked along the edge of the grounds hoping to see Ray's face in one of the windows.

No.

It was clear, then; the past night was their goodbye.

Ray had been out with Ginny Fredericks but had got in early, around 10:00 o'clock.

"Ginny's sister was in from Thief River Falls," he said. "I felt like a third tit. Or a fifth," he corrected. "She's going wacko."

"Who, Ginny?"

"Mom. She doesn't want you to go."

Luke shrugged. "She's the one who's been pushing me. Not that I don't want to go."

"Yeah, but you know Rose Anderson."

They both paused, Luke trying to think of his mother as Rose Anderson. "Know what?"

"Nope."

"I wish we could go skating."

"Skating...you? The arena...."

"No, I mean winter skating, just you and me. Right now."

"Well, pardon me while I go outside and change the season."

"It's always the wrong season according to Warroad Time."

So they walked instead past the high school and down Lake Street, and it was dark and still and they didn't say much.

"Luke?"

"Yeah?"

"I got some Russell Stovers."

"Lucky you."

"No, for you. I mean, from you. For Mom. Okay?"

Ray had gone out, on his dinner break probably, to buy a box of candy for their mother, from her thoughtful son, Luke. It would be this way forever, wouldn't it? And part of Luke resented that presumption, the mind-reading that never actually read Luke's mind but rather a flattering reflection of its own. He felt this even as he was thanking Ray.

"Yeah, and don't worry about my verdigris. I'll shine when the time comes."

It was no big deal. People went away all the time, especially young people, especially these days, Warroad Time or no Warroad Time.

And it was no big deal. Brothers. Willie Olson had four of them until the truck accident. And when they all went to Christie Olson's funeral there was just one brother less, that was all.

Luke continued on past the factory. His parents would be worrying if they didn't leave soon. Luke looked back.

Pick up a window, Ray.

Lift up one of the demos and put it against the wall.

But the blank wall remained, and Luke chided himself for having looked back, and then he picked up his pace.

LANDED

THE BLIND: RAY: 1964

*M*y father always says a man's got to carve out a living. He also says a man should do what he's cut out for. He uses a lot of words about cutting and hacking, but, even so, the Thanksgiving drumsticks get pulled off in the end.

He likes to tell me how hard it is because, I guess, it's hard for him. He's not what you'd call a patient man. Somehow, though, I don't get on his nerves. At least, not as bad as Luke does.

Luke. And even my mother. They don't jive even when there's a hive (under them). My father actually said that once. It strains him and it pains him (that's me) to have people in the house who don't say good morning and goodnight to the same day he does.

"It's going down the drain," he says.

Us, the world. He said it over at Ruddy Hardigan's, and Ruddy just nodded and handed my father another beer. I sat there with my single bottle. I knew, somehow, that I wasn't supposed to talk, that even though I was having my first official beer with The Men, I wasn't a man and should keep my mouth shut. You get a lot of practice at that around my house. Beer drinking, too.

I kind of wished Luke could have come along, but my father said no, said it was my big day and Luke was still a school kid—he said that like there was something wrong with it—and how maybe next year Luke could come out for a beer, too.

It just would have been better with someone else 'cause my father and Ruddy Hardigan can talk a blue streak all day, and I had to get cleaned up for the graduation ceremony. I was trying to think of how I was finally out there and how I'd be working before I knew it and pulling in real money from a real boss instead of my father, and all I could think of was my father saying the world was going down the drain, and Ruddy Hardigan agreeing.

I don't want to be a guy on a veranda someday saying something like that. Really. I'd rather I didn't have a house, or anyone to say it to.

"Chip off the old block," Ruddy Hardigan punches my shoulder.

Luke says if I go to work at the window factory I'm crazy. Like there's a lot of other places in town. Besides, I like it, there's lots of my friends there. And what about carving out a living?

Luke doesn't go for that. I mean, he doesn't fall for it, which all of a sudden sounds bad, like my father is trying to put one over on me, like it's my father's fault how you have to pay for Cokes and smokes (my father's—always in relation to an allowance—"what, so you can go out and spend it on Cokes and smokes?")

Luke says our father didn't have any choice, but that I do and he does and we better choose right. I asked Luke what was going to happen when he finished up. That'll be next year (I failed a grade). He'll be in the same spot as me, sitting on Ruddy Hardigan's step with a bruised shoulder and a beer, listening to how the world's going to hell in a handbasket.

It made me mad. I felt like saying, "Oh, YEAH?" Which always worked when I was a kid.

They all know it's so I can stay here and play. That I'd be wherever the Lakers were.

What choice have I got, Luke?

The Lakers play here. The Arena is here. So, what? I'm going to go over to Thief River Falls or Beaudette, when I play for the Warroad Lakers?

My father thinks I'll get put on a good line. I think so, too. He's up there in the stands all the time, watching, as if I do everything right on the ice. Alex asked me if my father's our mascot, which is a funny way to think of my father at any time but especially when he's up in the stands cheering and waving his arms whenever I handle the puck.

Ruddy Hardigan says it must be great to get into the boards and mess up a guy a little.

"What? You mean check him?"

"I mean kill him!" Ruddy Hardigan bellows, and he and my father laugh at their beers.

A defence man's gotta be careful. His body is what he's giving the game, not his fancy stick handling or his overtime goals. He just can't go in and damage a guy, which is what the people ten rows up don't seem to understand. You have to know how to shield yourself, how to fall and how to inflict the necessary punishment without destroying the other guy.

Even my mother knows this, thinks it's "the one unfortunate thing about hockey", and wonders how those peace-loving Canadians could have thought up such a thing. Couldn't we just play it like touch football, like the President had with his family?

I think my mother had a thing for the President. Nothing strange. But, like, like I think she wished we were the Kennedys down by the water....

"We live by the water!"

Down in Hyannisport, there, with all the other Kennedys. Somehow, I don't think it'd work in Minneapolis where Mom's from. And, I think you have to have about a dozen more Andersons for a good game.

The thing about hockey is you get to go places with the team. Up to Canada for the odd game, a little east and west.

"Not Asia," Luke says. "Not Russia."

"No son of mine's going to goddamn Russia!"

My father's not original when he's jumping into a conversation.

Asia. What would I do in Asia? Or Russia? Tibet?

My father says Luke must have gotten switched at the hospital which really upsets my mother no matter how often she's heard it. I don't know if Luke's ever heard him say it, though I expect he has.

Funny, 'cause he does his share. And more, sometimes, 'cause he'll put in time out at the cabins, then come home and help my mother peel apples for a pie. I'll be taking off to go out somewhere, and my father'll be in the shed or out on someone's driveway, and Luke will just be about to leave, himself, and he'll see her sitting there and go back and break out the cribbage board.

I don't know. My father, maybe, doesn't like good ideas unless they happen to come from himself.

And he's got a million of them.

I remember the last time we ever really did anything together. It's a couple of years ago now, one of those perfectly clear mornings during duck hunting season.

So, we're in the blind. Me, Luke, our father and Dan Nelson. Actually, it's just this old tarp thrown over us, except for our heads. I don't know how long we're supposed to lie here, but there must be an easier way to get a meal. I haven't even looked over at Luke 'cause if I do I'll laugh, and you don't want laughing when you're duck hunting, which is one reason I don't like duck hunting.

This isn't my idea; that's all I can say. And it sure as hell isn't Luke's. Strange, I think it was our mother thought up this one. She's always trying to get us to spend time with our father. As if summers at the cabins and working on projects after school isn't enough.

Luke said he'd heard him talking to himself, going on about how we didn't know a thing about duck hunting, how we'd slow 'em down and jinx 'em, too.

But here we are.

I've never worn this much junk before. The hip waders make me walk like I'm lock-kneed or like I got a load in my pants.

And Luke looks...never mind. It's so stupid; I'll just start laughing. He's got these giant waders on; they're probably killing his crotch, and this field coat of Dan's with more pockets and loops....

Oh, and to top it off, he's got his hat pulled down low on his forehead, reminds me of a Robin Hood hat, like this bumbling Sherwood Forest duck hunter.

And then I think it's funny that all this gear is made out of something my mother calls cotton duck. Like maybe we're big cotton ducks to them as they fly over, long lost giant cousins or something.

I sneak Luke a look. Hah! Something out of Sears Roebuck. Or Halloween. I catch his eye, and he mouths something at me which I don't get, and then we are in the blind.

Quiet.

I think maybe everybody's sleeping. Like if you took a helicopter over and looked down you'd see these four guys dressed like army ducks, sleeping in the marshes, ducks flying over, duck shit landing like rain on Robin Hood hats.

I think my father and Dan Nelson don't think about anything when they're out here, that maybe the reeds moving back and forth just make a brownish-green wavy nothing that passes in front of their eyes.

Sometimes at the table his face will go like that, like he's concentrating on nothing and trying to catch the pattern of it. Usually then Luke'll say something, or my mother, and he'll focus down hard on them.

Luke and my father; guess it's just one of those things. Not that I have a lot to talk to him about, either; we just kind of spend the time. But with me, I think he just feels I'm not saying anything. With Luke it feels like a judgement.

Splash over near Luke's end.

"Frog," he says in the low voice he uses when he knows someone think's it's important.

I can hear them off a ways. Everybody else must have heard it because my father and Dan Nelson tense and shuffle, splash, slosh, click, and Luke looks over his shoulder at me.

They're a *V*, an almost-perfect *V*. No, it is perfect because one side is longer than the other which I guess is the way you'd draw it if you were trying to draw a *V* streaking through the sky. A moving *V*.

Then my father and Dan Nelson are muttering about which, which half of the V, and I've got this useless gun in my hands that my father says was his best one before he got the new one. I look over and Luke isn't even getting ready; the gun might as well be a splint or a walking stick. Then he's holding it up and squinting, but like you'd do with a telescope.

I guess if my father was paying attention he'd be pretty mad by now, but he's not because he's got this face, a cross between his Christmas face and the one when we finished the cabins. It's nice. It's actually nice.

Crazy shrieks and honks. A traffic jam up there.

My father answering, loud excited mallard sounds from his call. He blows....

And the ducks call back.

"Shoulda brought the dog," Dan Nelson growls thinking, I guess, that he's actually going to have to wade through to pick up his kills. His dog, Mick, usually does the dirty work.

Luke's probably trying to see the stars, or the Milky Way. Too bad it's daytime.

"Here they come," a low voice. Luke's.

Dan Nelson blows on his call.

The ducks answer.

"I think that one's in love with you, Danny."

Some of the ducks are coming in close for a landing.

My father's smile gone strange.

"One...two...THREE!"

We're up and firing.

We're firing.

My father and I are recoiling and shooting and it's hard to tell what's going on. Luke's like a statue; he's aiming and aiming.

I'm blasting away at the reeds in front; I got a bullrush, its powder explodes in front of me.

"Hooo!" Dan's going.

"How many?"

I'm watching the rest of the birds as they keep going. Strange, they don't close up the broken *V*, they just keep flying with the space, there, for the fallen one.

"That's three! Three I took!"

Then there's quiet again, but the echoing-off kind like we're all inside the arena with the sound hitting off the walls.

Then Dan and my father are plowing through the bush saying how they wish they'd brought the dog, and Dan says why don't we use the boys, and my father calls back at Luke and me.

He hasn't moved. He looks like he's listening hard to something. The gun is off to the side. He won't look at me. He won't answer my father, and my father hates that.

"COMING!" I call and get these waders going left and right.

"CAME DOWN OVER THERE!" I'm pointing.

Great. He's got me pointing. Maybe I should pull it out and do it with my tail.

Dan's got one by the wingtip; the wing opens and spreads like that souvenir fan of my mother's.

I troop my way through the reeds. There it is. I'm glad ducks don't have expressions because I'd sure hate to see the one that reads: flying over Lake of the Woods, agony, falling, stubbly guy in hip waders....

"Here...over here."

Slosh, slosh.

"S'beauty!" my father booms.

This is one of his.

"Take 'er, Ray."

It's limp. If you can call something with tight feathers and a hard beak limp. It's awkward to carry.

I can hardly make out Luke. The gear must really work. I'm sure if I was a duck I wouldn't have seen us; which, I guess, was the whole point.

"S'a matter with you, boy? Your gun jam?"

Luke and the old double-barrel shotgun from my father's leaner days.

"That happened to me once. The Missus was fit to be tied."

Grunts or chuckles.

"Luke! I'm talking to you!"

He looks up. It's the expression the duck should have had.

"Here, gimme that one, Ray."

I hand over the bird.

"Open your coat, Luke."

He doesn't move.

"Open your goddamn game bag!"

And slowly the hands come up. Buttons, zipper.

"There, now, that pouch in back, your game bag, undo the snap back there."

My father's pointing to the lining, to the snap that holds the pouch closed.

"Goddamn it, boy!" My father wrestles with Luke. I don't know if Luke can take him at this point, but I bet he can.

Next thing, I see the bird being stuffed into the back of Luke's coat, and there's this bulge now, and my father's saying, "There. There!" to it.

"Do up the coat; that's how you carry 'em."

Luke looks....

"Listen," I say, "why don't...."

"You shut up!" my father warns. "Goddamn mamby-pamby here...."

Then he turns to me.

"Didn't hit anything?"

I'm thinking of the bullrush head, blasted to smithereens.

"Think I clipped one."

And he seems happy with that.

We're packing up. Dan Nelson is folding his tarp. I know he wishes he'd brought Mick instead of the two of us. He's got his ducks around him; a fat ring of warm birds around his guts.

Then Luke's walking behind us; it's pitiful, the single bulge in the back of his coat. I wish I could switch with him. He's walking solemn in his waders.

"Ah, leave him alone," my father says. I guess he thinks I feel left out because Luke's carrying one and not me.

We're off a ways when it happens. Other than the slosh there's been nothing, and then reeds shiver and there's a SPLASH and I look back and Luke's got the coat off and on the ground and he blasts at it with the shotgun.

BLAM! Luke jerks back.

BLAM!

"Ray!" my father yells.

I go slowly. He's out of shots, but I'm no fool.

"Luke, listen...Luke? I'm coming over...."

We both stand there hearing the shots echoing off the invisible walls. Then the gun goes down, right into the water.

"Shit!" my father.

"That's my friggin' jacket!" Dan, off in the distance.

"Luke?"

He's completely still; he's weaving a bit, swaying with the echo.

"It was moving. I swear, Ray, I felt it moving."

Nobody says much in the truck. Dan's already dunned my father for a new jacket even though the one he'd lent Luke was his old one.

My father is speechless. There's a first. I don't even want to guess what's going on in his head.

Luke's in the back of the pickup. Wouldn't let me ride with him; wouldn't talk to anybody. The messy jackets are spread out there and the ducks, too. Luke's, full of holes.

"He wasted the fucker," Dan says. "Can't eat it now, all full of shot like that."

Dan definitely has no plans to take us duck hunting again.

I remember how my father considered himself responsible. How he was the one with the useless sons. And how he didn't want my mother forcing us into things anymore, which mostly hasn't happened since. I mean, we still do one or two things. My father comes to my games religiously; he's a real Lakers fan. Next year, he says, he'll buy a portable movie camera to film me. "To show all those sisters-in-law in Minneapolis."

He says I should make foreman someday over at the factory, and he's already planning to re-do our windows as soon as some more cabin payments come in.

Ruddy Hardigan is pushing open the door with another couple of beers.

"Now, you get on home. Your mother will be worried. You gotta look good for the ceremony.... Graduating!" He turns to Ruddy. "My boy's graduating!"

I step down and start heading up the walk. He calls after me. I turn.

"You'll get your piece of the pie, boy!" he says, and they raise their beers, and suddenly I realize they mean it.

MEMORIAL ARENA: LUKE: 1968-1969

*T*he first time Luke said goodbye it was from the sprung-steel seat of Willie Olson's tractor. The dust and the topsoil said it for him, and Willie's glance, over his shoulder from the other tractor, said it. Luke was eleven years old at the time. He did not know what he had then and forever parted from.

Warroad was hazy in the uncommon spring heat, and row upon row of raised earth could be whispering if Luke was listening, which he was not, his thoughts far away from this town and this time, and his friend's sweating face grinning back from the tractor. Days could go on like this with only the evening fishing off the jetty; Luke and Ray and maybe Willie and Lon, sloshing their malteds down to the lake, to wrestle the massive walleye. One evening Luke did just that from the dock, crawled and scraped along the planks after his rod, after this fish half again as big as the one in his dreams, and it took Ray holding Luke holding the rod to bring it in. The fish thumped wildly, slapped the pier and the legs of the boys before it finally gazed up with a resigned eye and slithered to a stop.

Ray was ever-watchful, the extra pair of hands at the end of the rod. Luke may have noticed it the way he noticed the stuffed, mounted bear cub holding the sign for hunting licenses, the way he saw herons pick their way through precise patches of shoreline water. He might have felt it the way he felt the wind kick up from the seaplane landing, that tripped-up mixture of air and moisture deep in the fish-tinted reeds. If he did, it was no more and no less to him; his brother carried the rods while Luke toted home the magnificent dream fish.

A town grows the way that paradise grows, slowly and with attention paid to the needs of the unearthly inhabitants. A dirt road leading to perfect nowhere necessarily sprouts a shiny new mailbox. A blueberry patch—and a few old boards—become a blueberry stand. And another dream, and a pause, and another. A factory appears where red pine probably appeared, and paradise shifts boundaries and accommodates again. Luke's father envisions a Realm of the Most High, a place of almost perfect splendour where a body (and a soul) can enjoy the summer by way of either outboard or canoe. And he calls this place the wilderness and he calls his wife a proprietress and he calls his sons to work most days, and the summer rolls along as dusty and as porous as the bricks that hold in the idea of a schoolhouse.

Luke probably said goodbye in the blue-grey dead of a December afternoon walking from the high school to his brother's hockey practise. His brother played defence, skating backward as if it was forward, and always a wave to Luke between face-offs as if it was Luke who was doing something up there in the seats. Ray was always saying that, saying Luke was the one who had it going for him; Luke was the one who was using his head. Ray made the distinction; he engineered the separation, the hopeless rows of seats in front of Luke, the defence man down on the ice.

Afterward there was soda, and when they were older there was a beer. Ray and Luke in the Silver Dollar Saloon a few years later, a thousand years later, looking back at fossilized lives along the bay—their own, their family, the Chippewa medicine man in a white man's old-folks' home. KaKaGeeSick, ancient Chippewa healer, retired to the Warroad Rest Home; his sister, Laughing Mary, gone; the burial gifts she brought, and the vandals who watched and stole from the graves. The bay, Muskeg Bay, proclaimed and decreed to be here fore and forever KaKaGeeSick Bay to honour an old man in a retirement home. Ray and Luke sitting inside the Silver Dollar, tracing a mural with their eyes, its river and its ducks, its perfect symmetry over door frames and right angles, its two dimensions garnished with an occasional flying third; another dream necessitating another shift of boundaries.

Was he leaving this, as well, when he ordered two more draft? Luke knew that Ray had a dream just like they all did in Minnesota. Ray would play for the Warroad Lakers, pride of the north; Ray would play defence for the best amateur team this side of paradise.

Luke raised his glass, and his brother raised his glass, and Luke heard a click like the sound of a gun being cocked.

"Hey, Luke, think fast!"

Ray lifted a clod of earth with his blade and sent it rocketing toward his brother. It hit Luke in the back and sent a shower of dirt over his shoulder.

"Asshole!"

His brother's wide smile, the look of an off-duty defence man.

Ray's dream fit neatly into the postage-stamp town. The sun rose and shone in one serrated corner, and the entire world could be fastened to a letter sent to Luke. The way Ray stood in the uniform of the Warroad Lakers, and then fell, stretching his body out in mid-air above the ice, not gracefully or in imitation parachute jumps of flying squirrels, but brutally embracing gravity, the ultimate sacrifice for the man in the net. In the cold damp air moving swift across the ice, watching left and right and imagining behind, Ray understood the blood in his mouth.

When Ray breathed in, Warroad expanded. Yet on a good day, after practise, one breath took in the whole town.

Luke folded the letter and placed it back in the envelope. He ran a finger over the cancelled stamp, then picked up his knapsack and headed to class.

Ever since he had left for college, there had been this distance. His father, stuck somewhere in the Pleistocene Era, complaining about the ice sheets covering his favourite fishing holes.

"College! I been in the north all my life! I never needed anything down there in the city. All of that fancy crap down south."

Complaining about the winds, the water and the ice that were racing down from Canada to ruin his sportsman's paradise.

"But don't you like ice fishing, dear?"

Luke's mother's scent of gingerbread trapped and carried away in the ice crystals flowing over Roseau County. The stew and the cream pies that she made for an absent son. And Ray wrote:

"Dear Luke:
Ate your piece of pie again last night."

"Dear Luke:
You were right, you were right, you were right...."

And the inevitable:
"Dear Luke:
How come you never write?"

It was fading despite the countless letters from his mother describing Ray in uniform, Ray in the corners, Ray, for a while, in traction. Luke would read these letters, too, walking across campus and then deposit them in the trash bin at the end of the yard.

So it was the enactment of goodbye, carried out in detail. Words taken and folded and dropped into the air, falling into a receptacle among the soft-drink bottles, the chocolate bar wrappers, and, one rainy Tuesday afternoon, the protest flyers.

Luke traded the letter for one of the flyers and scanned the page as he moved along slowly nodding his head.

Defend. DEFEND.

Clowns on ice, toothless grins on their smashed faces, skating on pure hope, on bruised, taped ankles.

Stately guardians dressed in walleye scales with bright flat swords at the gates of paradise, casting out sinners, turning away Adam and Eve, pointing with sword-tip to a world just over past the window factory somewhere to the left and down a road that ends a few hundred feet from a lake. The waters are from the Pleistocene glaciers, but the water level is determined by the Norman Dam up in Kenora. The cries in the air are from seventy years ago, a Sundance out at Buffalo Point. The blood on the sword is type "O" or type "B", pure type for pure aboriginal people. This sword has tasted human blood...the better to designate, my dear.

Luke breathes in and holds and passes the roach along. And once again the boys are fishing off the jetty. The sword points at Luke, and in the evening sun the blade looks like a highway stretching out across the water, past the Red Lake Indian Reserve, past the Angle and the borders and on into the north. The boy beside Luke looks up and sees a gleaming hockey stick on the frozen ice of Lake of the Woods.

Ray's version of this period was concise. There were their trips out: Eric and Rose and a picnic hamper; three pairs of newly-knit wool socks for Luke; Luke, the son, who was in the university. The word "university" sat proudly in the air outside the drugstore as Rose and Nettie Hellman discussed their respective children. "Universe-city", Rose proffered, and Nettie countered with one "Foreman" and two "Honours Students" although these last were only in high school.

Ray wrote that one university could safely beat two foremen that year. At least, in the north. Who knew what was happening down south? They were all reading about the trouble on the campuses. Young people not appreciating how their parents had slaved; young deadbeats, not working themselves, mind you, going around criticizing honest, working people. Ray wrote that Rose was proud of Luke, but she was becoming careful about the word "university". Ray, on the other hand, had his job at the factory which paid okay; he wasn't complaining. And he had the Lakers.

And they had him.

Ray.

Luke shook his head.

The hamper Rose packed was to contain all of Luke's favourites: her chicken, her blueberry preserves, her gingerbread. That is, his.

Luke had known since he was three or four that in the hierarchy of maternal love he had edged out his older, friendlier brother. He had beat the all-in-all more caring, helpful brother. Luke's father, on the other hand, had gone the traditional route and embraced the boy with the hockey-puck bruises.

Rose and Eric had planned to surprise Luke that weekend. It was, after all, Thanksgiving, and for the first time in three years he wasn't coming home for the holidays. Ray stood beside the car saying, "Are you sure?" and "Have a good trip." Eric grumbled but started up the Ford, and Rose ran out at the last minute and grabbed a handful of grass from the shore.

"What, for his litter box?"

Rose ignored her husband and gave Ray a list of instructions that included plans for the construction of a bomb shelter, and Ray kissed his mother on the cheek and hit the roof of the car, for his dad.

Ray's version of the rest wasn't as pleasant. Rose and Eric told Ray that they had been betrayed.

It just wasn't possible that Luke wouldn't be there. They'd driven all the way from Warroad! But the registration office was closed, and the residence office was closed, and the students at the dorm had never heard of him. When Rose finally located a boy they'd met the year before, he frowned and told them the news: their son, Luke, wasn't at university this year.

Of course they didn't believe this...this Ted person. They'd sent Luke letters and addressed them here.

"Maybe he picks them up."

Their son had never once mentioned...and where was he if he wasn't in school?

"He drops by now and then when there's something going on."

So Rose and Eric waited in the city until the holiday was over and the office re-opened, and it was there that they confirmed that Luke had not registered for the 1967-68 school year.

What followed was a manhunt—phone calls back to Ray for clues, notes left for students who could possibly know their son.

"Luke? Tall, black hair?"

Rose nodded, wobbling the tears under her eyes.

"Isn't he that guy who travels?"

And quick glances back and forth among the students, and dead silence.

So Rose sat outside the university where she received several stares from the young, long-haired bums, as Eric referred to them, but this didn't stop her from rummaging through the picnic hamper and pitching spoiled food into the bin beside the bench.

She phoned Ray and begged him. Eric got on and threatened him. Ray didn't know; that is, he wasn't sure. Luke didn't write him much either, after all. But there was something, some inconsistency, and there was someone named Libby who might be able to help.

"What the hell's the matter with you? We drive all the way down here...!"

There was a silence on the phone that was different than the stone wall the students had erected.

"Sorry," was all Ray said to his parents.

They finally discovered Luke's whereabouts. There are only so many places a son can hide from his mother Rose later told Ray. And he hadn't even looked like Luke. He had ragged clothes, and his hair was long and curly, and he looked like a lost soul or one of those apostles in the Last Supper pictures. Ray smiled when she said that and tried to give his mother a hug, but she pulled away from his grasp.

"Dear Luke:
You probably should have told them."

"Luke:
Just give them an address where they can reach you."

And the surprising phone call in the middle of the night.

"There's no point. Besides, they'd only get hassled about me."

"Why? Luke?"

And a silence that filled Ray's ear and the entire kitchen.

"Hey, Ray? Look outside for me; what's out there?"

"What?"

"Just look out the window."

Ray glanced over his shoulder.

"Nothing. What...there's nothing!"

But Luke closed his eyes in the phone booth and saw a black lake spun with gold lights and heard the low, gold sounds of cormorants deep in dreams.

"Never mind, brother. Thanks. And, hey, take care of yourself."

There was a click. Ray hung up and went over to the window.

This was the year Rose read the newspapers. Ray said his mother bought the Duluth paper, and the Winnipeg paper, when she could, and she listened to the radio and picked up news from Minnesota and Canada. She also read the Warroad Pioneer so she could keep up with news at home in case Luke wanted to know.

She no longer mentioned university at the drug store. She had Ray, whom she was told was doing a good job with the Lakers. He was becoming a star defence man, which always beat out a single university in Warroad.

Ray admitted he'd had a good season in '67-'68. No major injuries and an impeccable record. Eric still went to all the home games, and if the car hadn't acted up that winter, he'd have gone to more away games, too. Rose still refused to go to any games; it was her chance to listen to classical music on the radio.

Luke sat in the diner with his third cup of coffee. His contact was supposed to have shown up the previous hour. Somebody slipped a coin into the machine, and everyone listened to The Turtles sing "Happy Together".

And it was Ray and Luke in the Silver Dollar Saloon noticing how, for the moment, there were only the two dimensions. Only the duck seemed capable of flying out of the painting, its single three-dimensional wing flapping crazily in a mid-air profile.

It was the year of the cryptic message.

Ray managed to get a letter through using the old connections. The letter arrived two months after Ray had written it.

"Dear Luke:

The Medicine Man is dead. They're going to bury him in the Indian cemetery with his brothers. He was over 120 years old. Remember?

And Luke read the inscription Ray had copied:

Whereas, Ka-Ka-Gee-Sick, who is the senior citizen of Warroad
and who has been a lifelong resident of over 100 years on the
Lake of the Woods,
And Whereas, Ka-Ka-Gee-Sick is a well respected
trustworthy member of the Chippewa Tribe, the Village Fathers of this village
of Warroad feel it fitting and proper that
permanent recognition be bestowed upon our beloved Medicine
Man.

NOW WHEREAS, Ka-Ka-Gee-Sick has resided on the shores of Muskeg Bay of the Lake of the Woods for over a century, be it hereby resolved that the name of Muskeg Bay be retired, and from this day forward this geographical area be called KaKaGeeSick Bay, in this English form of spelling, and for the record let it be known that the proper Chippewa spelling in the days past was "Kah-gah-ke-shig" translated to mean "Everlasting Sky".

In testimony, whereof we have hereunto set our hands and seal this 4th of May, 1965, A.D.
[Morris C. Taylor, Mayor *et. al.*]

Luke read down the page. His parents, apparently, were renovating. His father was cleaning out the work shed.

Your old boards are gone, the ones you were going to make that cart with. She almost started crying when he threw them out.

Luke noticed that the waiter was trying to get his attention. He knew it was time to pay up and leave.

Luke, I know what you're doing. It's good, I guess. That is, I don't know. I don't know anything. And I make sure Mother and Dad don't know either. But since you're going to find out anyway, I wanted to be the one to tell you, to say it straight out. I've joined up. I enlisted, Luke.

The arm of the guardian is pointing again, and the walleye scales fan out in an arc colouring the landscape in a wash of grey-blue translucence, and for a moment all is Pleistocene ice.

Luke paid and left pulling his collar up against the rain and walking through the roadways of a Japanese embroidery, two-dimensional mountains and ornamental gardens on top of his dripping head. The wind bit and he remembered his fishing jacket back home.

There was no contact for a while after that. It was beautiful in its purity. Luke marvelled at how Ray, in one perfect gesture, had cancelled twenty years of comparison. How did he figure it out? Lying in bed at night thinking maybe I'll join the NHL, maybe I'll go to Philadelphia, or the Bruins. Thinking, as he smelled the cinnamon-scented air: maybe I'll join up.

Asshole.

And cancelled his brother out.

Now Rose Anderson would be able to keep her head up at the drugstore, run into Mrs. Olson or Mrs. Lavery.

"My Willie's in the service, too," Mrs. Olson reminded her. They're sending him overseas in a week."

And Rose Anderson closing her eyes at this, perhaps trying to place the country on a map inside her eyelids.

"What about your Luke?"

And the eyes jolt open, and there is suddenly a prescription to be filled.

Ray at night, out on the porch, never questioning why he's still at home on a parents' porch, never considering a night of frantic lovemaking up there in his little boy's bedroom. Where did he go for that? In a town with the eyes and ears of Warroad.

Yet it was the perfect gesture. There would be photographs, of course, just out of basic training. And the beers with the old man. And the walk along the shore with their mother, Ray walking for two sons, talking for two.

When he lost him, then, was when he got the letter. Or when he heard, that late night through the pay phone receiver, of his brother's departure.

"His unit left yesterday. We were hoping you'd have called."

They were hoping that Luke would somehow, miraculously, have known, the way he always seemed to sense his brother nearby even when they were playing out by the water.

"It's uncanny," Rose would say, and watch them from a distance, eight-year-old Ray and six-year-old Luke, and Luke always turning and expecting his brother to be there.

"He picks up one end of something; he just *knows* Ray's on the other end."

Luke listened to his mother ramble on. Her legs were bothering her; his father had bursitis.

Was he eating enough? He still had the long hair?

"Ray told me to tell you he understands. Understands what, dear? I'm not sure I...."

Luke saw Ray in his hockey uniform, sweating in the heat, taking off in a small plane from the Warroad Airways landing, circling, whirling with insects over the Lake of the Woods.

Luke is holding his arms out in front of him. They look like the train tracks at the Warroad depot except they're moving, the parallel lines joining, crossing at will, meeting and separating, together, apart. Train coming, Luke. Together, apart. Hold on, Luke, hold on...!

"Hey, man, you okay?"

Someone is laughing hysterically, someone....

Blankets.

The sound is distorted from where they are sitting. Luke and Val are in the centre of the city of people. He has been with Val since he met her at the group house. She had been Libby's friend until she met Luke.

"You okay?"

He nods and pulls her closer. All around are dark blankets with people stretched out on them. The blanket edges touch perfectly, seamless seams, it seems—Luke starts to laugh—and the bodies are bright stars on the flag of a new United States.

He has been to the tents of Movement City; he has talked to the Crazies, the Yippies, the yogis; he has been offered food by a young woman with a burn scar shaped like the tip of South America. And the talk is of Nixon's War, Apollo, and bad drugs.

"We're on the moon. We're on the fucking moon, man! Like, fuck the war!"

"Fuck the moon, too."

In April, when the number of troops in Vietnam had peaked, Luke received a letter from Ray.

You know, it's getting crowded over here; they want me to share my knife.

And Luke smiled, remembering their mother's admonition: Your fork is your own, but you may share your knife, boys.

In May after the Berkeley shootings, Luke sent Ray an angry letter which Ray never answered. Then, when Apollo landed in July, Luke again wanted to talk to Ray, but he knew a letter would not suffice. He could hear Ray's comment, a concise summary of years of planning, of billions spent, of two men trooping around on the moon, "reconnaissance" Ray would have called it, all to collect a few lousy moon rocks. Luke could hear Neil Armstrong proclaiming: "That's one small step for man," and Ray's quick "but, like, I had to get my rocks off."

America.

He didn't know what his brother thought now. The few letters he received from overseas were relentlessly upbeat. Ray did say this, though— keep your nose clean.

Arrest? Activity?

He didn't elaborate. He was too busy describing the farming techniques over there.

"Can you just see it? Old man Christianson and a water buffalo? 'Course, that's a bit redundant even as a picture."

Keep your nose clean, Luke.

Keep in the clear.

Clear. Clean.

There hadn't been any more letters.

Val pulled Luke down beside her on the blanket. This woman, this Canadian, who had escaped a Montreal university, who had emigrated to the United States of Woodstock. She said she'd come down to be where it was all happening.

Luke frowned, remembering again how things always got forgotten, how once it was, all of it, out on the lake. The northern pike, the walleye feeding, and Luke and his friends lying along the jetty half-awake, half-asleep, listening to Ray talk about a crazy man out at Buffalo Point.

Luke and Val made love on the blanket-flag of the new nation. With people all around them, they were perfectly alone. They were David Thompson, and Tiarks after him, surveying a line that would become an international boundary, a nation and a colony divided along a lonely frontier wood, along a stretch of moving water flowing north into Hudson's Bay.

As Val kisses him they merge. Someone is singing in his ears, harmonies he's never heard. There are invisible borders in the Lake of the Woods. There is division in the heart of a stand of red pine. Luke on a rock looking past the boundary into the mist, and somewhere beyond the mist and the islands is Canada. Canada, warm, wet, miles and miles of unguarded border, unbelievably delicate ports, her lips. Hidden pools, Angle Inlet, cedarwood air, fire, cinders, spitting sparks, fireflies, fireflies.

Val is smiling at Luke as he raises his hand straight up, twirls it a couple of times and holds it there.

"What are you doing?"

Duck wings flapping inside a paint can, drumming the sides, splattering the wall as one bird emerges, forced in spent colours to stick to a painting; one wing working free and flying forever in the two-dimensional mural in the Silver Dollar Saloon.

That was it, then. The anger or the frustration or whatever it was that had marked the attempts to communicate with Ray. The impossible events of 1969. The way Val was slowly working her way into his pre-dawn thoughts, replacing—no, dismissing—any other woman he had known, taking her place alongside the permanent things in his life. Val had begun to appear in family snapshots taken years before he had known her. Luke could see her with scabbed knees, with pedal-pushers and a lime-green t-shirt, crackling her way over twigs through the forest to sit beside a younger Luke at the evening campfire. When he rubbed his eyes, the pictures disappeared; Val could be smudged away from his closed eyes, but then he would open them and there she'd be, her light brown hair over the pillow, her naked back and buttock golden against the sheet.

He had not needed to meet Val now. In fact, the timing could not have been worse. He was on the road a lot, not knowing where his activities would take him. Yet Val said she approved of his anti-war stance, and she, too, was busy with the other members of the house planning activities. Cooking, too. Someone always had to cook. She was learning to use the organic ingredients found in Libby's kitchen, and she.... And he would find himself doing it again, getting side-tracked with thoughts of her when there were other things to consider.

This timing. The Bad Timing of the Impossible Year.

Luke had received a notice from the Selective Service System saying that he had been upgraded from "2A" to "1A".

It seemed like centuries ago, that registration day when he'd dutifully filled out all the papers placed before his pen, the forms, the deferment, a young student, after all, young American going to "universe-city" to study history and philosophy.

"It's my philosophy that history won't get you a job!" his father responded when he heard Luke's majors.

This was during the Pleistocene Era, and Luke slid out between the sheets of ice.

And now the deferment was gone. He was 1A. And given the current events, Luke knew what 1A meant. Sure enough, the next morning Val walked into the bedroom with his "Greeting" notice in her hand.

Greeting. Fellow Earthling.

Like he'd somehow been away. Like he hadn't been living here, a full-time citizen of these United States of Stupidity, watching all of America leave it to Beaver. Leave it to Ray and Willie and Luke, to high-school dropouts and inner-city stalkers.

And Luke started smiling at this picture, this vision of Val in a kaftan and kerchief, some displaced pale peasant who'd been conscripted by the United States Postal Service, who stood, quite legitimately, between Luke and the draft board unless this 'family' deferment, too, would be ignored, which it would because this was 1969 and whether you were in school or had a wife or had to spoon-feed your old man, whether you had a goddamn *life* going on, you were going to be visited in true Holiday fashion, your presents wrapped in duffel-bags, your tree cut and all your cards saying: "Greetings, Boys, Men, Whatever. Compliments of the Season!"

Luke read the letter he had received from the President of the United States.

GREETING:
You are hearby ordered for induction into the Armed Forces of the United States and to report to....

It was identical to the scores Luke had seen, some held before his face by shaking hands, some thrust at him by angry, hostile hands. What are you gonna do? Can you help me out?

But none of then, until now, addressed:

"To Mr. Luke Anderson."

"What are you going to do?" Val asked, one hand clutching his shoulder.

He felt the hand, but he didn't hear her. He was thinking of the vinyl pool; no, it might have been rubber because it was certainly that long ago, the swimming pool stuck under a swift-moving glacier, the ludicrous square of frozen water and the perfectly preserved bodies of five-year-old Ray and his little brother, Luke.

Was it rubber? He had forgotten. It must have been vinyl, but a thick and heavy precursor of the pie-crust thin liners in today's wading pools. The bottom was green, a dark hunter-green, and when the pool was filled with water the bottom looked infinitely deep and mysterious. Never mind that his knees or thighs or buttocks were always touching bottom, or that he could see Ray dog-paddling along the bottom in front of him. The green through squinting eyes made the pool as deep as the Lake of the Woods.

The sides, he remembered, were lemon yellow and thick enough to need no external casing other than the rectangular tubular frame. And Ray or Luke could undulate the yellow walls from the outside and cause small tidal waves within.

"*You, now!*" Luke would shout, and his brother would hop over the edge and slap the side of the pool.

There were four red metal seats, one in each corner. They were triangular and somehow—and Luke found this miraculous—the hard metal edges never put holes in the rubber, or vinyl, and never got rusty and never got scratched. This backyard, a world that belonged to his brother and himself. Their father might come by and kick the wall to make a wave; their mother might leave large glasses of lemonade on one of the red triangles, but inside the four-walled world was big enough only for Ray and Luke.

His brother breathes in as he drinks the lemonade and cough-sputters the contents into the green lake of the pool.

"UUUUccck...!" Luke screams, then stops, seeing the wild face his brother makes as he tries to breathe again. Eyes red from the water, sunburned nose peeling straight down the middle, wheezing sounds as the chest rises and falls in rapid bursts.

Luke studies his brother's face, afraid to be afraid.

"Water's got stuff in it," Luke complains and stands up, his bathing suit halfway down his hips.

"Yeah," Ray shivers, "I peed in it, too."

Ever since the October commencement of the Draft Lottery, the group's anti-war activities had been somewhat curtailed. It was the unofficial 'Why bother to protest if you get a lucky number?', a perfect sleight-of-hand designed to keep the troops rolling while breaking the back of the resistance, and it had dented the resolve of many marginal protesters. Now Luke's own number had come up in the draw.

"You're crazy!" was Val's initial response. "What's all this shit you've been doing, then, if you're ready to...willingly!"

Luke thought of his brother probably hitchhiking to the recruiting office, probably driving in with the old man. Smiling. Stepping up and offering.

"You can do more these days from inside," Luke said as Val stormed out of the room.

The group could not believe it. Libby said he wouldn't last a week, wouldn't last boot camp. "It's not spring training, you shit." And while she agreed with the idea of working from the inside, she had a single summary comment for Luke.

"You're not the man. You're too quick. You wouldn't pace it like you have to, and you'd just wind up in the stockade, or worse. And the stockade is full of people who don't need convincing."

Somebody mentioned trying for C.O. status and someone else reminded them if its near impossibility. Somebody challenged the C.O. deferment, and Luke said he agreed.

"One thing I am sure of, and that is I don't want some other poor fucker going in my place."

An army of men in hockey uniforms swatting the jungle into submission with their sticks, bullets bouncing off Cooper protective gear, helmets, and the shining blades.

Dear Ray:

I don't know when you'll get this. Looks like they caught up with me. So much for my luck with lotteries. I've been called up, have to report for induction...I'm going to step forward, Ray.

It felt strange to write the words. They flowed so simply from his pen onto the soiled steno-pad. The words accommodated the coffee stain and the muffin crumbs. He could be writing out the muffin recipe for all anybody cared. He could be writing his mother, or his girlfriend. He could be dropping his brother a line.

Snake, listen, why don't you write me? I could use a little of your real life.

Keep your nose clean, Luke.

Luke carried the letter in his vest pocket, and sent it from somewhere in upper-peninsula Michigan.

He wouldn't understand the significance of the training. He would be paraded around like this, made to shine brass and to oil rifles, made to spit-shine boots until he glowed back from their toes, and yet he would not understand the sameness of the humiliation, the need to number his two pairs of combat boots, the need to be wearing the correct pair during inspection. Alternate. But alternate at the same time as everyone else. Eat at the same time, sleep at the same time, shit right alongside everybody else.

And he would look at himself in the mirror and see a twenty-two-year-old recruit replica of someone he was supposed to know, suddenly hairless, suddenly appearing no older than nine or ten. They were all like that, a few a little older, thirteen perhaps, with pimples festooning their faces; twelve, with that amazing awkwardness of movement; ten, like Luke, curious eyes stamped with that unhealthy awareness. One named Sheldon was being made to endure more than his quota of abuse. He was Luke's bunk mate, he on the top until he nervously approached Luke about the prospect of switching.

"They'll probably send you over!" Luke marvelled.

"L-long as t-t-there's not-t-thing higher tthan a ttop bunk."

And Luke, much taller than Sheldon, loping up the side every night, climbing the rock to his lookout perch.

To watch them all. The men snoring noisily and wrapped around their pillows, his father out in the boat on his way to the cabins, his mother in the yard hanging her third load of wash. If he looks back he can see it sashaying in the wind. He can see his mother, too, if he looks back. And his brother fresh from an afternoon's fishing, knowing he should fish in the early evening yet successful all the same, holding up his catch as he approaches the rock.

And then, there she is in the wrong time again, Val Leighton, bumped back into the Ice Age, Luke never asking her permission to do this. Val now ten years old holding out her hand to Luke, expecting him to help her up, stepping, unsteady, and then pulling herself forward to stand beside him on the rock that holds only one.

What was duty, and where did punishment begin? The guardian at the gate tickling them with the sword-tip; out, stay away from this place, find someplace else to live. To be wrong. To be right.

To be wrong to be right.

Living on nuts and berries and starting over.

He was making contact with the 'element' in the army. The soldiers' coffeehouses, UFOs, underground pamphlets and papers, the AWOLS and the friends-of-sisters-friends who were spiriting across information and alternatives. R.I.T.A.—Resistance in the Army, A.C.T.. The army was a busy place.

But was he getting anywhere? At least on the outside he could make arrangements—a false I.D., a ride to the border, midnight promises over tokes and cans of beans. In here he only had his voice, and the army's voice screamed louder. Sitting in a UFO watching new boys talk like troopers, the same, same stories over and over.

There were those, though, who were listening. A few even had outside contacts—pamphleteers, the paper strewers, the troubadours of kill-the-messenger Bad News. And bigger fish. Even Libby, though of course, he could not contact her now. She had been moving to strategic locations. She and two others had been talking higher stakes around the time Luke left for boot camp. She'd given him a look, then, that asked for this one last favour: no questions.

Who did she know with experience in plastics?

A 3 a.m. eruption: warehouse, recruiting depot.

No questions. Luke nodded.

They each have their way. Luke eyes two men over by the pool table then edges over to get into a game.

It was Regis' idea to take Luke along. The two of them, fresh booted and heading through the coffeehouses and parks. Regis toting *Stranger in a Strange Land*; Luke looking sideways up and down the streets.

Luke and Regis made an unlikely team. Regis had pretty well the same opinion of the army that Luke had, but unlike Luke, Regis wasn't there for any ulterior purpose. The only one of his family who had finished high school, Regis had been drafted three weeks prior to beginning his first class at university. It seemed to be the way things went, so Regis couldn't understand why Luke was always setting himself up. Everyone knew the army was fucked, and if you didn't know it now, you'd get a hint when they shipped you over. You'd get a hint when you learned about the Presidio 27.

"Yeah, but shit, man, it ain't just the army. What about the Convention? And Martin? And Bobby? And Peoples' Park and Mayor Fucking Daley?"

Luke just stared at Regis.

"Presidio," Luke said. "They were court-martialled for singing "America the Beautiful".

"So, ev'body's a music critic".

Luke had been invited to Regis' family home to share a little southern hospitality. Regis had a brother and a couple of sisters and a Mama who still sent him Bible quotes through the mail. His father had died during a drinking competition. "Technically, he won by default. Turns out th'other guy's drink was watered."

Luke had planned to get onto the campus. There would be someone he could contact there. As a Traveller, he had credibility underground. If anyone would still believe him, Luke's eyes now staring out of an army boy's face. They'd have to believe him.

"You...you just a shit-disturber, ain'tcha boy," Regis said imitating, or not imitating, a sneering good ol' boy.

Luke grinned. "Yeah, well I heard there was a lot of shit down here, you know?"

They had hitched rides for the past three hundred miles. Strange, the people who would, and would not, stop. The soldiers' clothes were casual, but the hair was a giveaway. The sunglasses helped, but the drill march gait didn't. Or did, depending on who you wanted to ride with.

"I hate them hippies," Regis spit after a painted van zoomed by and gave them the finger.

"Regis, what's a hippie?"

"Huh? You know, one of them long-hair types with all that jangly stuff all over them."

"Regis, they happen to hate the army."

"So?"

"So we're the army."

Which shut them both up. Luke couldn't believe he'd said it. The words sounded so...real. WE ARE THE ARMY. Regis, who was travelling a thousand miles to eat grits at his mother's table. Luke, who was hoping to infiltrate a couple of coffeehouses and convince people that he, Luke, was a fool to be in the army. Regis who wanted to see his sometime girlfriend

MaryBeth and engage in a little R&R: re-engage, retreat, re-engage, retreat. "She thinks it won't get her pregnant like that".

Luke was thinking about Val and the last time he'd seen her. She was too young. Her idealism was too...idealistic. And yet she was the one to cough out the big lines. "You're afraid to love. Okay, Luke. So you're some emotionally backwards BACKWOODS boy from Minnesota. Big Deal!"

And, indirectly, she reminded him that he was also young. It was an advantage, in a way. He had the energy; he had the mobility. "Sure, the young ones are always the best to sacrifice. Just like the army, babe." Libby. Who had not backed his idea of going into the army even though she agreed that he'd make more contacts there. Libby who had gone from walking with Luke to sleeping with him to brushing past him in the station. Well, not quite. But that was coming. Libby who knew Luke very well. Val who loved him and actually had the guts to say it.

"This is it! Man, there's no place like home!"

Luke followed Regis down the dusty path half expecting to see Aunty Em emerge from the house.

Luke sat in the bright kitchen scribbling a phone number with Regis' ma, Mrs. Lemay, watching as she picked up around him.

"Got a girl?" she asked pointing to the paper and nodding.

"No...uh, yeah," Luke said. "She's travelling right now. We're going to meet in a few days."

"That's nice. She from up there...up Minnesota way?"

Luke smiled. Mrs. Lemay was a nice mother in a kitchen.

"She's from Canada."

"Canada! Why that's right up there at the top of the world...how in the name of...how'd you meet her?"

Luke slipped the phone number back into his wallet.

Drying dishes with the protesting Mrs. Lemay, Luke felt as good as he could remember. The muscles in his neck, always taut and alert, loosened. He found the flowered plates and the green bowl for the dog, all of it, absolutely right.

"Mrs. Lemay...."

"You might as well call me Betty Lee on account of nobody's gonna know who you're talkin' to."

"Betty Lee...I want to thank you for taking in a stray."

At this her head jolted up from the sink. "Don't you ever go sayin' that again, you hear? When my Regis brings somebody home, that somebody is *Home*, you understand me?"

Luke found himself doing something he had never remembered learning. He reached down into the soapy water, took Betty Lee's hand and kissed it.

That night, out past the grove of fruit trees, near the pecan tree, Luke sat with Regis on the edge of an old wagon. Regis was going on about how big the place had seemed to him when he was a boy, how the sky would drop right down and tap him on the head until he looked up, when it would be forever out there and away.

He would have stayed longer if the army hadn't called him up. Now he figured that by the time he got out he'd have to work hard just to catch up. "G.I. Bill should pay for college, though, right?" And Luke said he thought it would, and Regis reminded him that he was the only one in his family who would be going.

"How 'bout you?"

Luke paused. He hadn't let himself think about Ray in a while now. Regis knew Luke had a brother over there but also that Luke seemed reluctant to talk about him.

"Yeah. Yeah, I'm the only one going, too. My brother...Ray...he works in the factory back home."

Regis said he couldn't believe there were factories that far north; then he hopped off the wagon and went to meet MaryBeth.

Luke stared out on a stretch of southern farmland. It was getting dark; soon the stars would appear. He had not been in touch with his mother in months. His father would be out at the cabins most days, or with a group out on the lake. His mother would be sitting in the kitchen with the radio on composing long letters to her son. Baking piles of cookies for her boy in the army.

Luke shook his head.

They were both in the army.

Ah, yes, but one was doing his noble duty and one was plotting to pull all the pins. Two boxes. Four dozen cinnamon-raisin cookies. She knows how to get one box all the way to Vietnam. But she does not know how to forward this red box to her son in America.

Sometimes it rose so suddenly it surprised him, and he found himself fighting to keep from calling out and leaping for the lake, crazy loon cries all the way to Minnesota.

No. Better this way with all of it still intact. Better the old man boasting two patriots in public and privately amazed that the odd duck commie had learned to fly straight after all. Better all the fish lined up in a row, the hooks dropping one at a time, plop, plop. To hook a fish on the backhand pull of a false cast, better that than to sit late deciphering messages left at dusty bus terminals, brothers' bodies indistinguishable in the rapid-fire night.

Ray, hunched over in the heat, which is also cold some way he can't understand, cold sweat freezing to his shirt, cold packed just like it was in the reeds, in the woods out by the cabins. A flash brightens the sky to the left and Ray crunches down further into himself. Just like the cabins, Ray, just like the woods. Come into the canoe, Ray, it's over at the edge of the landmass. Over there, Ray, look at it! Tipping in and waiting for you.

Another flash.
The earth blisters.
There. Hah! Missed.

Ray the canoe

Two small ones on either side of a drift of snow, strangers' hands reaching through, shovels clanging beneath the snow, blades, sticks, all the while the snow is falling, drifting, glaciers on manoeuver, retreating and advancing, absurdly dancing in the dark cold, in the bottomless cold.

Luke felt the sun going down, the cold moving along his arm. He watched the stars in the southern sky. They were so bright, so final. Luke breathed in and it was the air inside the saloon back home, the faces and all those silver dollars embedded in the bar, specimens moulded into the counter, put your arm on it, s'okay; just lean right up there, maybe some of that luck will rub off on ya....

No stars tonight, and it sounded like a prayer.

No stars tonight for Ray.

Luke had been in Advanced Infantry Training, and now he had received his overseas posting orders. It was nearly Christmas. He would be shipping out following the holiday. He had been granted the trip home for Christmas, one of those "see the folks, clear up any loose ends" visits.

He took one last look around the base. He had not done much here; that was a fact. There was too much to do, and every few days, from somewhere, the army was shipping troops out. And Luke with his papers and his names and his codes. What he did was never enough. Would never have been. Would never be. Enough.

He had not actively considered going over. His decision, as always, had been a means to an end. Like how many other decisions?

"It's not that simple!"

"Leave me alone."

"Luke, c'mere. You can't walk away like that!"

"Says who?"

And his brother's hurt face, eternally hurt over some small deviation in the shared corners of paradise, the two pairs of boots worn down in tandem. His brother played defence because that is what he saw—not the Pleistocene sheets that had nearly decapitated them rolling over other slabs of ice and engulfing their home. Just this, ice. Just ice.

Amazing.

He stopped at the first hunting and camping supply store and bought a plaid jacket and a cap.

"That it, soldier?"

Luke did a double-take. "Uh, yeah...thanks, that'll do."

This one was partial to soldiers. He wouldn't necessarily get this reception elsewhere.

He hadn't been gone that long, but it felt like it. Things looked different: trees were bare; the firs stood out; the chip wrappers shone through the dusty grounders under apple trees.

He drove to the prearranged spot. Luke was, of course, no longer welcome at the house.

"Can't make it too easy for them, can we?"

Luke sat in the restaurant with a bowl of chili. A painted Mexican sun bled down the wall. Val and Libby entered to the sound of the Chipmunks singing about hula-hoops.

She seemed thinner. How could that be?

"She's been sick," Libby intoned. "I warned you."

Val seemed to want to tan under the unreal sun, to hang around the kitchen entrance, or, at least, to stay as far away as possible from Luke.

He stood up, realizing that he must look different, too. He pulled off the watch-cap to reveal his bristled hair. Libby let out a shriek. This was funny. Ray would have something to say about this.

Val approached slowly, looking at his hair.

"The closer she gets...."

Ray's voice.

"The better you look!"

When he held her, she felt like a stick figure under the bulky coat. She said nothing other than to excuse herself to the washroom.

Libby sat down opposite Luke. "She's still sick a lot," Libby said. "And scared." She reached out and felt his hair with the palm of her hand. "What are you gonna do, Luke?"

He didn't need the question.

"You've sent a lot of people the last couple of years; why not take a ride on the train yourself? You know, Easy Rider of the North.... Look, Luke, I can't babysit her forever. Besides, she's thinking about heading home. You want that? Then you'd only have me again."

Luke remembered Libby, making love with Libby. Her red hair and her breasts like raspberries, not strawberries as he had imagined, and the surprising strength in her legs wrapped around him.

She must have remembered, too, because she leaned forward across the table and they kissed. He remembered her scent.

"That's for luck. You take care of her, okay? Oh, and...I never saw you. None of this took place."

And Libby, and two years of Luke's life, walked out the door.

None of this took place.

Luke could see the comic side of it. Ray would have, anyway. The call to his parents with "I'll be home for Christmas" playing in the background. The hurried plans and his final "I'll be bringing a friend" lost in his mother's baking litany. Further amusement was, of course, imminent. He hadn't talked to his parents since he went in, and while they had been notified that he was in the army, they didn't know why he was there. And now he would appear—without hair and with a girlfriend.

Val was recovering from a cold and was not very communicative. She was still upset with Luke. The fact was she had only ever said it once, "don't we mean anything?" spoken into a rice salad. That was before he had decided to be inducted. No wonder she hadn't told him.

"When do you think it was?" he asked handing her the bottle of ginger ale.

"Woodstock," she said, and closed her eyes.

Warroad was white, snow stacked along the sides of the road, the tracks clear and the headlight of a train in the distance when Luke drove through town. And silent, the train whistle stifled in the cold air, a single cry and then the toboggan-drop back into silence.

Val was asleep, but even if she had been talking Luke would not have heard. He was distracted by the surface. Not just the surface of the road, which was slick, but the way the scenery had been propped up, pine trees with fold-here tabs, a car stuck by the side of the road, the *Red Owl* supermarket surreal against the edges of his eyes. And, most strange of all, the

Memorial Arena, a semi-circle curved in space, hard and stiff and flat against the sky. Luke slowed the car near the arena resisting the urge to get out and walk around the building if only to confirm that it *had* an around. Then he woke Val and drove on to the house.

What followed could have been written by Ray in one of his "meanwhile back at the ranch" letters. The preparations had, indeed, been made for the return of the prodigal son. The tree was tall and slender the way that Luke preferred. His mother had emptied the local stores of baking supplies and had made four different kinds of seasonal cake, each to be devoured "depending on your mood." His father had exercised the supreme restraint of not reaching over and yanking off Luke's hat, waiting patiently until Luke finally removed it before dinner. And neither parent had said anything to Val.

Oh, they spoke to her politely, asked her where she was from.

"Canada!" Luke's mother said with the impressed tone one reserved for the truly absurd.

"Up there?" Luke's father said.

Up there.

They ignored, or tried to, her long beaded dress and the complexion too-pale for a healthy girl from the north. And they did not once stare when she wrapped her arm around Luke's waist even though they had never seen any other woman so casually do this.

There were errors, of course. Ray would have been toting them up. The first, the mention of Ray in the service.

"He's a point-man! Just like he is on the team!" boomed Eric Anderson.

There was the sit-down dinner and the holiday inquiry "Light or dark?" which elicited an "I don't eat meat" from Val and a wringing of hands from Luke's mother.

There was the observation post at the edge of the kitchen with the decoy radio atop the refrigerator.

"They're watching us," Val muttered to Luke, and looked back to see Rose changing the station again.

There was the way the news of the pregnancy broke: no labour, no pain as Val said it while declining the alcoholic sauce that went with the Christmas pudding.

"Have to think of the baby," she patted her stomach.

And Rose and Eric Anderson looking at one another and saying things like: "Oh look, dear, she's going to have a baby!" and "Oh, how about that; our son has gotten this girl pregnant (if it's his), and we're going to have a little bastard for a grandchild."

Val was tired and went up to Ray's bedroom to rest.

Ray would have said something about that. Actually, he wouldn't have. Unlike the rest of the family, Ray knew when to keep his mouth shut.

Luke listened to another hour of how the army was supposed to be making a man of him, and, while he had obviously proved that in the battlefield of the bedroom, he had responsibilities, and was he going to make an honest woman of her? And was she the most honest woman he knew, anyway? And Eric having too much to drink, and the Mormon Tabernacle Choir squashed into the little radio on top of the fridge, and Ray's handmade cotton-batting snowman hanging from a branch on the tree, and Luke's, which hadn't held up as well, on a branch lower down, "Remember? From when you weren't taller than Ray?" And his mother hoping, squeezing her arms together and hoping, and Ray's Christmas letter on the mantel, just read it, go ahead, Luke! And Luke, unfolding and listening to his brother's voice once more, a voice that was talking sometime before Christmas, somewhere, filling their heads with all of his talk. *Go support the team, Dad, they need you.* And to his mother: could you *please send a picture from home*?

Tell Luke, he said.

The tree shimmering in the firelight.

Tell Luke I'm going to haunt him with the Ghost of Christmas Yet To Come.

What?

Take care.

New socks. New Years.

Take Good Care.

Luke pulled on the scarf at his mother's insistence, and she gave him a hug, there, on the stairs.

"I'm so glad you came home," she whispered. "It's almost the same, isn't it?"

Luke held his mother and breathed into the sparkles on her Christmas dress.

"Sure, Mom. Sure it is."

He stepped out into the night. He hoped Val was asleep. He hoped his parents were okay about all this. He walked over snow drifts on the side of the road. He decided to walk along the tracks.

He was going to be haunted by the Ghost of Christmas Future? How had Ray known he'd be home? Of course, he hadn't. It was something to write in a letter.

Luke found himself walking toward Lake Street in the direction of the Silver Dollar Saloon. He knew it wouldn't be open at this hour, on this day. And a thought hit him: this was Ray's town. It always had been. Ray grew up in it and loved it and told its stories. It was a simple familiarity. Is that all it took? Somewhere out there in the Indian Cemetery, old KaKaGeeSick was buried in a blue suit instead of buckskin. Perhaps it matched the blue tattoo marks on his forehead. His frozen ancient body going blue-white in the cold, Pleistocene blue like the everlasting sky that was his name, blue like the veins that protrude with the years, like the tips of things that are nearly, not quite, perished.

"Luke!"

The voice shook him. He turned. He knew the face.

"Willie. Willie Olson, what the hell are you doing here?"

Willie Olson, back from a tour of duty, preparing to re-up after the holidays. Willie Gung-Ho Olson with whom Luke had lost all contact. Who would not be speaking to Luke right now if he knew where the lines were drawn.

"My mother heard you were in."

"We just got in last night!"

"No, I mean in the army. News travels fast."

At the drugstore, no doubt.

"The Dollar open?"

Luke shook his head.

"Why you standing out here, then?"

They walked down the street together, Luke and Willie, pausing before store windows and shaking their heads. Luke knew that he couldn't afford to talk to Willie, yet the man didn't seem to mind the silence. It was just a bit like it used to be when they were fishing and concentrating on the lapping sound against the rocks.

"I saw Ray."

Luke stopped, muffled in his mother's scarf.

"You heard me, I saw Ray. Before I shipped back. Scared the shit out of me."

"Is he okay? Willie, is he all right?"

Willie walking on ahead.

"*Damn you!*" Luke whirled him.

"Whoa...okay, Luke! He's okay...he was when I saw him. He's seen a lot of action. Been out on point duty a lot, and in hot areas. There's...you know...not a big longevity thing there, and yet he's doing real good, you know?"

Ray clobbering Viet Cong with the butt of his hockey stick, poke check, hook check, body check. Body....

"Listen...I got something to do here. Ray, he didn't know if I'd see you. I told him probably not; I mean, we know you don't come home for Christmas. But he made me take it all the same. That is, he made me swear I'd get it to you somehow. So you just made the job easy."

"What are you talking about?"

"I got it at home. You'll have to come and pick it up. My mother'd like to see you anyway, now that you're in...."

Luke was going to strangle this walking stuttering bag of....

"It's his combat pay. Actually, it's money he's been paid back on loans from his combat pay. He's been saving it up."

"So, what do I want with his combat pay?"

"Hey, I don't know! Look, you're the brother! He wouldn't tell me. Fuck, I only saw the guy for ten minutes! He...he had it in cash and it's from his combat pay and he said it's for you and you'd know what to do with it."

"How much money are we talking about?"

"Three hundred dollars."

Luke heard something click in his ear. "Willie, do you know if Ray got my letter, the one about me going into the army?"

"You bet. He told me before I could tell him. Anyway, would you come back with me? I want to get this over with."

They walked to Willie's where Luke greeted the family and waited for Willie to come down with the envelope. Luke could not endure the suspense and tore it open there. There was no letter.

"No time, I guess. It was kind of spur of the moment, you know? He just shoved it at me."

They parted with the usual words, and Luke walked back along Lake Street the way he had come. Goodbyes were getting easier. He wouldn't feel a thing.

Three hundred dollars. Three hundred. How did his brother know?

Three hundred dollars would ease an immigrant over the border.
The magic number.

Seed money. Start-up. In Canada.

He stood outside the Memorial Arena now huge against the late December sky. He stood with no letter in his hand, with no phone receiver at his ear. He tried not to notice the blue uneven light, to imagine the stone eagle on the wall of the school, its beak hooked in ice. He debated making a snow angel, but instead just stood there in the dark and wished the bells were ringing at the church down the road.

PART 2

LICHEN

*P*ink light. A church window and light frosted, stained, a strand of air dyed pink and pale, stretching from the window across the length of the body.

Cold light. It is not just the frost at the window; it is the light itself, glowing luminescent like the remains of a Roman pot unearthed on a chill October morning in Cologne.

Luke opened both eyes now. The light had found him on the floor in his sleeping bag; a movie projector was threading a light into the room, and he was the projection. A naked man lying in a sleeping bag. He sat up, and the light fell across his chest, caught the detail of each hair. But it did not warm.

It must be early. He should probably let Val sleep. Honey and Clyde had been good enough to let Val take their son Jason's room, as she had been exhausted when they'd arrived.

Honey and Clyde. He'd almost laughed.

Deciding he could afford to lie there a while longer, Luke continued to watch the Canadian winter sky. It must be a northern light, he told himself, although he knew that Warroad was north as well. Mornings in Warroad were like this if you got up early enough. Luke had always been an early riser, but he rarely was up before his mother, whom he would spot out in her flowerbed or sitting on the porch. Sometimes he headed down to the lake, but he always felt she knew that he had seen her and that they had noticed, together, the early light.

Val had grown up looking at city morning light which was filtered through wires and poles and the windows of other buildings, other peoples' glances, coffee and bacon-scented air.

Her parents' house. He did not want to have to deal with her parents and had told her as much. It sounded cruel, even to Luke, but there was nothing he could say to those people any more than he could explain anything to his own parents. It had all happened so fast...even though its causes had not.

It had come about after a few years of causes, hadn't it? A couple of years of holding the lighter while the young kid burns his card, both of them watching the boy's history and his future curling in the ashtray. A few too many mysterious phone calls, odd messages left at diners and laundromats. And a couple too many hours abed with their daughter to deny or explain what was happening.

Maybe he could just follow this strange religious light and wander after it in a silent pink procession.

"Hi."

Luke twisted around. A small boy in cowboy pajamas stood over him, one hand dragging an enormous blue elephant by the trunk.

"Hi...you're Jason, right?"

"Uh-huh. Who are you?"

"I'm Luke."

"You came last night."

"That's right."

"I know because my mommy took me out of my bed and put me in their room in my old baby bed from before."

"I know."

"You gonna live here now?"

Luke smiled. "No. We're just staying here for a couple of days until we find our own place. What's your elephant's name?"

"Reginald. But I call him Stuffing because of the hole. You wanna watch cartoons?"

Here was the reason for the early morning hospitality on the part of his pint-sized host. Luke was lying lengthwise between the coffee table and the television.

"Yeah, okay. But first, take a look at that light over there on the table leg. You know where it's coming from?"

"The window."

"No, I mean, follow it with your eyes and your finger until you discover exactly where it comes from."

The boy let go of Stuffing's trunk and solemnly traced the path of light.

"It ends...over...there!" he pointed up to the left corner of the window.

"Right!"

"Can I turn on the T.V. now? It's *Roadrunner*."

Luke shifted, unzipping his sleeping bag. "Yeah, go ahead. Wait, just let me get some clothes on, here."

Luke stepped into his underwear.

"I see your bum."

Bum. Luke paused. This must be Canada.

When Luke and Val left Warroad they were ostensibly on their way back to the base. Luke had not informed his parents that he was slated for Vietnam feeling it would be impossible to explain any subsequent actions. So Luke and Val climbed into the car while Rose and Eric stood on their porch waving, and Luke saw them like that, framed by the porch, lit with a yellow bug light.

That's what Luke thought of as he backed the car out onto the road, how his father hadn't changed the bug light even though it was winter.

The car sputtered. An old boot of a car Val had bought for $150 on her last trip to Canada. She had felt the group could use a new vehicle and had actually thought the Canadian plates might be less of a distraction. Luke turned to Val, but she was bundled into herself. Or her baby. He tapped his fingers against the cold steering wheel and blinked the headlights for goodbye.

Val had called ahead and made arrangements with a couple who would put the two of them up for a few days.

"Straight?" Luke demanded, realizing how paranoid he was becoming.

"No...they know. And they said you better remember the point system at the border." Which had been working against people the previous year. Ever since the leaked MacEachen memo, which had left it to the discretion of immigration officials whether to let a deserter in as a visitor or as an immigrant, there had been a game of wits at the crossings. There were favoured officials, and hated ones, and the information came down the line. Since May, things had eased up thanks, mostly, to NDP pressure. Now Luke would not officially be discriminated against providing he met the immigration criteria. There were still the points.

"Why am I thinking of *The Sound of Music*?" Val asked.

"What?"

She pulled her head up from her chest. "You know, that line of little kids singing 'Goodbye, goodbye, goodbye...' until there's only Julie and von Trapp left and there isn't a dry eye in the place."

"I don't know. Why?"

"I don't *know*! Probably because...."

"Because you and I have the luck of picking the worst moments to describe our worst moments."

She looked at him, and, for the first time in days, smiled.

POTENTIAL POINTS

Education:	20
Occupational Demand:	20
Age:	20
Skill:	10
Language:	10
Relatives:	5
Destination:	5
Personal Quality	15
	100 points

"You have to score at least 50."

"Well, I have the language. *Skill?*"

"Pain in the ass," Val said.

"*Relatives?*"

"Mine."

"Great. *Occupational Demand?*"

"Anyone who's looking for a pain in the ass, I guess, in which case," she added, "you're taken."

"*Destination?*"

A sore point. For although Luke did not want the intrusion of Val's parents, Luke had wanted Montreal because of the political activity there. And although Val had emotional ties to her family, particularly to her brother Freddy, she wanted somewhere else, some place with no questions and no guilt trip. Some place safe and quiet for the baby. "There's too much going on in Montreal. I don't have a good feeling about the French situation."

"At least there is a situation! At least the French are standing up and being counted."

"Yeah, well, I don't want it to be a question of who counts and who doesn't. I don't want to stand up. And I don't want to be counted. I want to go somewhere where this," she patted her stomach, "child can get a break."

Destination: Ottawa.

Ottawa had been good to the dodgers, as had Toronto, Montreal and elsewhere. But Ottawa had been particularly good to deserters, a distinction Luke believed might be useful. Ironic, Ottawa, the front yard of the nation, deserters sprawled about the city, marching in sandals past monuments and MPs.

"*Personal Quality?*" he asked.

"You wish...."

It had been cold, and the defroster wasn't working right, so Val had had to keep leaning over to scrape Luke's window. There were two cars in front of them. Luke flicked on the radio. The Byrds.

"Hey, turn it up."

They sat, close-windowed, listening to "The Ballad of Easy Rider."

The officer glanced down at the Canadian plates.

"Anything to declare?"

Luke was not prepared for this strange goodbye and hello.

"I'm...I'm American...."

Val took over. "I'm Canadian. This is my car...."

"Lucky," the customs official said.

Val glanced at Luke. "I'm heading back home with my friend here."

The officer turned to Luke. "Identification?"

Luke handed him his driver's license.

"Luke Anderson. What makes you want to visit Canada in the middle of winter?"

"We're...."

"I asked *him*, lady."

"My girlfriend's parents live in Montreal."

"How long are you planning on staying?"

"I don't know. 'Til they throw us out."

Wrong. Val nudged Luke.

"Sir....Actually, I'm thinking of immigrating to Canada. My girlfriend misses her Canadian home—you know, blue skies, clear water...."

"You see any blue skies in the vicinity, Mr. Anderson?"

Fifteen points for personal quality based on the border interview.

And all the rest of it.

Education, Language, Age, Skill. And the other law that made the world go 'round: how much money you got, kid?

Luke carried Ray's $300 in a passport pouch inside his shirt, a precaution probably unnecessary up here in Canada.

Perhaps it was the Holiday Season, or the odd pains Val began having during the interview, pains that felt, she guessed, exactly like those of a child kicking—only wasn't it too early?—the thumps punctuating the officer's questions.

"What's wrong with the little lady?"

She smiled for the officer. "I'm pregnant. I'm not feeling up to par. You know how it is."

Perhaps he did know how it was. Perhaps the Season of Goodwill, or the quick check of the tiger-eye ring on the wrong finger and the officer with a daughter around the same age.

The interview improved.

While there was no great camaraderie shown to the deserter and his pregnant girlfriend—chick, babe—the officer did not comment on politics or morality. Val looked over at Luke and they both looked at the officer.

Maybe all he wanted was to have a Jimmy Stewart Christmas. But Val and Luke were in the car and the engine sputtered and she saw a hand wave them by. The hand looked like the one that waved from atop Santa's float in the parade. She remembered standing on St. Catherine's Street with Mrs. Molloy, her baby-sitter, waiting for that wave. St. Catherine's with Santa Claus. Montreal with bombs and separatists. Canada with border guards.

They ate a quiet breakfast of bread, cheese, yogurt and dried fruit; washed it down with tea; and set out. Over the next few days, Luke was gone most of the time meeting contacts and being greeted by people who had merely been names to him before. He went to the house on Eddy Street, over in Hull, and spoke with Christian about the situation in Ottawa. And, in between his meetings, he tried to find a place to live.

"Alex says we could rent his basement for a while," he said, and saw the look on Val's face.

"Look, we'll probably have to share...."

Why was she being so difficult? She'd been living in group homes ever since she left Canada.

"What do you want to do?"

She looked up at him and seemed so young he didn't know what to do with her. But that wasn't quite right, was it , Luke? He had managed to get her pregnant despite her use of contraceptives. He had managed to get her involved in this half-life existence he had to live. She looked up at him like it was just an oversight that he hadn't found them anywhere to live. When it was her country!

"Luke?"

Little Jason pushed past him to the television.

"Wanna watch cartoons with me?"

They found an upstairs flat on Percale Street. Val was surprised at how few flats were available in Ottawa. She told Luke Montreal was full of them. Most people she knew, students, couples, lived in them. Theirs was not a big place, but it had a kitchen with a fire escape—"They've heard of my cooking"— and a living room which was connected to a bedroom by a long hallway. They had arranged the rental through a contact who had had to vouch for Luke.

"In Montreal, the staircase up would be on the outside."

"What?" Luke was emptying a box in the other room.

"Never mind. Well...here we are."

They looked around. Ice frosted the window on the fire escape door. Grimy ribbons along the radiator.

"Here goes nothing," Luke said and turned the knob.

Groaning, clanking, ping pinging, and then a whoosh and then another groan.

"This is gonna be fun...."

At some point, he knew, his parents would have been contacted. When the AWOL was noted? When the AWOL was clearly desertion? It would be brutal for his mother. His father, Luke knew, would hold forth with his answers. How he had always known Luke was no good, how Ray alone was his son now, how Luke's mother had been such a fool, such a damn fool—rising to his full height and singling her out when there was only her standing there—to believe that this bum had ever done anything worthy of their approval.

His mother? Well, this time she would be speechless. This time he would have his diatribe unchallenged, as she shook her head slowly like it was just something unclear, as if once the facts were known all would be understood, and her sons both heroes, and her sons reunited and their wives and children visiting.

Dusting. She would move the cloth along the mantelpiece, carefully picking up Ray in his hockey uniform, Ray in his soldier uniform, Luke and Ray beside the canoes. Dust, dust everywhere, blowing in from God knows where, maybe from the seaplane landing, or floating down from Canada, glacial dust tingling the air as it moves past, going north, heading north.

They set up the mattress, and Val put a blanket over the window.

"We'll need to get more stuff," she remarked, and Luke hoped she wouldn't elaborate, not tonight.

"I could go home, I suppose, and...."

"I thought we decided you weren't going back there for a handout!"

"It's not a handout! It's my stuff; Freddy could bring it if you didn't want me going to see my own goddamn parents."

Brother Freddy. Mysterioso Teahead Freddy.

Luke knew he was partly to blame for this. He had even suggested Montreal at first. That would have been even worse. They probably should have settled out West.

"We'll talk about this later, okay? Tonight.... Tonight, all I want to do is...well, then there's...."

"Welcome home," Val embraced him, and they moved down to the mattress. The radiator pinged; they made love inside a pinball machine.

She slept, breathing easily, beside him. She was sleeping more these days, or so he thought having never spent so much time with her before. The pregnancy was still unreal to him, and he wondered whether she understood what was going on either. It was like making all the moves on spec with no sure footing. It was like rock climbing. Not that Luke had had much experience with that. But he used to listen when Ray described his adventures out with Nolan Hartley. Nolan took vacations around rock climbing ventures and travelled across the country to do it. And Ray had gone with him twice and found himself to be a natural. Ray was built for climbing—a compact body, good coordination, strong arms and solid legs.

"You have to read the surface," he said, with a glint of the excitement still in his eyes. "Balance climbing, nothing like it." No ropes at first, Nolan going up and securing then belaying Ray from there.

"Three-point contact, Ray!" Nolan would yell. Three points. One limb free to continue the climb. A push on rock. Now a pull hold.

"Nothing, *nothing* like it, man. Where's your next move, read the rock face, an indentation? a lip? a fingernail hold? Traversing, Luke, sideways up a sheer face of rock!"

"Where's your next move?"

Luke listened to Val's breathing, then to the radiator which he would have to bleed in the morning, then to the tinny rattling of the old, old stars.

And then it was Ray climbing a glacier, ice climbing so different, he supposed, and yet Ray climbed it as if it were rock without regard for the shifting ice and the drops, grinning back at Luke; hey man, get a load of this! His cries sounding far off echoes of avalanches. Luke watching. What is he *doing* there? Is he a member of the team? Ray free-climbing on ice, what a fool, and the dry ice smokes, looks like a rock concert. Ray, Ray! Disappearing up into the smoke, far out, man, you should see the view, and higher....

"Ray!"

Val shook awake beside him and abruptly sat up.

"What?"

Luke's eyes searching the dark room left and right.

"What? You all right?" her voice was half concern, half annoyance.

"Yeah....uh. Sorry...."

"Right...."

"I had a dream."

"I gathered that," she let out a long sigh and stretched and turned over. "Your brother."

"Yeah."

Jesus.

He had no hope of sleeping, so he got up and made himself an instant coffee in the dark, spilling hot water all over the sideboard and wiping it up with a sweatshirt sleeve.

Snow pellets swirled, hitting the kitchen-door window and almost sizzling there, he thought, almost like a sizzling sound, like clothes in the rinse cycle in laundromats across the country, well, across *his* country. He didn't know about Canada.

Luke dressed quietly, slipping into his pants and jacket. He grabbed his watch-cap and the scarf his mother had given him and closed the door. The boots were cold. He would have to remember to bring them inside instead of leaving them on the stairs. The outside door made a gritty sound as he opened it; he pushed it and toppled a small snow drift that was forming on the porch.

Canada.

The new Land of the Free.

Cold, though. And salty. Stalagmites up the sides of his boots.

He wrapped the scarf around his face and turned left up the street. *AWOL* on an Ottawa street. National disgrace on a late night stroll. He was a lot worse than *AWOL* now. How was he supposed to feel? Cold. He was cold.

Where Ray was it would be steaming. Luke wished he could send Ray a handful of snow pellets, or better yet, a snowball right between the shoulder blades. Heads up, Ray! Snow disappearing into the hot night air.

There was a deserted school yard up ahead. Luke stepped through the drift and into the yard. There, a naked basketball hoop ringed with a halo of snowy light, the bricks on the wall swept with snow. Luke leaned up against the wall to get out of the wind, *AWOL* at the wall.

Hah.

And then it happened. From the middle distance, behind the snow pile at the fence, a man appeared. Luke stood rivetted. His history in the movement had made him watch for detail, and his feet were already poised.

The figure walked slowly, hands out of sight. Luke didn't know what this scene meant in Canada, but in Chicago, or New York, it meant trouble.

Luke had size on the man, but it was hard to tell anything else, except that the man did not appear to be too bundled up. Luke began to wonder about those hearty Canadians taking 2 a.m. strolls in their pyjamas.

And then the man was in the light.

Moonlight glances off a shoulder, the overhead playground lights dance across the chest, and some other light, not identified... and it is....

"Ray...?"

Movement that is neither graceful nor clumsy, steady purposeful steps.

He is dressed in a shirt and tie. Civilian. He is wearing a white shirt and a dark tie, the left hand is not waving.

"Ray...?"

Real as to touch, and if he does his shadow will fall across that light. So he does not move, watches until it passes across the yard and beyond the far edge at which point he wants to scream out to it to hold it still.

She would not want to hear about it. She simply glanced at him, propped up at the kitchen table with his coffee, and brushed past him to the bathroom. Maybe he dreamed it. He might have, walking around in a cold half-sleep. It wasn't impossible that he just had that old thing between a dream and a vision—some mild drug-induced visitation. It was possible. But, either way, she wouldn't want to hear it.

She had never come right out and said it, but Val didn't like Ray; that is, she didn't like his presence, or absence, the way he crept into their conversations and their lives. It had happened just the other day when they were talking about the baby. Val had said she wanted Luke to meet Freddy so that Freddy could be the godfather when the child was born. Luke had absentmindedly muttered something or other and then she exploded. He couldn't believe the anger. "Your goddamned brother is good enough to be spoken of in hushed whispers, but mine doesn't even rate, eh? Shit!" And a door slammed in the home of the new neighbours on Percale Street.

Val.

Who was she? Could she be as sure about all this as she seemed? Sometimes she was like his own heartbeat to him, it was infinitely strange, this grafted-on feeling. Like they shared their actual senses. Other times she would turn to look at him, and he was embarrassingly aware of the loneliness in the room, this curious stranger smiling his way, ignoring his pot of coffee for her metal box of herbal tea.

"Sightseeing?" she said too casually.

And Luke, who had experienced the visitation, agreed.

Val spent a lot of time waiting for it to warm up. She told Luke she had done this for most of her life.

"Not an outdoorsy type, I take it?"

She admitted she had liked the usual winter fun: skating, tobogganing. But she had had frostbite on one ear and two fingers, and she knew that the weather didn't play games.

"Of course, I never used to wear a hat."

"Why not?"

"I thought they didn't suit me."

"And frostbite did?"

Val smiled ruefully and shifted her weight on the sofa.

Could this all be as strange for her as it was for him? At least she was in her own country, a couple of hundred miles from her hometown if she felt the urge. At least she was used to sitting around in the winter instead of ice climbing, hiking and tracking.

Luke looked over at Val who had closed her eyes. There was this baby. Totally bizarre. There was this child of theirs growing in her.

Luke knew about frostbite, and being trapped in a whiteout. Blue-green glaciers, glaciers with lights refracted in panels, mirrors of light, long diamond panels of light. And quick cold dusted his face.

Then it was May. It was to have been hopeful. Luke had a part-time job, and as soon as it warmed up he'd be working full-time. Outdoor landscaping, mowing, weeding. All of the boyhood jobs from home. Luke had tried not to think about home. A couple of letters had arrived during the winter, and Luke read them and felt his mother's anguish. And felt as well the extra burden she had to endure, the anger of his father.

Son:
Your father and I.... I want to say....

They were brave attempts. Luke knew how brave, sitting up in the kitchen at night, the lake black, mysterious, encroaching on her porch. She had talked to him like that once, stumbled forward with her load of dreams and fears.

"That's why I never dressed you up as Indians."

"I thought it was out of respect for old KaKaGeeSick."

"...I didn't want to look out this window and see you and Ray in feathers or buckskin, dashing between the trees. I...was afraid. I was scared I wouldn't know what time it was."

"*GOOD MORNING. IT'S SEVEN-THIRTY!*" the radio sang.

And Luke had understood. And she thanked him with the pressure of her hand on his shoulder as if she were ashamed of this tiny little fear of time, this lifeboat of chronology.

Mother.

What could he say? If it was just her and not The Voice of Judgement as well, could he explain?

I don't expect Dad to....

In her letters she said that she hadn't heard from Ray in a while. Surely this was the supreme torture. To send her boys out into the world and to receive nothing, no reminder that they had ever existed. Had she invented them? There, on the mantel, the two of them soaked and sandy from the lake, dangling their fish for memory's inspection. Had she made them up?

Luke loosened the earth around a juniper bush and wiped his forehead with the back of his sleeve. From his vantage point he could look out onto the Ottawa River, the old lifeline, old artery. Slip a canoe in the river, slip a canoe in the river and paddle away.

He had walked into the apartment to find Val glued to the radio.

"What's up?"

Her face sent waves of pain.

"Nixon. He's sending troops into Cambodia."

And now the cry. Now at last, from the nondescript and the uninvolved came the cry. The animal beaten, sat on, made to carry packs and drag carts, and now, nose flared, comes the unbelieving wail.

In the universities—demonstrations and clashes. The President tells protesting students they are a bunch of bums. American bums, worthless, not bared Canadian buttocks. And Luke is following Kent State especially because it is one of the contacts he had, because Libby was from there, and could be there again.

A war observer from a neutral zone? An astronaut watching the planet from space?

What was he doing here?

Each day of that weekend they followed the Kent State demonstration. The burning of the ROTC building, the easing off, the tightening up. Then on Monday. Then he is looking at Val as she stands by the radio.

"They shot...they kill...."

He grabs her and she falls into him.

"They arrived and they fired right into the crowd and they killed four people. At least four. They did it, Luke. They fired on us."

He had gotten out. He had escaped only to become a not-so-innocent bystander. He understood, now, how Val had felt when she left Canada "to be where it was happening." He was standing here in the country of bystanders watching his country implode. Like a sudden vacuum, his country had sucked in these four. No wonder the Weathermen blew themselves up making explosives in Greenwich Village. Even an explosion counteracted the void. No wonder Libby had asked Luke not to ask anymore. Questions were the enemy now, and that was most dangerous of all. But understandable. Hopeless and soulless and understandable.

Over the next few days he read the accounts of the killings on Blanket Hill. Kent State was not a Chicago street; it wasn't a Berkeley or a Columbia. It was nice little Kent State. And Luke knew that part of his job would have been to meet with the people who would have fired up this group, talked to and coached the movers of that swaying crowd of young, young bodies, until.... Alison and Jeff and Bill and Sandy fall down once and forever.

One, two, three, four!
We don't want your fucking war!
Whose war? Whose war did they mean?

Two, four, six, eight!
We won't live in a fascist state!
And so you will not live at all.

Luke, who had been a Traveller, even at the time knowing he could not do it wholeheartedly, watching the Regional Travellers and knowing how they worked, not wanting, himself, to fire up a crowd only to disappear into it the moment the police arrived, not wanting to come onto some kid's campus and tell him what to do. When he went, the information he gave was good; the opinions he offered the draft-aged were real. But when he was expected to tell the boy, the teenaged girl, to run up against a cop in riot gear or to take a baton across the back, he had declined, taking the blow himself. Luke's bruises from Chicago had lasted for months. And even now his right shin bothered him whenever he worked too long outdoors.

But it had never hit home quite like this, the actions and their consequences. Before, Luke's covert jobs had resulted in a smiling, relieved face at a truck stop, a new identity invented on the way to the border. False papers. Improper IDs of Promise.

These four, wandering around on the campus. A student's head blown apart, his face bleeding into the pavement, his records in the admin building, marks, essays in files somewhere, his name in the system that was Kent State University, his lost face in the pavement of the country that was America.

An anguished father across the radio waves of America, his daughter taken forever from him. "She resented being called a bum because she disagreed with someone else's opinions."

Luke, the Traveller, on the street outside the Canadian Parliament. A young, scrawny man complains to the sky; a young woman screams at the walls of the American Embassy, the American flag waving proudly across the street from the Canadian Parliament. Canadians with their military equipment that will go to Vietnam, not-so-innocent bystanders.

And Luke, who knows how to organize some of these people, moves around past the embassy and Parliament and is heading over to the river. River's rising. Water moving faster in the warming climate; trees in bloom, in heat, in verdant rapture.

Weathermen. Dylan's volley.

Weather. Men. And the wind.

—ɯ—

It wasn't so bad. It was not going so bad she thought. Luke had found a job through some contacts, and they had a few friends: Ronnie, Celia and Dan. Or, she did. Luke spent time with them, too, of course, but he was forever heading back to the temporary houses to meet the new arrivals. Which was okay, too; Val wasn't complaining. But it seemed to her that if you wanted to settle in a new place, you should make a real effort to adapt to that place. All of this hanging on...but he wasn't keeping in touch with his old life per se, was he? He hadn't even finished a letter to his mother yet, and Val was due any day. She had reminded Luke that his mother was probably frantic.

So—what—she was pushing him toward his old life and pulling him away at the same time? What was wrong with her? Aside from weighing 4000 pounds. Was she ugly, or supremely beautiful? Or were they the same thing when you felt this weird?

Her trip home had gone better than expected. Perhaps because she had expected the worst and was slightly surprised at her parents' response. Maybe because Freddy had run interference for her. She had intended not to go home until after the baby was born, but one late winter storm saw her trapped in the flat re-reading an old copy of Time magazine. Luke was at a meeting, and the radio was on, and Sly was singing "Hot Fun in the Summertime", and Val was overtaken by a powerful desire to walk familiar streets with friends, tramp around record stores, have a hot chocolate up on the mountain. She wouldn't, of course, do any of these things, but for that moment she forgot she was pregnant, and with Luke, and here, and before she knew it, she had called her home number. Fortunately, Freddy answered.

It was nice. It was so nice that he was growing up alright. They had had nothing in common for so many years and then, wham, he slapped himself awake, and they could talk.

He warned her of the press she was getting within the family.

"Black ewe, babe."

And of the lectures and etcetera that would occur if she came home.

Of course he hadn't known that she was not coming back to stay, or about the pregnancy, or Luke. She hadn't seen any point in telling him in advance.

She arrived in Central Station with her big coat and a brocade bag. And it was amazing. It was a sudden shock to see herself reflected in a long shiny shop window for she had become...a voyager. All those times as a young teenager when she had traversed Central Station on the way through to St. Catherine's Street or Dorchester, there they had all been. Longish hair, canvas jackets and jeans or flowered dresses and sandals. And they sat on the ground whenever they waited for trains, sat anywhere, in a corner, one and then another of them, flopping down, and the boys fell around them and they held a campfire without the fire. It was the knapsacks and the cloth bags that she always remembered. And she thought of them, romantically she realized, as voyagers, her Anglicized mental picture of the old Quebec *voyageurs*. And weren't they? Val looked again into the Cantor's Bakery window. And wasn't she?

Years later, perhaps, she'd remember the startled look on her mother's face and be able to place it. It was unlike anything she had ever seen, and yet it reminded her of something, standing in her sandals and socks, her cloth bag by her side, carpetbagger in front of her own home. Her own....

"Hi, Mom."

Eyes terrible in abject...something.

She is ushered into the front hall like the beggar who came that time at Christmas, who sat at a card table in the front hall and ate a full Christmas dinner by himself, the noise of the family in the dining room, the clatter and the chatter as he folded his napkin and departed in silence.

"Valerie."

Sadness? Absence?

"Oh, Valerie."

There is almost a hug. The baby getting in the way so that her mother must hug her around the neck, off to one side, and Val catches the sound of the stifled cry as her mother's lips brush past her ear.

Her father wanted all the facts: who the lout was; why weren't they married; why had she left university? Who, what, where, when, why.

"Back home with the journalists," she said pulling up a chair at the kitchen table.

Freddy nodded, then shrugged and held out his hand. Val took it. Her little brother, long hair now, and a fu manchu.

She never spoke of Luke, never directly tried to put him into words. She wished she could; maybe then they'd understand. She could see his tall, hard body bent over a clump of bushes, his hands cross-hatched with grass stains, his nails caked. And again, at a bus stop, in a diner, his arm around the shoulder of a tired, dirty kid about the same age as himself, his voice calm, saying: take the paper on the table; take the money; call the man named Jim. And just that brief glimpse, the Christmas tree in Warroad, his childhood dangling from the branch. She didn't dare admit it at the time, yet in that one act she was forever connected to Luke's mother.

But she couldn't explain any of it.

"I like him a lot," was the best she could do for explanation, which was enough for Freddy, but not enough for her parents.

—⁂—

One day while Luke, stick in hand, is peeling clumps from the bottom of a lawnmower, his child is born. He feels a sharp yank, or pull, on his shoulders. He almost hears Val's cries over the roar of the other lawnmowers, cries that alter the uniformity of the precise, cropped rows. He is mowing down tall green, turn, mowing down tall green, and a small voice is crying, too, now, over the sound of the machines.

When he finds them he is still earth-snared, grass stains ribbing his hands. She is weak and white, and her thin straight hair is slick across her forehead, and she is sleeping so childlike that no one would believe that she is not the child herself.

"Mr. Leighton?"

He does not know a Mr. Leighton.

"Have you seen her yet?"

"What?"

And Val opens her eyes.

"Have you seen her?" she repeats, and it is curious how they are both looking at him like this, Val's eyes especially, and he shakes his head even as the nurse takes his arm.

He is brought to the nursery.

"You might want to wash up after you take a peek because I'll be bringing her to the room soon."

But for now there is this wall and this window, and boxes with little shining faces and souls. She is there, the third baby; she doesn't look at him. Eyes jammed shut; fist in the air. He almost laughs. Little radical. Tiny wristband. Under constant surveillance.

Luke lifts his fist to the window.

Hello.

"Did you see her? Isn't she terrific?"

Val pulls him over to kiss him and winces as he sits on the bed.

"Was it bad? What happened? I wish...I'm sorry I wasn't...."

But there is time for revision and retelling. Now they are staring at the round fuzzy head of their daughter who nuzzles in close to Val's suddenly motherly breast.

Stuck in the No-Man's-Land of chlorine and ammonia; safe in this uncomfortable metal bed.

"Aurora," Luke says, and the child stops sucking.

"Aurora," he looks at Val.

For the northern lights that danced in a child's imagination high above the Lake of the Woods. For the wind-snowy night of departures long past.

The child lets out a wail.

Aurora.

Mother, Father:

Mom and Dad:

I know I haven't written. If there had been any way to make all this easier, I would have taken it. I thought it might be a little easier on you if I truly disappeared for a while. Fewer messy questions for you to answer.

We have settled in Ottawa (look east). It's just over a hundred miles from where Val grew up. Val and I want you to know that: you are grandparents! We had a baby girl last week. Her name is Aurora, and she's beautiful. We'll send you a picture soon.

Don't feel comfortable writing about much else. I want to know how Ray is. I guess no news is good news. Please try to understand this, as well, regarding me.

Take care of yourselves. Bye for now. Luke.

P.S. I'll send the pictures as soon as they're developed.

—w—

The child was crying again. It seemed as if she would wait until Val had just sat down, then she would cry her small heart across the room to see if there were any takers.

Oh, Val knew how that worked. "You're a little shit-disturber, aren't you?" she asked and picked her daughter up again.

It was that stupid and delirious. It was wholeness in stocking feet, raining outside and dancing inside. Val hardly dared to look around to register the yellow kitchen curtains and the splotchy linoleum. Was that the same window that had stuck every day she lifted it to throw out crumbs for the birds? Was that the useless radiator that had radiated no heat?

Luke walked in. He smelled like mown grass. He put his arms around her and the baby, and Val closed her eyes and breathed in deeply and thought: Remember This.

The summer had passed quickly. Luke was working, and Val was kept busy seeing to Aurora's needs, so it took her a while to notice the change in Luke. It wasn't a change so much as it was a blurring, a slight ghosting that she sensed, as if his precise angular lines were eroding. She actually found herself blinking hard when she looked at him, cursing her vision. "Damn your eyes!" as Mrs. Molloy used to say.

"Something wrong?" she'd ask knowing that it was not the right question, then smile and lift up their daughter as an ancient offering.

So she had taken to skipping the questions and offering up Aurora exclusively. Sometimes they took her out together in the evening. Val aware that some people on her street were watching the peasant-dressed woman with the baby strapped to her, the man with the long hair and the battered canvas jacket.

Sometimes they would go to one of the cafes Luke knew; there they would find others like themselves. Val knew the faces, but Luke knew all their names, and he'd sit with this one and buy that one a coffee, and Val would watch as Luke's wallet appeared and a five dollar bill was extracted.

Some still carried the nervousness, the darting eyes of the deserters she'd seen in the States, losing their names, practising bogus signatures, always with those quick careful eyes. Luke seemed much more animated when he was with them, talking and doling out phone numbers. He'd talk until Val wanted to leave and was forced to remind him that Aurora needed to get home.

At that, at the mention of his daughter, he would stop, close his notebook or whatever was before him, say one or two last words and then join Val over by the door.

She didn't want to nag. She didn't think it was nagging. Their daughter needed to get home, and Val needed to get...and why weren't they at home in the evening, anyway?

"You want me to take her?" he asked.

Val realized she was panting.

"Here, just give her to me."

And lifted the child from her arms, holding her strongly and gently with hands that were beginning to blur at the edges.

Percale Street. She hated the place, the scraggly curbside trees, the bicycles on the corner. When they were better set up, they would move to the country, and Val would get a job in a health food store or a co-op. Someone Celia knew was thinking of starting up a commune. But no. Val realized she would not fit into a commune. With her lost-ghost man and her crying baby, and—yes—her feeling that the three of them belonged together as a family. No. Better to wait 'til they could afford to do it on their own.

The apartment was stifling. Indian Summer. Indian Summer used to mean walks through the park with Mrs. Molloy, or adventures with her brother when he was a little older. And he'd wring her wrist, and she'd wring his, and they'd both hold up reddened arms and announce: "Indian Sunburn!" in the middle of Indian Summer.

There was mail today. Val missed her family but was afraid to admit it to Luke. After all, she was the one going on about how it was the three of them who were the family now. And Luke had only sent the one letter to his parents whereas Val had had the trip to Montreal. Val sorted the mail. Phone bill, hydro bill, a letter from the States.

Val picked up the letter and dropped it on top of the cookie tin on the fridge. She had arranged to have a friend of theirs, Jess, look after Aurora, and she had washed her hair and put on a dress she'd picked up at the clothing exchange. It fit her nicely, now that her figure had more or less returned. More had returned, it seemed; her breasts were fuller because she was nursing Aurora. Thank God her thighs had behaved, and her ass was still good. There was just the smallest stomach bulge which she could make disappear whenever she breathed in deeply. She hoped to do a lot of deep breathing that night, she reminded herself, as she adjusted her earrings.

Luke came home tired. She could hear him kicking his work boots off on the stairs and taking slow steps up. His head poked around the door, and Val gave him a smile.

"Don't bother looking for her; she's over at Jess and Rod's. Come here."

Grass, earth, gasoline. "Anything new today?"

"Aurora isn't home. I have this dress. And we have three whole hours."

He smiled back, then....

Val blinked. Damn. Damn her eyes.

He always listened to the news when he got in. The war news played every evening on TV, but Luke preferred the radio on top of the fridge.

"What's this? When did this get here?"

"Uh...just today. It just arrived."

Luke shot Val a glance.

"I guess my mother got the baby picture," he said, too casually. Val hadn't realized it, but they were keeping a silent tally of these things now.

What followed would be relived many times in Val's memory. Was it that he was falling and had reached for the first thing he could? Cupping the small radio and flinging it across the room so the voice consoled itself against the wall.

Ghost face, like Val and Freddy used to make at the table when report cards were due.

"So...." She wants to join in, erase the haunted eyes.

But he says nothing, and she is not even sure he is there except for the faint grass and gasoline smell which she has come to know as this man.

He pushes past her from the kitchen; he is gone without a word.

—⁂—

Tick-tock.
Tick-tock.
His boots hitting hard flat pieces of the Shield.
Tick.
It sounds hollow. He jumps two-footed onto a shelf.
The whole thing sounds hollow.

Ray.

This is the aftermath of the ice sheet. Here is where the glaciers came, right through this provincial park, massive moving glaciers sometimes two miles thick. Scraped the earth like they were flensing it. And this is what was left.

Tick-tock.

Sound of man, sound of feet on the Canadian Shield sharing the sound with timber wolves and goldeneyes, sphagnum moss and leather leaf, pondweed, sedge and shining willow. Human sounds, not of hammering or fucking, sounds of wooden feet, marionette feet, blocks of wood hitting against each other as the strings are manipulated, as the puppet starts to move as if it is almost.

Tick.

Tock.

Almost alive.

Muskeg.

More muskeg than anywhere else, Ray. Bogs and escarpments, mammilation and the great grey owl.

He is not allowed a fire here, but he makes one all the same being careful to keep the wooden feet from tripping into the flame, the strings from catching and sending fire straight up through the shoulder.

There would be a fire in the fireplace at home. His father would be out by the shed sorting wood, his old Christmas pipe between his teeth, his stubborn face frozen along with his suddenly blasted spirit.

She would be...she would be....

He didn't know. She might be sewing another cover for the sofa, caught up in the measurements and cutting. She might be hanging a cold wash out on the line or screwing a light bulb into the socket on the porch. Her arm over her head, turning, turning, rotating the bulb until it shatters in her hand.

Son.

Her penmanship.

The old man would never have written having relinquished any claim on his second son, branding him with a last look that spoke generational shame.

It had had to be her, who could afford the reality least.

These are the seasons on the Shield, the time of the quaking bogs. This is where we wait to hear the Tennessee Warbler and the American Redstart; Americans in feathers, here on the Canadian Shield.

They said he didn't...it wasn't right away. His foot got
caught, one of their horrible hidden traps. He bled to death
before they found him, Luke.

Luke knew about their "horrible traps" and had seen the foot of a vet who had survived one. *Punji traps*, nails or fire-hardened bamboo, spikes on a tilt that could rip the foot to shreds.

The man who sent the letter was a friend of Ray's.
Kenny Jackson. He said Ray was a good soldier.

The strange thing about the foot of a puppet is that it could survive a *punji trap*. It would splinter, probably, maybe crack if it was dry enough, but the strings would still be able to pull the puppet away in escape.
Tick.
Tick.
Favouring the stumpy wooden foot.

How it is. How it is to see Ray walking ahead of him to school, Ray with his friends on either side; one is punching him in the arm, and Ray hits back, and they scuffle together and then resume the slow easy saunter.
Luke is behind and walking alone. Sees Ray along the side of the road, sees Ray almost perfectly moving with the day as if this is the correct thing to do with a day and the school has been built for this purpose, today, so that Ray and Lon and Rick can skid and trip and wrestle their way through the streets of the town, to arrive in the school yard a moment ahead of Luke. The school yard merely a destination.
How it is to have a destination, walking behind your brother.
Ray the hockey star.
Ray of the Warroad Lakers.
All of it in the world that rides on his shoulders, the whole cloud of dreams that clings to Ray's head.

Luke pauses, suddenly out of breath. Crouches low on a lichen-covered rock and listens.

Are we best friends, Mom?
Who, you and me? she smiles and turns to him like he hasn't just walked in over her clean floor, like he isn't scattering leaf dust in his wake.

The error has made her happy.

"Uh, no, I mean me and Ray."

Her face only shows the barest hint of disappointment, a spark and then just wood smoke disappearing to the right of her eye. She pulls him close into her plaid skirt.

"Do you feel like best friends?"

He doesn't know. He knows only that his errors sometimes make people happy, and then he must correct them.

He thinks of Mr. Ellison sitting in the Silver Dollar, his elbow resting on an encased 1953 dollar.

"If I didn't have the cancer, I'd be laughing."

Which, curiously and horrendously, makes everyone laugh, even Mr. Ellison as he holds up his empty to signal.

The *Warroad Pioneer* obituary saluting back a few months later.

Warroad, "The Future Metropolis of Northern Minnesota", Warroad as seen through the window of the pharmacy from the vantage point of the soda-fountain stool.

Follow the feather moss and moccasin flowers up through the woods, past the landings, to open ground, a border stripped. David Thompson has been by.

"What do you want to be, Luke?"

Ray's voice at once so serious.

"Where do you want to go?"

And Ray's.

"What do I want to go to Tibet for?"

Or Russia. Or Canada. What do I want to go anywhere the Warroad Lakers aren't playing?

Saigon. Cambodia.

What do I want to go to Cambodia for?

This is the old world. The voices are younger. He hears only these, Ray with the crack in his voice when he's excited, their mother admonishing their noise half-heartedly.

"Ray? RAY!"

Voice skims off the flat Shield rocks, round and round, off the walls of the escarpment.

Luke looks up. A difficult climb, too difficult. He will not get all the way up.

Toe-hold, Luke.

He sees it. Has the wrong kind of boots so he jumps down and unlaces them. Work-socks caked in mud, he begins. Sees the sliver of ledge above, an almond protruding from his mother's banana bread.

Great. Look up. Lateral, Luke.

Another hand pull. His fingers almost buckle.

Hold.

He is sweating profusely and tries to wipe his forehead against his shoulder.

Ahead, a crevice, dark slit to jam a fist into.

Push off. Grab.

Skin peeling from knuckles as the hand is wedged into the space.

Luke feels the pain in waves; he holds to the rock-face letting the waves wash over him, their rhythms filling him, the geese flying above him.

Someone pulls the strings, and the marionette moves again, shoulder muscles tight. He is in the canoe now, Ray in the stern this time, their father in the middle and Luke in the bow pulling forward in even strokes.

They are paddling into a "V" of white suspended in the sky. Below them, grey water, patches of twilight blue, but ahead the horizon is split open in a white V.

"...It's beautiful," Ray ventures.

Their father turns back to look at him.

It is beautiful, Ray. The old man looks out and sees only the distance to the cabins. But there, or there, the falling down green, gold showers tumbling into the lake.

Ray toe-testing a jungle floor, blade of his skate slicing vines as he passes. Hot? Or freezing? Darkness overhead? These greens too beautiful for you to bear?

Removes his shirt, his hairless chest gleaming, removes the skates and hangs them in a tree. Tender underfoot, crackle of a twig, look Luke, I have lichen growing on my toes! Jungle rot, dizzy, red fungus on his toes, take some medication, point-man, take some "Number Tens."

Barefooted wrestling in the front room until she tells them no. Barefoot in the little pool that mirrors the muted lake. Tiptoeing out the window and tree-frogging it down to the yard.

"It's growing on me Luke." Small nervousness in the voice. Point-man, point-man in a Warroad Lakers uniform, athlete's foot or lichen legs, "Hey, Luke...!"

Does it snap?

And silence.

Ray!

Can't hear. Puppet's wooden ears.

Feels himself hanging from a rock-face. Smells blood his....

How long did Ray hold, foot in shreds, useless blood, sweat in rivers down his back? And how long did he remain silent so as not to give the position away. Silent point-man.

Breathe.

Wave of pain.

Breathe.

The Lord is my shepherd....

Skating a trail of blood in intricate circles in the Warroad Arena.

"Anderson, take the guy into the boards—Anderson! Fall with him! Do it, c'mon, roll, damn you. Fall!"

Luke is on the side of the escarpment. The fingers of his right hand white, the left hand jammed into a fissure, leg cramps, the left leg beginning to tremble. He doesn't remember.

C'mon Luke, don't lean in. Keep the weight over the feet. Pull back.

Luke tries it.

See! Can't kiss it and climb it at the same time.

Three-point contact. He pulls his left hand free of the crevice, the skin curling red at his knuckles.

Next move, Luke. Rope-climbing?

I'll belay you. To Canada? I'll send you my combat pay.

Ray.

"What you going as?"

Brother to brother, Luke already feeling a little too old for this make-believe, but his older brother is going, so....

"C'mon, Luke, it'll be fun!"

Wandering door to door with children dressed like *The Lone Ranger* and *Howdy Doody*.

"What you going as?" Ray repeats.

Luke never knows. One year he wanted to go as old *KaKaGeeSick*, but his mother said that would be in poor taste considering the old man was still in town.

"But I want to be more than 100 years old!"

"Then go as one of Ray's jokes," their father said slapping Ray on the back of the head with a rolled up *Warroad Pioneer*.

And when darkness filtered the lake to black, the two boys could be seen leaving the Anderson home, Luke in long-johns emblazoned with decals and badges, an unlikely astronaut without a bubble helmet; Ray uncomfortable but beaming, in a wire contraption decorated with pine boughs, immediately recognizable as Warroad's famous Lone Pine.

Luke hazards a look down. Too far.... He will have to make the ridge.

"It's cold," he says, to no one. To the rock. It's cold here, he thinks, as if it is the first thought.

They are shovelling snow. Luke hears his brother through the drift, the heavy, clanking rhythm. They will meet in the middle, Ray has said. They'll split the profit and each get to the movie.

Minnesota snow.

Endless Minnesota snow.

The sound of hand-held metal squaring off borders, and then the grunting heave over the shoulder as acres of it, chunk by perfect chunk, are picked up and flung, glacial masses forming to the left, to the right.

"Luke?"

A white balloon goes up, just like in the comic books.

Luke waits.

"Hey, Luke?"

Another one, bigger than the last.

Luke picks up a wedge with his shovel and pushes it skyward.

"Yeah?"

"Could you watch where you're throwing it?"

The moon on their shoulders.

Too cold to talk about it, fingers wet and stiff against the handle, mitts permanently fastened to the metal, mouths under scarves wet from breathing in wool.

Luke stamps his feet and rearranges his scarf, the shovel resting across his chest. He looks up at a wall of white.

The glacier rumbles and starts to push its way across the stretch of Roseau County.

"Holy...."

He turns. And faces the wall with a snow shovel.

—m—

Val was frantic. She called Danny and Celia, and Lonnie. She even thought of calling Libby in the States although she knew he would never be stupid enough to think of going back...and besides, Libby was underground now.

"Hello?"

She had answered the phone once today. The call was meant for Luke. And what to say to someone who had just lost a son while Val's own daughter was wailing into the receiver?

"He isn't here."

And the hope in the woman's breathing, that irrational breath that fools the woman into thinking he will be home.

Val was aware of the almost physical harness that connected her to Aurora across the room. Her hand shaping the curve of Aurora's head, a hand cupped even in sleep. This woman had held her son like that, her boy's face leaning into her lap as he slept, his damp hair smelling of yeasty soap bubbles.

Val's arms ached for this woman.

"I'm sorry."

The two most useless words.

When the phone rang again, she nearly knocked it out of its cradle.

"Yes?"

The voice on the other end sounding every bit as nervous.

"Val. Are you okay?"

Her mother had her phone number. It was the Night of the Living Grandmothers.

"What? Yes. Why?"

Had she not heard the news?

"The Cross thing? Yes. Are you...okay there?"

The James Cross kidnapping.

"No. Laporte. They've got Laporte, too!"

Val could picture this room full of diplomats, pudgy politicians, game show hosts, the weatherman from local T.V., all held captive by the FLQ.

"They're just scaring them."

"Valerie! You *approve* of this?"

"Nobody's asked my approval, mother. I just said...."

"You approve of this kind of thing; is this what your radical friends think of as an improvement?"

"I just said...."

"You, with an infant! This is the kind of world you want for her?"

Val listened for Aurora, but the child was sleeping undisturbed. Val could hear her mother's breathing through the receiver.

"I'm sorry, mother...truly. Listen. You sit tight, okay? Just sit tight and don't go out more than you need to."

Her mother sitting beside Mr. Laporte in a little back room on a side street.

"Where's Dad?"

"He's in Cleveland on business."

"Well, call Freddy. Make sure Freddy stays with you."

Val filled the empty 7-UP bottle and proceeded to water the plants.

So it was happening. The Revolution had come home and was knocking at her door. It was marching past the *dépanneur*, tripping through her former school yard, picking up local children like the Santa Claus Parade did, the miniature multi-coloured troop saluting in salty mittens.

Luke.

He wouldn't.

He...not with her here, and Aurora.

"I'll kill you if you're there," she muttered as her daughter latched onto her breast.

—⁓—

Blood is drying on his hands, his knuckles caked with blood and dust. From the top of the escarpment he can see the old farm roads in the distance, thin strips of brown cross-hatching the land.

The air is good up here; he inhales deeply, slow deep breaths. Sitting on top of the world, or as near as it would pass for in this part of the country. Sitting on top of the glacial shield, Pre-Cambrian patterns tattooing the inside of his eyes.

It's as if the other country had broken away and floated off. One more continental divide and here he was, left here on this side of the chasm, looking back. And looking back was useless now.

Luke looked at his hands, hardly recognizing them, and watched as they reached down beside him to pull at a piece of lichen. It came away from the rock easily, its greenish colour impossible to describe, its delicate construction like brain fissures. Fungus and alga, lichenized alga, the only way these things can live. He twirls the lichen between his fingers. A perfect system—two hopelessly unalike components forced into necessary collaboration, producing something that looks like...neither.

Crawl along toward the light; leave your dead limbs behind you as you go. The lichen on the edge of the rock has become a dusty shadow, yet closer to Luke it is healthy and alive. It goes on like this, ALGAE + FUNGI, and the thing they make together clumps and holds to the shield forever.

He was hitching into town realizing he looked like a man who had just been in a bad fight, his plaid shirt in strips wrapped around his hands. He would get the odd crazy glance from a young girl in a back seat. Young. Maybe only five or six years younger than he was, but she seemed really young, looking back at him with a quizzical expression through the dust and exhaust.

He got a ride in a Volkswagen with a French guy, Simon, from Hull whose leather vest was festooned with buttons and medallions. A kid who wanted to go west with his buddies, who wanted to go south to the U.S.A..

"*Mais, ma langue*...my language...*ce n'est pas possible.*"

They listened to the radio a while, the driver drumming on the steering wheel, "*comme Charlie Watts!*" he enthused.

The news report interrupted the drum solo and was redundant even in its brevity. Pierre Laporte has been found. Pierre Laporte is dead. The body of Pierre Laporte was found, murdered, the FLQ has murdered, has taken responsibility for murdering the body of Pierre Laporte...!

Silence.

The radio switched off and an uncomfortable silence in the car.

"Christ!" Simon said suddenly.

Luke waited.

"*Maudit Christ! Moi, je suis pacifiste, mais....*"

Silence, and a stare sideways at Luke.

"I haven't been following the news...," Luke said. "Who is Laporte?"

And a look now between rage and plain frustration, Luke apparently unable to understand the confusion and pain.

"You're a pacifist? And these men are what, separatists...."

"*Toi, tu comprends rien*! Listen, okay, shut up. Just shut up!"

Silence the rest of the way into Ottawa. Simon let Luke off near the bridge, and Luke found himself entering a city on military alert. He felt his muscles tightening as he carefully approached and then passed a gun-carrying MP. Luke was filthy, suspicious-looking in the way that tired, unkempt people looked suspicious. He would be questioned if stopped, and he had no identification on him. Luke felt the old instincts clicking into place.

—ᴧᴧ—

The baby was crying. Val picked Aurora up from her crib and sat with her on the ugly sofa, lumpier every time it was sat upon, a donation from a student Luke had met.

So.

Val couldn't help notice the four walls because for the first time she saw them as exactly that—four walls, and the outline of wall adjacent to wall, and the little box that contained Val and Aurora small and specific in this building, on this street, in this town, in this country, on this planet. Yes, she thought, the old verification, the name stippled along her brown paper notebook, the blunt pencil working, defining, outlining. There were four walls and one door. And in that door stood Luke Anderson. Leaned, really, and then she saw those hands....

"Luke!"

He waved it away with one of the hands and wordlessly approached.

She should be pissed off, she was starting to realize; she should tell this son of a bitch what he put her through.

A scab encrusted hand moves across her daughter's forehead.

"She's been good," Val whispers.

He is tall and straight she thinks. He has a way of staring and a ticklish spot on his left side, and, somehow, that is all I know.

"I'm sorry about...."

And the blood caked hand waves again.

"Your hands, Luke...."

The hands lift Aurora into the air, raise her slowly until she is the highest one of all.

Walking Backwards on Feathers:
Fragments: 1970-1974

*O*ctober, 1970
Dear Mr. and Mrs. Anderson:
I want to say how sorry I was to hear about Luke's brother Ray. It came as a real shock especially because, as Luke says, Ray would probably have been coming home soon. It seems so unfair.

I know we've been on opposite sides of the fence over this, but you must realize that this is precisely the loss we had hoped to prevent—for you as well as for thousands of other families in America—and over there. It is what, in our own way, Luke and I have been fighting against.

But this isn't the time for that kind of talk. I have no idea how you can bear...that is, to live without. I'm sorry. You see why it is I'm not much good at writing.

Your granddaughter Aurora is a very happy baby. Sleeping through now, which lets her parents get some sleep. Luke says she looks like your family, but I don't know. I've enclosed a recent picture.

I know Luke will want to write to you himself. I'm not very good with grief, and I don't get a minute to myself too often, but anyway, again, I'm very sorry.
Sincerely,
Val

—m—

Son:
I don't know why, but I hoped anyway. I looked for you along the street, in church, and over at the cemetery. I kept thinking it was all a dream. I kept thinking you'd both arrive together and walk me to my place like you used to. But you didn't come, neither of you.

It was very nice, Luke. Everyone said afterward how it was such a nice service. I guess you don't know the new minister, Reverend Heller. You'd have sworn he knew Ray all his life. He talked about Ray's selflessness—and his bravery. And the flowers.... I ordered red roses and white carnations, and the spray, or pillow or whatever it's called was lying to one side, and I kept looking at it the whole time Reverend Heller was speaking to see if it would fall off.

Your father. Your father was a rock of support to me. It's now, though, he doesn't seem to be doing too well. He's trying, God love him. It's just hard. That's what he always says to me, that it's just so hard to believe anymore. I'm worried about him. You know he's not an easy man to get through to.

I'm going to pull up those shrubs along the back and plant some bulbs there. I think a flower border will look fine, what do you think? (You know where I mean, along the back by the shed?) Your father said whatever's right by me.

The Olson boys were asking about you. And Ruddy Hardigan, and Mrs. Clyde. I don't know what to tell them, Luke. I don't know anything anymore.

Kiss our little granddaughter. Your father says he can't believe her either. Love to you, my son, and your family.
Mom

—*∞*—

Luke:
 WHERE ARE YOU? ALL HELL IS BREAKING LOOSE! AURORA AND I ARE OVER AT CELIA'S. CALL THERE.

—*∞*—

Oct, 1970
Val: Just a note!
 I don't want you panicking, but I think you maybe better sit tight for now. Montreal is a mess with this Laporte thing— bad time for a visit. Besides, they're arresting everyone who ever even offered an American a lift. Not to mention all the Québecois with separatist leanings. Chèz Hélene this ain't.
Peace, sis.
Freddy

—*∞*—

<u>Oct 17/70 LUKE STILL NOT HOME</u>:

I hate this journal. You should never write anything they can hold against you later. Freddy says I should stay put. What am I supposed to do? For all I know he's back down in the States, and if he is, well, that's it. I think he wants to go back, get himself caught, or shot.

This is why I hate journals.

Gotta go down to the cafe, see if anyone there knows anything.

The news just said. Jesus. Laporte is dead.

—⁓—

<u>OCTOBER, 1970</u>:

Luke is back. Sort of. We've been getting into it lately. Like the other day when we were talking about the Québec situation; and he said he could understand being pushed to the limit, being trapped. And suddenly I could tell he wasn't referring to the FLQ. So I said you want to talk about it? Which apparently works with some people. Luke? Shit...his hands...a whole other story. Missed two days work over them, too.

—⁓—

November, 1970
Dear Mother,

I've begun this letter so many times. I'm sorry I haven't written sooner. There is just no easy way, for you or for me, no way to make this better.

I'm not much for letters. All those letters back and forth didn't do a damn thing for Ray. Like you, I keep expecting to see him. Sometimes I think I do. It would be....

—⁓—

January 3, 1971
Dear Luke:

I wanted to wish you both (you all) a Happy New Year. I'm afraid my heart isn't really in it this year. (Your father and I were very low-keyed throughout the Holidays, Luke. Your father went down to the Silver Dollar a couple of times with Ruddy, and I went to my Tea at the church, but that was it). I did, however, feel it important to let you know we are thinking of you.

Thank you, Valerie, for the latest pictures of Aurora. I hope the sweater and booties I sent will fit her all right. You must wear a lot of sweaters up in Canada. Luke, I wonder if you noticed the little "P.S." I put on your Christmas card? The one asking you for a recent picture of yourself? I don't mean to bother you, dear, it's just that it's been so long since I've seen you. I was down to Minneapolis for Cassie's funeral (Did I tell you? My old girlfriend from school days had a stroke and passed away in December). Anyway, while I was there I bought a lovely picture frame, mahogany, and there's a place for both of you. You and Ray. I've got his army photo in there now (it's the one your father wants. I like the one Ray gave Margaret better—the dear girl sent me a copy after the funeral—he looks like he just stepped in the door after winning a game. Truly, it's that same smile. Margaret said her brother Phil took it).

I'd really like to put my two boys up on the mantel together, Luke.

I haven't got much else to say, so I'll say goodbye for now. Kiss Aurora for us. We would love to see her.
Mom

—◦◦◦—

1971:

He's very cold. He's cold with them; that's all. Not that I'm any better with my folks; I mean, I understand that. But they've lost a son, and Luke is all they have left. Except Aurora. Who can blame them feeling hurt? They could come up. I mean, they know he can't go back, but they could come up. Yet Luke just won't.... It's none of my business. I am learning that all the time.

I was listening to some albums the other day, the old stuff that used to sound all the right notes for me. Celia was over, and we were smoking a bit. Aurora was sleeping. We were sitting on the floor and just getting off on the music, and suddenly it seemed, it was absolutely sudden, it seemed like it was ages ago. All of it. The States, the movement, the music that played as the soundtrack of my life. It was a different country. And I was different. And I knew then that I didn't feel the same anymore. Was it just me? Was it just me who'd moved away from all that? Back then Luke was...and there was no Aurora, or rundown apartment, or Celia, who was going on and on about men, how she was sick of men and the way they took charge of everything. She didn't mellow when she got stoned. Then I was replaying the whole thing, the music, the moment standing in that kitchen in Libby's place and turning around as Luke walked through that door for the first time. And the days that followed, that tense, tense trip to the river, the picnic/information session, everybody naked and running to the water, and me watching Luke and wanting him so bad. Watching. And then I was the only one not stripped down. What? Canadians! Libby snorted. Laughter all around. It seems we were prudes and boring. And everybody waiting and gawking while I slipped out of my jeans and t-shirt. Naked in America I said. More laughs. We all raced to the river.

Maybe because I was stoned, remembering, but I was seeing it very clearly, the legs, all those funny, bony knees moving back and forth, and I started laughing and looked up from this set of knees, and I was looking way up ("way way up" like the Friendly Giant used to say) at Luke. And it was like we knew, without saying it, like we both knew we were lovers running to the river.

The memory was so sharp I almost started crying. Celia said I did, which disgusted her.

The river was especially bright, I remember.

I remember he took my hand.

—⁓—

March, 1973
Dear Son:
What do you know, I won a contest! It was this cleanser company; they wanted me to write in twenty-five words or less why I like their product. Well, I'd only just tried Starbright the one time, but it seemed to work as well as any of the others, so I wrote:

> *I use Starbright*
> *so my rooms will look right;*
> *my toilet gleams so white*
> *I can find it in the night!*

It was more of a lark than anything. Your father says I have a knack for it. Anyway, I won! Not first prize; that went to somebody who used it "for all her needs". But I won a trip and a year's supply of Starbright.
About the trip, Luke....

—⁓—

LUKE! VAL!
GREETINGS FROM THE UNDERGROUND, DOWN UNDER, DOWN AND OUT. POSTCARD POSTHASTE; YOU HEARD ABOUT FORD'S CLEMENCY? THINK. NOW, THINK AGAIN.
- LIBBY -

—⁓—

My dear Son:

Thank you for your letter. Your father was quite surprised when he opened the box and found it there. Things haven't been easy for him, Luke; I wish you realized that.

I understand about your not wanting us to come visit. We wouldn't want to make any trouble for you. That's, in fact, one of the reasons I'm writing. You've heard by now that the President will be offering some form of "clemency". I don't know if the details have been worked out yet, but do you think it might allow you to think about coming home? I don't know how Valerie feels about Minnesota, but surely you'd want your daughter to spend some of her formative years here, wouldn't you?

Aurora is so sweet. Thank you for the picture. The one of the three of you walking beside the water. Who took it? Too bad I can't see your face, though. Valerie looks very thin.

Oh. There was a choice about the Starbright prize, and we've decided to take the money. Your father says we could fix up the shed and have the chimney re-done. Besides, we're getting a little set in our ways, and there's an awful lot of crime out there in the cities.

Give my love to Valerie and, of course, my little Aurora.

Love,
Mother

—⁓—

Dec. 12, 1973
Luke:

I don't know how you're going to take this. Your mother said it should be me who writes about this envelope here. A fellow the name of Johnstone or Johnson came by out of nowhere, says he's had this thing sittin' in with his stuff the past couple of years. Says he only noticed it this November when he was going through his gear. Says he does that on Memorial Day when we're out saluting the soldiers.

It's a letter to you from Ray. I don't know when he wrote it, but this Johnstone says it couldn't have been too long before Ray was killed since they'd gotten letters out before that.

In case you're wondering, no, I didn't read it. Nothing for us. I asked the guy was he sure there wasn't another letter? Nothing at all for your mother. Maybe you can put into words what Ray said or send her back the letter or something. I keep telling her he meant one for us.

Your father

—⁓—

Shit, Christ, Luke.

Fucking hell. Fucking shaking twisted, man. Looking at my hand and it's this old tree, twisted, warped. Elephant pills, and I got hair growin' out my face, dig it, and fur on my feet, Jesus, walking backwards on feathers, man.

I remember you. I remember you crying over time like a lost bicycle. I remember you with an abscess in your mouth, sucking at all the pain, walking through scrub grass and reeds by the shore, the old Indian in the bushes with his traps.

Wilderness. Rat-tailed pines criss-crossing, tipping over, hey, man, it's funny...it's so hot here and I shake all the time.

Margaret, you remember to tell her, you tell her.... She was okay, y'know? She wore these skirts. She smelled like soap.

Time to go. Soft lights, man. Going walking.

Ray

—◊—

APRIL, 1974:

Libby in Montreal for contacts and meetings. Luke and I went. She's changed so much. Wouldn't talk to him; wouldn't go near him. Radicalized beyond friendship, beyond men, she said. Wanted to see me, talk, talk. I was telling her about Aurora; she didn't want to hear it. Wanted to talk about me. I said okay. We met after her meetings. I'm not so interested now, I guess. I mean, now that the war isn't so much a part of my life. And she doesn't even care about that anymore. Says it's men doin' men, and they can go ahead and do the lot of them.

We shared a lot of things down in the States back then. But she's come up for air in Canada and is thinking of turning herself in. Says when she goes back she can maybe get off with only a short prison term. Then devote herself, up front, to turning women around. Okay. Okay, I said.

I don't know. She really hurt Luke, I think, not acknowledging him. I mean, they used to be lovers. They used to believe in the same things. Now she hates men.

Even Luke!

"Especially Luke. And Charlie. And Lenny...."

I left before I heard the entire retinue.

Libby. And Celia.

I feel like some kind of leper. Because I like holding Luke, trying to talk to Luke. He told me he'd meet me back in Ottawa and then left without another word. Didn't even get to meet with Freddy who wanted to see him about a job or something.

Freddy's okay. Does a lot of dope, though. I think it's getting in the way of his work. Still, the painting is going well; he's got this tremendous new series with all these different media, took my old bus pass and some used Q-Tips. He wanted a tampon, but I said no. But he's got all this sacred and profane stuff going, just wild! The caretaker job at the church seems to have really paid off.

—m—

GRAMMA GRAMPA

1 2 3 5 5 6 8 9 10

Aa Aa Aa

                                        Bb Bb Bb

Doll. Bird. Tree.

Aurora.   Aurora.
                               Hello.

MACHINES: VAL AND LUKE: 1977

Val did not remember whether it was the chicken or the egg, whether Luke's inattention lent credence to Celia's theories, or whether Celia's pronouncements undermined any credibility Val had in her relationship with Luke. The angry comments that were a part of Celia's outlook, the fact that she had booted Dan out for being a lazy sonofabitch, and Celia's latest revelation—a girlfriend named Marika—surprising proclamations in Val's kitchen in the afternoons.

Celia seemed to delight, in particular, in putting down the men she knew, and more than once Val had asked her to refrain from discussing Aurora's father while the child was in the house. Celia, who adored Aurora, would muffle her complaints only to resurrect them at the next convenience.

So it was especially confusing to Val to walk in one afternoon from a job interview and find Celia and Luke together in bed. Celia parked like a Buick on the soft shoulder, and Luke pumping her full of gas. It was...it was almost funny because all the comments, the barbs, came spilling and toppling back as Val stood there watching this amateur car maintenance; Celia's red head and her perfect little breasts bobbing like the ornaments hanging off a mirror. And Luke, looking more intense than Val had seen in a long time, all over her neck with his tongue, his body dolphining hers; this was too much, this....

They saw her. The engine turned over once and died.

Celia shook her red mane to clear the ecstasy from her face and appeared not a bit embarrassed. And Luke...Val couldn't look at his face just then. Luke...Luke hid himself, pulling the blanket around his waist, hiding himself from his own wife....

"I'll be going," Celia said hopping up and marching her bare ass into the bathroom.

Val looked at Luke trying to register the degree of darkness in his eyes. And he let her do this almost as his punishment, it seemed, let her look into his eyes with an expression of her own that must have been terrible. It was so confusing. At that exact moment, with Luke twisted up in the covers, his chest sweating for someone else, eyes not avoiding hers, at that moment she wanted him so badly she would have thrown herself into that same bed. It was insane.

"I'm sorry about this," Luke said.

The laudromat hummed when all the machines were going, but Val preferred less of a crowd so she did the clothes early in the morning when she could hear each motor separately. The whites, the colours and the dryers which would take them all and dry them *en masse* in linty lumps. Like Val and Luke's clothes when they were on the road. A few coins pooled between them and their clothing— including anything they could remove in public— tossed together in the hole, the tiny package of soap snowing over the garments.

They had been together then, side by side waiting for the rinse light, chewing stale licorice until their teeth ached. Sometimes he held her hand, absently; other times he was wild and absolute, breathing his plans into her attentive ear, hugging her shoulder in confirmation. She could barely remember. She pressed her knuckles in the back of her neck.

She'd gotten Aurora off to school. Luke had slept on the couch and left while Val was in the bathroom; she heard him singing to Aurora.

As Val unwound the sheets from the washer, she could see Luke and Celia wrapped around each other, Celia's bony shoulders, Luke's hand lost in red hair.

"Something wrong?"

The click...shit...shit! "Stuck," she sputtered.

A sweatshirted arm helped her pull her sheet from the washer. Tears of stupid gratitude. As a man handed her a bed sheet.

"The dryers are tricky, too," he warned as tears brimmed her eyes and ran down her face.

Someone had brought in a radio, and Val listened to Paul MacCartney sing "Silly Love Songs" to Linda MacCartney. Val shook. The windows on the dryers were portholes, and she was out on the tumbling sea.

Celia came around a few weeks later to straighten things out which was more than Luke did, though he lived with Val. To be fair, he had asked her if she wanted to talk about it, but at the time she simply couldn't and thought that any false word on either part would be tragic for both of them. And that was it, Luke apparently assuming that she never wanted to talk about it at all, that things were somehow "back to normal".

Celia was nominally contrite. Not about Luke, of course, but about any pain she might have caused Val.

"This...uh...thing with Luke...just proves my point."

Logic Val couldn't see.

"What about Marika?"

"Marika's cool. Besides, it's not worth it most of the time. Oh...I didn't mean Luke by that."

Which hurt more? That he was a lousy lover and she hated it, or that they were great together?

"I guess he told you how it happened. How it was an accident."

Val paused and then couldn't help herself.

"Accident? Like...uh...falling down stairs with a cake in your hands? Slipping on ice on the goddamn laneway out there? Or like coming over to someone's house when she isn't home and screwing her old man?"

"See? See, I *knew* it! He hasn't told you anything! Fucking typical!"

"He wanted to! He said he wanted to!"

What was she *doing* defending Luke to Celia? Jesus, how did she....

"Mommy?"

"Oh...."

Aurora rubbing her eyes in the kitchen light, her pyjama bottoms hiked up to her chest.

Celia swoops first.

"Angel! You're awake? How about CeCe reads you a story, okay? While your mommy gets you some cocoa?"

Celia's arm around Val's child.

Val is in the kitchen making cocoa.

—⁂—

Luke couldn't blame her. She didn't want to discuss it. Who needs to hear excuses when you're staring that in the face? Besides, he wasn't convinced he would have had any to give.

Celia had been a regular around their house for several years. Initially, she had been exclusively Val's friend, one of the band of people who appeared to welcome new expatriates to town. He had been grateful for them, all of them, and especially Val's women friends while she was pregnant.

Celia and Dan had been mainstays in the little community, and their apartment had always been open to visitors who arrived without identification. They had been great, and they were welcome in Luke's home.

Then Celia split with Dan, which surprised everybody since they'd taken on the role of mom and pop to a lot of people. And Celia's politics shifted radically which was even harder. When she came around then, she began to ignore him, to concentrate exclusively on Val and Aurora. She was condescending; she was loud in her opinions; she was maddening because she would not discuss anything; she asserted.

"Back it up!" he tried vainly.

"I'll back you up!"

She began to drive him crazy. He liked Val's calmness, her ability to deal with the here and now of their situation. She rarely complained. She could be counted on. She was even going out to look for work now that Aurora had started school.

Celia came by that afternoon looking for Val. There was a lecture she wanted Val to attend. When Luke informed her that Val was off on an interview, Celia's disdain was clear.

"Now she's going to have to support you, too?"

Forgetting, of course forgetting, the disposable facts.

Her stance, her proximity. She moved in close to him, a technique she said men always used. And it worked. It intimidated—Luke was alarmingly aware of her crushed velvet shirt, the pants that fit so well. Alarmed, too, when he looked into her eyes and saw a look that he understood immediately. That energy, that fight was passion, and passion is what these Canadians didn't have and it came at him like a roaring truck and he grabbed on as it passed.

Luke and Celia in the kitchen by the refrigerator. The old fridge chugging along. He looks up and sees the sign *Frigidaire* and laughs, is laughing; she is so absolutely there, but not laughing— matching, testing, challenging. New breasts, new arch of inner thigh, new taste, something intoxicating in the stumble to the bed together, panties ringing her ankle, his penis pointing the way.

They were...what could Luke say now?

They were alive.

To feel alive when everything was dead around you, to feel ...thank you for breathing in and...breathing, thank you for having another day to do this, I love this, I love....

Celia?

No. And she could barely stand him.

Celia!

Come on, Val, think of what we mean to each other.

But why should she?

He might as well have been a hunter out back in the woods. She might as well have been a white-tailed deer, deer eyes staring down the barrel of his father's rifle, classic death scene right out of *Bambi*.

Why did she have to be hurt by him?

Or. Why did he have to hurt her?

Or.

Fuck it.

Luke shifted the mower into high gear and headed for the long grass.

On August 10, 1977, Eric Anderson died. Luke hadn't known his father had been ill other than the chronic emphysema. The broken heart. Luke's mother wrote periodically and always tried to sound upbeat the way Ray used to. They were really very much alike.

Then the phone call, answered by Aurora.

"You're not my Gramma. My Gramma talks like *Kermit* to me."

Luke took the receiver from his daughter.

"Hello?"

He wished he could have spared her that, at least.

"Aurora," he motioned to her, "come here. This is your other Gramma. This is my Mom."

And a faint lightheadedness when he said it.

Aurora gladly retrieved the phone and rattled on about her friend Tommy's turtle until Luke cupped his hand, demanding back the phone.

"Here's Daddy!"

Such a curious exchange. Luke frowned.

"Mother, how are you?"

Eric Anderson had died that morning. Eric T. Anderson, the T was for Titus, something very few people knew.

"Oh, Luke...."

Luke sees a stocky, well-made man against the evening sun. Sleeves rolled up and a bat in his hand. Luke sees himself, young, scrawny, and then his brother, who looks like the father, tamping down the outline of a triangle in the grass in the backyard. The man is teaching them how to throw; he shows them head on and in profile. He even delays his movements so that he is in slow motion. Now they can witness every step.

Slowly the windup and then the extension, the pitch at the end of it as inevitable as that.

"Just like that, like a well-oiled machine," he says into the history that the day is becoming, and just like that two boys in shorts and T-shirts throw a ball back and forth through the setting sun. Their father moving in slow motion, watching his own shadow like a sundial across the grass.

"How...?"

"He couldn't breathe. Oh, my dear God, he started gasping and wheezing, and I tried to get him over to the couch, and then we fell...."

"We...are you okay?"

"He fell beside me. I just knew this time he wouldn't get better."

His mother's slender shoulders, his father's head bent back in a scramble for breath. I knew he wouldn't get better.

This time. All the other times.

Ford coming at them in '73 and '75 offering his bad fruit. Explain to the President that this is what Luke wanted back. All of the other times.

"Are you going?" Val asked, too casually.

He had thought about it. And about that breed of man who would frequent funerals to arrest the sons of dead fathers. And of the border. And, even, of his mother.

"What good would it do?"

"She's *alone* now!"

"I couldn't stay there anyway! I couldn't spend time with her at the house, or fix things for her, or anything! I can't bring him back!"

"You could stand by her when she needs you!"

Who were they talking about?

"If I go back it's for good. You know that."

"So...?"

"So, think about it."

And she did. And she stopped.

He thought about his mother. Maybe she would move back in with her sisters. There must be one or two of them left in Minneapolis. He would have to talk to her about that.

"I'm going to order flowers," Val said as she left with Aurora, Aurora's boots like flippers along the floor until Val reminded her, "Feet all the way in!"

He watched them from the window, Val in that stride she had when she was angry, and she was angry a lot these days. Aurora grabbing onto Val's hand and racing on her tiny legs.

Keep going, little girl, he nods. Your mom's a hard one to hold on to.

That night Luke sits quietly on the floor as Van Morrison keens and wails behind him. The marijuana that has been sitting too long in the ceramic jar is hardly affecting him, or maybe it is and the room isn't singing. He listens to Neil Young, too, that untamed voice in the wild. How Canada used to sound to him when he first made it his home.

Val and Aurora are sleeping, Aurora's little night-light is a star down a distant corridor, a star lighting the way to Bethlehem. Or the bathroom. He chuckles.

His brain is a grid of the mower's patterns, the squares and rectangles of the paths he cuts. Weeds and grasses. He takes another toke. Weeds and grasses.

History and philosophy.

"It's my philosophy that history won't get you anywhere."

Olé, padre.

Looking out the window until the world has altered all around you, 'til the front door is the back door and the back door opens nowhere. Hanging on to this ship of state, state of the union, rubber-stamped silo of grains and grasses, of grasses and grains.

"Daddy?"

Silent, round-bottomed feet.

"Daddy, don't be sad."

They sit like that; her head falls to the side. Small limp body curled up in his lap, breathing his air, thin fingernails scratching at dreams.

—m—

His father had died, and she couldn't get him to talk about it. He'd disappeared when Ray died; that was bad enough. But he was stone silent about this. People had to deal with their parents. One way or another, you had to deal with your parents. This was impossible, this silence.

She wanted to wake him up out of this...stupor...to tell him, hey, this is it. Your father. You only get to grieve over him once, and if you don't do it right you spend the rest of your life doing it wrong. It won't leave you in peace. Mrs. Molloy had proven that to her, the old woman shaking her head, but never shaking out the memories of her wrong grief.

Oh, Luke, be careful, she wanted to say.

Be careful my friend.

Val walked home along the bus route just in case she wasn't able to make it on foot, and, sure enough, the dizziness returned and she was happy to sit beside the man with the wheeze.

This is what it felt like to be wandering home picking up scraps of your life like mail at the door; you remember your daughter on the corner and Luke as you are walking to the door.

—m—

Aurora pulled out her *Etch-a-Sketch* and demanded Luke draw her a picture.

"Please?" she wheedled standing on tiptoes, craning her neck and holding the toy up as if it were a tablet of Moses.

"Pleeese?"

She hopped up on Luke's lap and settled in noisily.

"There! Now draw, please, Daddy."

"Where did we get this thing?" he called to Val.

She poked her head around the corner of the kitchen.

"Your father. Last Christmas."

His father. Great.

"Okay. Here now, watch. Now, what am I making?"

"A line!"

"No, look harder."

"A line with a hat!"

Thank you, father.

They drew together, Aurora on the left button, Luke on the right. They had a few false starts, each one picked up, turned over, and shaken clear.

"See? My mistake's all gone!" she triumphed squirming in delight and nearly castrating Luke in the process.

"Sit still, will you?"

They drew a garden. Square, and square, and little pathways through.

"Is this like where you cut the grass?"

She's looking at him with little daughter eyes. Your father is a mower. Your father mows.

Later, when it is story-time and Aurora is again camped in his lap, she proffers new tablets: *A Trip to the Zoo; The Three Little Pigs*—"Never mind, I don't like them." ; *Toy Rose*, a British book that Val had sworn by; *Green Eggs and Ham*.

But Luke holds Aurora in place and crab-walks over to the bookshelf, pulls down a book from over his head.

"Oh, no...." Aurora says hanging on as they crawl the sea bottom back to the chair.

That evening Luke reads Aurora the Mower Poems, Val's old college copy of Andrew Marvell's poetry splayed open before Luke and Aurora.

"No pictures."

"Just listen. Then we'll draw our own pictures."

Aurora listens, playing with the button on Luke's shirt. Luke listens, too:

I am the Mower Damon, known
Through all the meadows I have mown.

And after Aurora has been tucked into bed and Val is in the kitchen making another batch of tahini, Luke takes the book out onto the balcony. The light from the kitchen window is dim, the twilight is over all of the rooftops.

"The Mower's Song," Luke begins quietly.

My mind was once the true survey
Of all these meadows fresh and gay,
And in the greenness of the grass
Did see its hopes as in a glass;

When Juliana came, and she
What I do to the grass, does to my thoughts and me

And he hears the scythe sweep across the field and the motors of lawn mowers, the noise of the seaplanes, his father's bellowing, his father's cough from the shed echoing off the walls and corners of the alley, the right-angled Etch-a-Sketch corners of the alley, rising to the first floor, to the second.

NORTHERN LIGHTS: AURORA: 1978

*A*urora skidded along the sidewalk, slowly making her way home. Ever since she had started school, she had walked along here alone, but only after her mother made her memorize PERCALE STREET.

"Can you say it, Aurora? Can you memorize PERCALE?"

Of course she could. Like the names of the kids in class, the whole class turning around as *her* name was called out.

Her mother said she worried about Aurora. But then her parents worried about lots of things. She heard them at night in the kitchen. Names would go by that sounded like regular peoples' names except her parents would say a name as if there was only one "Bob" in the whole world, when there were Bobbys all over; there were two in her class! But her parents would breathe in and out on those cigarettes and say "Bob" to each other, and the word would float down like a balloon with a slow leak and land by the boots in the hall.

They were busy; they didn't know that Aurora worried about things, too. Like the animals she tried to tell her mother about, the Animals of Doom that came at you on the street and in school by the fountain in the hall.

"I'm not buying you any new toys. You have a perfectly good collection of stuffed animals, and I'm the one who has to pick them up, and ...."

Her parents had their own Creatures of Doom. The pigs came and ate up some of their friends. They were fierce animals. Some friend of her father's would be sitting at the table, and he, too, would talk about the fucking pigs.

"I don't want to go in today," she started, promising herself that today she would tell them about the Animals.

"None of that. You're going."

Her mother with a cough, and a cigarette, told Aurora to feel good about herself, then gave her a bag of nuts and raisins and sent her out the door. So,

Aurora was walking home on another afternoon of bluish snow, going along a different street.

Where they lived things didn't work. First there was a door that creaked open no matter how many times you slammed it. Her father bashed it closed once and it didn't open at all after that and he had to butter knife it just like with a dime on the ice, and when he finally got it loose, he shut it gently. It creaked open.

"Be here 'til fucking Doomsday!"

The Animals lived there. And the door always opened. That was when Aurora first knew. From then on her father's big lace-up boots stood guard in front of the closet door.

Then there was a medicine cabinet that fell right off the wall. Right as her mother was at the sink, she looked up, "Christ, with a face full of soap," and saw it falling "right into my reflection."

The mirror broke in the sink. Her mother began seven years of bad luck. Aurora marked it on the calendar in green, just a little star, to mark the beginning of her mother's luck.

The shower on Percale Street didn't work properly which was more than too bad since showers were the best thing the girl knew. Aurora used to get up quietly, go into the bathroom and close the door. Then she'd drop her flip-flops beside the tub and her towel on the clothes hamper. She always liked showers because behind the vinyl curtain, inside the steam and the mist, she could be anywhere she wanted—she was in her grandmother's house in Montreal or the smelly spitting shower at the pool. Under the warm spray she was where she wanted to be.

She screwed the taps to the left. There was a groan, and then somebody was hammering on the pipes; then a ghostly wailing inside the walls. It was that man in the Christmas story dragging his chains through the stained enamel tub. It was the Animals crawling out along the sidewalk, lurching, sniffing to find out where she lived.

"Stop!"

And one of those rare things occurred. The noise stopped; the water ran smoothly.

That's better, she thought. For a moment she watched a spider weaving a web under the sink, then she took off her bathrobe, pulled back the curtain, and stepped into the shower.

Warm hands moved slowly down her neck to her chest. She turned around, and someone was touching her shoulders. Then she was lying face down in make-believe Minnesota with her pretend Grandpa telling her another story, with hay and clover rising all around her. She had never met this Grandpa, nor had she seen the blue lakes of Minnesota. They belonged to the world her father sometimes whispered about when the room was all smoky and the people were gone.

"Do they know about me?" the girl would ask.

And Aurora's father would look at her mother and make a tired grin.

"They knew about you before you were born. We tell you that all the time."

"Then how come they never visit me?"

She knew better than to ask the opposite for there was no possibility of going to Minnesota.

The Animals must live there Aurora thought. Her father said once that it would be a cold day in Hell before he went back to the States.

A cold day. In Hell! Aurora was sorry that her Grandma and Grandpa lived in Hell with the Animals. And that her other grandma had to live in Montreal where even the frogs were unhappy. It must be everywhere Aurora thought.

Once, a long time ago when she was little, they were on a trip somewhere, Aurora forgot, some place in Ontario, and they stopped at a restaurant, and the lady brought the toast, and there were all these little squares of butter.

"Land o' Lakes," her father said softly, really to himself, and held the small container like it was as important as the quarter in her pocket. He didn't say anything else, but Aurora remembered. Over time, she found out in a story about the Land o' Lakes dairy in Minnesota, and the name on the license plates, and the lake her father used to live beside.

"Are my Grandma and Grandpa still there?"

And her parents always said yes until the summer after the Christmas they sent her the *Etch-a-Sketch*, when the Grandpa got eaten by the Animals and left the Grandma all alone.

Aurora watched her father then, pacing the carpet, looking out the window like she sometimes did, herself, and she went up to him and latched her fingers on his belt, and they watched bugs dancing all around the streetlight.

She let him tell her bedtime stories. She let him because of how he'd sit on the edge of the bed and then lie next to her so that his head was near her knee, and she couldn't see his face. He was just a voice, then, and that's when his stories were best. These stories had the same kind of adventure people that her books did, but these people had ordinary names like Jimmy or Lon. They were just people, but they got to stay up at night and see the shooting stars. And the stories weren't all happy ones, not like in her books, but there were places to go in them and lots of things to do, and music, and lakes, and everybody running. Canoes, too. And things that smelled like the woods. And Aurora would lift her head and look down at her father, stretched out talking to her knee, or to nobody at all.

So she learned of a place called *Land o' Lakes* that had grandparents and silly boys out on adventures, that had cold cold winters and nights of skating and the best Christmas trees in the whole wide world.

"Is that where you and Mommy loved?"

And her father's head came up, and he had on the saddest face.

Thump!
Owww!
Water thundered out of the hole; she saw the faucet head at the bottom of the tub and grabbed wildly for the taps.

She was disappointed a lot. Sometimes it was nothing more than the absence of cereal at the breakfast table. Her parents didn't believe in any cereal they couldn't make themselves which automatically ruled out *Cap'n Crunch* and *Cocoa Puffs*. No *Fruit Loops* and no *Sugar Crisps*, just some lumpy oatmeal, or some hard fruit and nut pellets that her mother made every two weeks.

Some mornings they were smoking the roaches. Bugs smelled bad when they burned. Mornings like that Aurora usually skipped her breakfast.

"Don't forget your fruit!" her mother would call, then some other person would chuckle, and her father would say something she couldn't hear, and Aurora would leave without the fruit.

Maybe it wasn't disappointment. She had had the feeling so often. There was a cramp in her stomach, or she felt light-headed all morning long, or maybe a kid would give her a candy, and that would be enough. Other kids had parents who lived in houses that had garages. Aurora had longed for a bicycle as far back as she could remember, but her father said it wasn't practical in a second-story flat.

"You had a bicycle when you were a kid."

Which was different she was told.

Everything was different. She didn't make friends easily, and when she did find someone she liked, she'd stop and think: I can't bring her over; I don't want her to come over. And the few times she went to a girlfriend's house there would be a mother who was older, or more like a mother than Aurora's own slender, long-haired mother. Sometimes the mother would be home all day, and sometimes she'd be a mother who came in from work, but there were always Oreos in the cupboard and Pepsi in the fridge, and Aurora could never believe the toys the kids had in the basement.

They had a basement.

Wasn't fair. She walked through the snow, her boot laces untied, and the tongues lapping up snowflakes. The lights were on in the front room as she came up the sidewalk. The curtain glowed orange, and there were shadows behind it.

Aurora beat her toes against the step and kicked her boots off inside the door. She climbed the stairs, already hearing the visitors. Four people were sitting on the floor with her father; the music was on. Everyone nodded as she walked by.

"No. No T.V. tonight," her mother said in the strange quick voice as she stuffed things into sandwich bread.

"I could bring...he could bring it in here...or *in my room*!" Aurora protested.

"No Aurora! T.V.'s bad for you. They lie to you on T.V.. Now, go in and take your bath. I'll bring your supper in to you after."

I don't take baths Aurora cursed, bumping her shoulders along the narrow hallway past the poster of that guy her mother called a gorilla, past the pile of coats that looked like dead bodies.

She closed the door to her room and fell on the bed listening to the muffled music and the talking; then she pulled the cover up and bit into the blanket, sucking the cotton flannel wadded in between her fingers.

They stared at her; they always stared at night when their faces would change from smiles and "woodland whimsy", her mother called it, into wild bright eye-slits and raw white teeth. Aurora didn't, she wouldn't be afraid of them. All of these animals had been given to her. "You can keep them," her mother said.

These...these...Animals.

Aurora reached out and grabbed one from the row, teeth already gnawing on her arm.

This place with the broken shower was where her father said goodbye. Aurora was cleaning her room, balancing the toys on the top of her upright suitcase-shelf. She snapped the flowered bedspread and slid it over the blanket, fluffing up the pillow and laying it on top. She liked the pillowcase. Her mother had made it for her when Aurora was seven, tied the colours in with elastic —"you don't tie them *in*, Aurora"—and let them dye themselves. And she liked how the colours wound around and around like little knobby hearts.

He was silent in his stocking feet, and she didn't know he was there until she turned around. He just stood and watched her, so she went to him and put up her arms.

"You're too big."

But he put an arm around her shoulder and drew her to him.

"I'm going away," he said.

She made her arms go rigid and wouldn't hug back.

"Did you hear me?"

The room smelled like cat faces.

Animals.

She heard her mother slam the outside door.

And then Aurora, too, was going down the street squeezing the buttons and rocks in her pocket, unravelling a mitten while it was still on her hand, watching the sky change from frosted silver to lemon-tinted, white-edged afternoon.

Playground swings were gone, the chains rolled around board seats and shoved into lockers somewhere. See-saws without the see or the saw, blunt stupid bar to dangle your body from. The jungle-gym was still there and the monkey bars, too, and she mounted and slipped and almost lost her footing; then she was hanging upside down in the deserted street-corner park.

White on top, now, buildings in the middle, sky on the bottom. Easier in winter, when the sky and the earth were so much alike.

Blood in the sky, on the snow?

One by one all of them hunted down, disappearing. Scraps of plaid and paisley, shreds of her mother's long purple dress.

She hadn't expected the earth to crash down on her head. She didn't realize, at first, what had happened. There was a dull pain.

"The sky is falling!" her storybook screamed.

She landed in a lump beneath the bars.

And now the earth. Aurora started to cry.

Three Ships: Rose: 1977-1978

She had never really liked crystal for all that her sisters had said otherwise. My Lord, when she looked at the things they made out of crystal these days, and she with a cabinet full of it, and expected to dust it over and over again. It was her sister who started her on it; Amanda gave her the first, the little linnet of light green crystal. "Greenfinch" her sister called it, who supposedly knew about birds and crystal, but over the years, at Rose's insistence, the bird became Rose's lake linnet.

And now dust everywhere, and her hands getting stiffer by the day. How long would she be able to go crawling into the cabinet like this without tipping and toppling the very shelves? Eric had reinforced them more than once with the sternest of warnings: this is the last time I do this. Neither of them ever believed it, of course. He said the same thing every time he fixed a trailer hitch for Ruddy or repaired that hopeless shutter on the shed. It was a way of making the time valuable, of robbing the day of its insignificance. This is the last time I'm putting this clothesline back up, you hear? Next time don't overload it! And the day was remembered.

They had a language, too, a significance which they had developed over the years. Rose believed other couples did the same. It was a strange thing to know, to know what Eric meant when he said "spindle and gruff". They, and only they, knew he meant the couple who rented the Lorrie house in summer.

"Days getting longer," Rose would comment from the porch, already planning the flowers along the side.

Eric knowing the next comment would be about fertilizer and tools in the shed and endless chores.

"Yes," she'd repeat, "the days are certainly getting longer."

"Ah, spindle and gruff," he'd fire back, and they would chuckle at the seasonal reference.

And after Eric, after Eric was gone, it struck her and she wondered what happened to all those languages, those languages that were spoken between couples. Spindle and gruff, Chickadee Pete and Blue Jay, did they stay in the air surrounding the ones who remained? Because they never could be spoken by anyone else.

It was different when you sent your words out, like boats, like she had done with the contest. She was still using that supply of cleanser from the *Starbright* company. Years after the contest had occurred, Rose's words muffled in a file in New Jersey.

This is the last time I'm tacking down this oilcloth.

How come she hadn't known? How come out of all the times, she hadn't *heard* it in his voice? His words sailing out to her from, Lord, incalculable distances; oceans and gulls, and it was their own language he was speaking.

Silence was awful. And annoying. Rose turned on the radio.

"And the temperature in the Twin Cities is....whoo...get ready for this one folks...."

He fell, and it was like watching a drowning man. It was totally incomprehensible to her. She had never seen Eric grasp at air blindly, terrified, and when he found her arm, he nearly pulled her in. All of him, all of his weight and fear, and words, words she couldn't make out.

Rose heard the kettle over the song on the radio and poured the water directly into the cup. Tea in cups. It had been a battle cry when she first moved up to Warroad. Her parents had taken tea properly and had taught the girls to do the same, so when Rose found some of the men up here taking their tea in mugs, men with greasy fingerprints claiming her mugs as their very own, she sounded the trumpet.

It had been amusing. She smiled even now at the vision of two or three of Eric's buddies crowded around the kitchen table, their fingers so recently separating worms or tying flies now pinching her splendid china cups, not two but three fingers held high in mid-air. Perhaps they did it to tease her; she had never thought of that at the time.

Tea in cups.

It meant a tea bag and a dash of hot water, now, the brown-betty too big. What had happened to her very language, the dialogue of tea and cup?

Oh....

She could feel the moments as they came on and was grateful for the warning. Self-pity, Rose..."tsk", she was about to add. Eric would have had none of it. He had always called her a woman of tall thoughts who had stood up to her family in order to marry him, who had come up here and made a life for them and the boys. A woman of tall thoughts with those symphonies on Sunday afternoons; happy as a lark by the radio with her mending, keeping an eye on the boys.

Oh.

The tea is black in the stained china cup. Starbright does not seem to clean it anymore. In the background is a song about "making out all night long". Rose goes over to the desk in the front room and pulls her writing pad out of the drawer.

Dec. 6, 1977
My Son,
The trees are bare now except for the conifers, which I can see much more clearly now. It is nearly the time of year when we would be deciding whose tree it would be this time, yours or Ray's. It really didn't matter to your father and me; we enjoyed every one you boys ever brought home. He enjoyed that so much, Luke, going out to the woods with you and Ray. I think it was what made him decide to get the cabins going. The idea of a man and his sons tromping through the woods...it was the way he'd been with his own father. He so loved you both. I know you may not believe that, but he did.

Christmas. You might wonder what a woman like me is up to here alone over the holidays. Well, let me assure you I have no intention of sitting around feeling sorry for myself. The church is planning a supper in a week or two, and Althea is asking me to come down to St. Paul for Christmas. So you see, my dance card is full.

What will you and Valerie and Aurora be doing? Will you go to Valerie's parents' in Montreal? You must drop me a line about it.

Please kiss my (not so!) little granddaughter and tell her Grandma loves her. I can't believe I have never seen her.

Or you, my dear, these many years. Take good care, Luke.
Love always,
Mom

Letters sometimes made her feel better. They transported her, briefly, from this room or that chair and gave her the quiet good grace to compose herself. There were few enough civilities left in the world. Rose sipped her tea. Althea's for Christmas, she thought; am I possibly that desperate?

Everyday around mail time Rose found herself hovering, which she hated, remembering it as one of her annoying traits with the boys. But no matter how she tried, there she would be with vacuum hose in hand, or up to her elbows in rinse water untangling stockings and would find herself waiting expectantly in the drip-dripping silence.

Afterwards she would always feel cheated no matter what had arrived: coupons, her *Reader's Digest*, her rebate from the porridge company, a letter. A letter! For they were rare enough. Her niece Althea, or one from Amanda's live-in companion, a woman as old and unreliable as Amanda herself. Very occasionally, a letter from Valerie. And, almost never, one from Luke.

This one day, a miracle in a large brown envelope decorated with primitive, brightly coloured trees.

Dear Other Grandma it began.

—Oh— a bird caught, hard, in her throat.

I am sorry that Grandpa died. I never saw him. Did he like me? I like you. Are you sad? I am in Grade 2 and I like to read my books and skate, too. I hope you are okay and be careful with the animals. My Mommy had to help me to write this. I love you.

Aurora Thyme Anderson

Wax-crayon miracles. Her fingers move back and forth along the page.

If only Valerie would relinquish Canada. It had to be why Luke remained there; President Ford and now President Carter had offered the boys a way home. Surely Luke missed his own country. Rose paused. So, could she then expect Valerie to give up *hers*? And little Aurora, smack in the middle. It was truly unfortunate.

Rose had never actually stated it, but she wished her son had found an American girl instead, which Rose realized was a perfectly selfish response to her own forced isolation. Hadn't her own family forbidden her to marry Eric? Which sent the headstrong woman hiking up north. Young women were so difficult to manage.

But young men? It wasn't supposed to work out this way. Of course she knew that you could never control young men and that, besides, they weren't the sort to run off with someone out of spite. Perhaps if she had just kept quiet.... But no, Rose, remember, now. When you met the girl she was already with child. So there was nothing Rose could have done, and she took some rueful comfort in that.

Ray's girl before he left, Margaret from Thief River Falls, now, she was charming enough. Rose didn't know if they had been serious though it had not seemed so to her. A nice girl, cheerful like Ray, worked in her father's store, if Rose recalled correctly.

All gone now. These things were slipping. Rose should really write them down. Perhaps one day Aurora would want to know about her Minnesota family, those spirited people from the north.

Rose paused and smiled again.

The child is Canadian. What could I tell her about the north?

Rose used her Starbright magnet to stick Aurora's letter to the refrigerator, and she was amazed at how one little piece of paper filled the room with people.

No card. No letter. Even when Rose was being honest with herself and admitting it was Valerie who wrote and sent the letters, she expected to hear...it was *Christmas*! Everyday the expectation and everyday the disappointment. She didn't want to have to call; she really didn't think it would be appropriate. Besides, she had her pride. The pride of mothers everywhere who one by one are broken down and beg for the love that they once sent out into the world.

A wintry night, wind blowing around the house and that shutter loose on the shed. Eric would have to....

She dialled. Number upon number like a ladder reaching up through the ice and snow, past the Indian Reserve, past the boundary, up into another country.

"Hello?" she always spoke too loud, CAN YOU HEAR ME UP THERE? How silly.

"Hello," the reply, so sombre. Canadian.

"Valerie?"

"Yeah. Who's this?"

Rose's china tea set handed down to this woman?

"Rose, dear...Luke's mother."

Rose could swear she felt a jolt on the line as if someone had jerked the wire all the way from Canada.

"Merry Christmas," Rose said, suddenly a tentative phrase.

"Yeah. Same to you."

Had Valerie been drinking?

"Are you all right, dear?"

Lord knows what went on behind closed doors these days.

"You calling from Minneapolis?"

So they had received her letter.

"No, I decided to stay up...down here. My niece has the flu, and I really didn't want to travel anyway, and, oh, I received the beautiful letter from little Aurora, and I wanted to speak to her, if I could...."

"She's asleep."

"Oh." Rose didn't really care if Valerie could hear her disappointment. After all, it was Christmas and not even a letter, not even a card.

"Then I'd like to speak to my son, please."

Pause. Shuffling cool wind from the north.

"He's out."

"Do you know when he'll be back?"

Another pause. The lines were probably frozen in this weather; Rose tapped the phone. Valerie?

"I don't know. When hell freezes over, probably."

She had been drinking!

"Valerie, I only wanted to wish you all a Merry...."

"Yeah, well it's gonna be really merry, okay? Luke barrel-assed out of here a couple of weeks ago, and I haven't seen him, heard from him since."

Rose, pinching the telephone cord between her fingers, the way the doctors pinched the cord that brought an infant into her arms....

"He's gone?"

"Flown. Blown. He's outta here."

"Where...?"

"I don't know! Maybe he's gone back to Minnesota. Maybe he's gone to the moon. Aurora cried and cried; I couldn't get her to stop." Valerie was crying, too.

"Maybe he'll be back soon," Rose heard herself say.

This is the last time I tack down this oilcloth.

What did any of it mean?

Rose wished Valerie well, hung up and stared at Aurora's letter on the refrigerator. The poor little girl. Her poor granddaughter. Yet even as she hated herself for thinking it at a time like that, one part of her was making plans for Luke's dinner, wet stuffing or dry. It would be the tall thin tree this year.

Oh.

Tall thoughts, Rose, she said over and over. Tall thoughts. As she tried to slow herself down.

Rose buttoned her long wool coat, her storm coat Eric had called it. "Look Out, Twin Cities, Rose's got her storm coat on." It was a far cry from the clothing she wore as a young girl in Minneapolis. Of course, everything was. What a strange expression, a far cry. Distances. Always distances.

She picked up the small axe from the shed, marvelling at Eric's organization. The shed had finally been tamed long years after the boys had left. Rose felt strange standing in the cold enclosure. This was where Eric spent many years of their life together. Rose wondered how many years. If you added up all the twenty minutes, all the half-hours out back, how many years was he in here surrounded by junk and license plates? Nailed to the wall, a plate from the early 40's, "Land of 10,000 Lakes" proudly inscribed...by convicts Rose wondered? The plates no longer said Land of 10,000 Lakes, and as everyone knew, Minnesota had more than 15,000 lakes.

We move on, Rose mused, busying herself with a coiled length of rope.

Eric had built a low sled to carry wood on. It was up against the wall. The rope, the axe and she was set. The shutter on the shed tapped gently as Rose closed the door and set out for the woods.

The old Indian used to tromp around the lake like this setting his traps along the trails. Rose could not really believe a man over a hundred years old still able to set and repair his own traps much less trek through the brush. Because it wasn't easy, no it was not a simple thing to pull a sled through the woods.

Rose stopped and breathed deeply. Enough. There was no need to bring it all the way in was there? How she wished she had gone on these outings with Eric and the boys.

Rose sat on the edge of the sled in the middle of a clearing. The snow heavily crowned the pines and outlined the bones of the maples. Ragged oak leaves, never knew when to quit. It was quiet except for woods sounds. Chickadees, wind through the red pine. If she had been quieter coming in, she might have seen a white-tailed deer. Rose was certain the old Indian never made noise like she had.

Up, Rose. She heaved herself off the sled and untied the axe up near the handle. Choosing the clearer of two possible trails, she set out beneath the canopy.

Tall tree. And not too bulky. And don't get big eyes, Rose, these trees are bigger when you get them inside. She could almost hear Eric instructing her, crunching needles and branches underfoot. She was silly ever to have been frightened by these woods. It was different in the olden times, of course, when the settlers were in danger. Rose could not imagine any settler putting up with that old Indian trekking around the land near a settlement, no matter how harmless he was. But that was because they hadn't all been harmless, had they? No, times had certainly changed, and Rose felt silly for having been frightened by the trees, and the growls, and the cries of the timber wolves.

She had found it. Walked as far around it as she could in the underbrush and pronounced it perfect.

Now, Rose, you'll just have to chop it down. She took off her mitts to get a better grip and took aim at the trunk.

One, two, three....

A thud, a chip of bark flying.

Rose was startled by the impact, and she staggered, then regained her balance. Two more swipes. Well, so far it looked like a beaver had been by.

She would be at it all day at this rate.

Hit on an angle. Use your body.

Hack, hack. If only Eric were here he'd have it down in a minute. Eric would....

She hadn't felt it coming this time.

Cold. So cold. Stupid clear Minnesota days can freeze a person to death, freeze them solid in hours. What was she doing? Oh, Eric. She was up here alone, and she didn't know how to chop, or how to be alone, foolish woman wandering the woods. Weren't these the same stories we unleashed upon children to make them behave? Wasn't she the creature that would leap from the bushes to drag off disobedient girls and boys? All the bogeymen, all the mad witches, a woman wandering the woods with an axe.

She began to laugh even as she was crying. Hot tears blistering cold cheeks; she wiped them with Eric's rough leather mitt. Her winter coat ballooned around her as she sat down beside the tree, a flabby skin too big for its owner.

Tall thoughts. But she was not tall. She could not see the sky from here, the canopy covered her view. Not even tall enough to see the sky, which was everywhere. Not even big enough for that.

She sat there long enough to notice some loss of feeling in her limbs. Her face was tight with dried tears, but her toes were numb. She wondered what time it was and then laughed once, loudly. Something skittered through the brush. What hour? Or what century? And if they found her bones one day, they would not be able to tell. Land of 10,000 lakes? Or 15,000? What time is it, what time is it?

Christmas Eve, 1958. The boys were out with friends but had promised to return in time for supper. Eric was down buying a few last-minute things for the feast, as he called it. The Christmas Feast. It made it sound as though they were the only people having this feast, when Rose knew that everyone was preparing to sit down to a Christmas Eve supper followed by drinks by the fire, carols around the tree, and an even bigger celebration the following day.

The Christmas Feast, Rose, he'd say waving his right arm ceremoniously. Was he conducting or about to bow? It didn't matter. He was sure to show up with a few extra baubles, an extra bag of nuts, just in case.

Rose was alone in the house enjoying the temporary respite, humming festive snippets as she watched the dinner rolls to keep them from browning too much on top.

There was probably Christmas music on all over the world. Rose flicked on the radio and slowly tuned the short-wave dial. Even the classical music was Christmas music this evening.

So it surprised her when she found the faraway station from up in Canada. There was a radio play about to start. Rose enjoyed radio drama as much as anybody, and she decided to listen to it as she mashed the potatoes. Maybe there'd be special guests on who would send out holiday greetings.

The play was called *Remember, Man,* and it was about this fellow who went up in space, up in a spaceship, and he stayed there a long long time. Only it wasn't a long time. It was all so confusing. Up in space it wasn't that long a time, but when he came back to earth everything had changed. The people he loved were dead and gone. No one knew him anymore.

It was bad enough to have to go away. But then to get back and find out that the world you knew had gone away, too. That must have been so....

She wouldn't even mind so much having to go away so long as she knew that everyone and everything would still be out there somewhere. In fact, it might actually be nice to be able to go away like that for a little while, so long as you could come back and nothing you knew had changed.

Remember, Man.

The man was frantic. Everything was gone.

"I dropped every damned one of them out on the driveway. Where are those boys? They can get out there and pick them up!"

Rose raced to the porch.

Eric was swearing about oranges.

It caught her throat to hear his voice.

Time to go home.

Oh, Eric, this is a wilderness.

She didn't know which startled her more, the sudden flash of light on the aspen across the clearing, or the swoop of wind which shook the trees as if all of them were shivering at once. She felt the wind, though; it pressed her skin against her face, held it wrapped to her bones. It hurt, like pressing against glass. A single shaft.

Light on snow in the Big Woods.

A shaft. Light entering a room, and a child entering her world.

Ray. She felt his hand pass against her face.

She left it all there, the axe, the sled. And most of all she left the tree, following her footsteps back along the arduous path, grateful for the needles from the red pines' lower branches which had dropped across the path and kept her from slipping. The wind was fierce. It pressed her face clean.

In her house it was Christmas Eve. There was a movie on the television, *A Christmas Carol* with Alastair Sim—which she was sure couldn't have been his real name. Perhaps it stood for Simpson or Simpkins. Wasn't Simpkins British? It was like that "Don Ho", the man on those television specials. Perhaps his name was Hogarth—or Holden. Rose liked William Holden although she'd heard about his reputation with the ladies and with drink.

Alistair Sim. He did a lovely job with Mr. Dickens's story, no doubt about that. He truly did seem nasty at the beginning, and then he went along, and life changed him, and he got nice. Tiny Tim helped to change him. Children do that.

Rose turned off the T.V., preferring the record player. She could put on Bing Crosby's Christmas record, she supposed. As Rose pulled the albums out one by one she found a few there from when the boys were still home. *The Beatles*, the *Rolling Stones*, with ANDERSON scrawled across the back cover.

Rose plugged in the machine. The cord was wrapped with electrical tape, a gluey knob next to the plug.

I know, I know, Rose nodded. That's the last time I'm....

But something was wrong with the machine itself. The turntable was turning but everything was wrong, too slow, and Der Bingle's voice wasn't crooning but bleeting or lowing. It was terrible.

Rose chuckled.

It was awful!

Eric would have squawked about the repairman who'd sent them the missing part. And Ray, he'd be imitating Bing, "MAAAATHHH-HEERRR...COOOUUULLDDD AAAAHHHH HHAAAVVVE MMM-MOOOORRRRE PEPPPSSSSI-CCOOLLLLLAAAA...." And Luke.... Her boy was out in the forest somewhere.

It was Christmas Eve at Rose's house.

It was Christmas Eve out there in the woods, for the animals, the tree she had nicked and chipped. The birth of the Baby Jesus, Hope of the World.

Rose turned on the radio. A choir filled her kitchen.

I saw three ships come sailing in
On Christmas Day, on Christmas Day.
I saw three ships come sailing in
On Christmas Day in the morning.

Rose, never on board any ship, always waiting for them to arrive. It is silly. I am foolish.

Sentimental, Eric would say.

I saw three ships....

Eric on the mantel, his strong arms holding high the prize walleye, his waders turned down at the cuff. Ray in the uniform of the United States of America, buttons polished, face as bright as day itself. An oval space where Luke's picture would go, a piece of matte board in mahogany.

Later, much later, after "I Saw Mommy Kissing Santa Claus" and Mahalia Jackson, Rose locked the doors and turned off the outside lights. First time no coloured lights outside, on all night to welcome the Baby Jesus.

Tomorrow she would call Althea and see how she was doing.

Good night Mr. Sim. Mr. Simpkins. Mr. Simpleton.

Goodnight, William Holden.

And God bless us, everyone.

PART 3

The Sheltering Lie: Luke, Aurora: 1988

*G*renge says everybody's more than a little fucked up in the head. Says it's not unusual for whole families to go that way, looking at me the whole time she says it.

Grenge is my best friend, the self-proclaimed geek of my high-school. But she's not, or I'd never hang around with her. She doesn't fit in there, and she just doesn't have time for it. Simple. Kind of like me, but at least I play the game well enough to get good marks, although this has more to do with the school's low standards than any big effort on my part, which says a lot about the school. And something about me, too, I guess. But, anyway, Grenge and I have that much in common. Which might have been all, at first. I mean, she used to play guitar in the corner of the lunch room. And this was back in Grade 9! I'll give her that; she was pretty brave sitting there with one or two other *Lost Horizons* (they called themselves....) and then all of them falling into retro-rhymes and harmonics.... Of course the rest of us were improving our minds smoking and scarfing down fries. Anyway, it doesn't matter. We got to be friends. She puts up with my clothes, and I put up with her frosted 60's lipstick.

She's the only one who understands why I went to Europe to see my father. My mother certainly doesn't. No, old Val had it all figured before I even opened the letter. Funny, it's like she knew what was in it. My mother, the psychic, with appalling taste in boyfriends.

"Aurora, that's enough!"

Yeah. Appalling taste in boyfriends.

I remember the first time Grenge picked me out of the crowd. It was: "What kind of name is Aurora?"

Like I'd never been asked that before. But she didn't have that edge in her voice so I told her.

"Aurora Thyme Anderson."

"Time? Like Time?"

"Like plants."

"Shit...," she shook her head. "Fucking thyme," and started choiring the opening of "Scarborough Fair". "Well, at least it isn't 'Parsley'," she concluded.

And so.

I let her come over to my place sometimes just to see my mother do the two-step. My mother is in what we call S.D.M.—Serious Dating Mode— although what I don't tell Grenge is that she's been in it for years. She spends plenty of time trying to hide the bags and sags from these totally depressing jerks who show up with sweet wine and tickets to curling playoffs. One of the Sleazoids even cornered me in the kitchen while mother was still deciding what to wear to the arena. I almost kneed him; then I thought about poor Mom and all that time in front of the mirror, and I grabbed the guy by his acrylic sweater and reminded him I was a minor, and reminded him that my mother was taller than he was and had a pretty good aim, herself.

Meek.

They're all so fucking desperate. Lord, spare me evenings with desperate men.

Anyway, so Grenge and I were just hanging around supposedly doing homework, and she, my mother, kind of casually mentions, "There's a letter from your father on the fridge."

My father! Now, there's two words that don't get cozy very often. My Father. Pop. Dad. Pater Noster. The Old Man. Old Luke Anderson, part-time Daddy Deluxe.

"You got a father?"

"Grenge, I'd like you to meet my Dad."

I held the letter out, and she gave it a nod. We both noticed that he had mercifully addressed it to A.T. Anderson.

"All right!" Grenge enthused causing my mother to look over from her zucchini.

I have a father. Grenge doesn't. That is, she did, but he got spliced by a drunk on Highway 401. Her father was drunk, too.

"I like to think they found each other," was how she summed it up.

The letter was from Germany. Berlin, to be exact. Luke Anderson had somehow managed to temporarily finance himself in Europe, and now he was wondering if his little girl....

"I take it he hasn't seen you in a while."

...would like to come over and visit.

"Does he know I finished school?" I looked over and my mother shrugged. "How does he know I'm finishing school?"

"Far fucking out!" Grenge approved before I could stop her. My mother has a problem with words like fuck which is more than a little funny since I learned it from her. "Mommy and Daddy" from the T.V. they weren't. I used to tell Grenge how my parents smoked dope and about all the people who'd drop by.

Grenge thought it was terrific.

"My mother lived in a *Tupperware* commune," she said. "Sad to see them, pale, ruining their health playing with those vacuum lids...."

"What do you think, Aurora?" my mother demanded.

She wasn't going to wear that awful green skirt again! Unless....

"Hey, you got a new boyfriend or something?"

See, my mother and I have a few problems. Don't get me wrong; I've seen her go through it over the years. And she kept things together after my father took off, him being no bargain to live with as my mother tactfully put it. Well, she called him paranoid, too, and sometimes manic-depressive, but 'impossible' is what we settled on, and it's how we remember him on holidays. I used to tease her, long after it was all over, a long time after when she was seeing men again, I used to say, "Well, mother, after all, he wasn't, you know...*Canadian*," as if being Canadian meant anything, and we'd laugh.

Grenge loved all of it. How Luke was an army deserter; how they'd run the border gauntlet with my mother hanging on to her stomach, a.k.a. me (imagine, a fetus with an a.k.a.). Most of all, she loved how I was conceived at Woodstock.

"Amazing!" she thundered. "I was an accident in a Biscayne after bowling!"

So, Grenge and I studied the letter pretty closely.

Dear Aurora:

"There's that name again."

Grenge actually likes my name except for the Thyme.

I don't know if you remember me. I'm the tall man with the unkempt hair who occasionally took you over to school. The one the teachers thought was a child molester, yes.

"They did?"

You must be different now. The green snowsuit must be too small.

"Ugh," Grenge moaned.

I'm different, too. I've been here for a while. I like it. I'd like to show you parts of Europe. I know it sounds strange, like receiving a wedding invitation from a stranger, but I'd like to give you the trip for your graduation present. It is this year, isn't it? I know it's this year, and I know you did well. You only had trouble when I was around. I think you'd love it here.

"Another psychic," Grenge shook her head. Grenge can be an absolute idiot sometimes.

I'm going to call your mother on the 20th of July, at 8:00 p.m. your time. Tell her, will you? And please consider the visit.

It's not like there were people breaking the door down to take me to Europe. It would have been great to have gone with Gilmer, though. Paul Gilmer, the most recent light of my life, but the bulb burned out about a month ago, and the new talent didn't look bright enough to negotiate his way to the airport.

Then Grenge said she'd come with me if she could, but she'd never get the money. Her mother was broke, and the only thing she was getting for graduation was an Oxford dictionary set that had belonged to her cousin, Reddick.

"I think we have some money, but she's saving it for our bypass operations."

Grenge is convinced she's going to die of a heart attack. "Either that or Arthur Murray urban guerilla dance lessons." Besides, Grenge had already decided to work at the *Pizza Hut* through the summer, so she could afford to go to all the concerts and comedy clubs.

Neither of us had plans for the fall.

—⁂—

Dear Grandma Down Under:

Well, it is a while since I wrote you. Thank you for the card and the money. I can't believe I've actually graduated. But something must have happened because—guess what?—Luke, DAD, sent me a letter! He wants me to go visit him in Germany! Last I heard he was somewhere out west. How about you? Has he written lately?

We Andersons are lousy letter writers. Well, except you. You are my only pen pal who has lasted longer than a couple of letters. Sorry I don't write more often.

It was funny what you said about that mixup with your pie. You should have told them. Now that other woman has a ribbon on her wall instead of you. My mother can't make pies, and neither can I. I am getting so I can shape jello, but why?

Gotta go. I'll send you a postcard from Berlin!

Love,
Aurora

—⁂—

My father—that is, Luke—was waiting for me at Tegel Airport. I arrived with my requisite one suitcase (his instructions) and with a slight hangover (the guy beside me kept buying me drinks; he was a dead ringer for a guy my mother dated a while back). I'd already been lost once, in the Frankfurt airport, which was not what I'd expected based on years of the *Heidi* movie every Christmas. Then again, that was the train station....

I was feeling real...I don't know...international, like something out of the European fashion mags I'd looked at on the plane, and I'm strolling around past these guards with machine guns.

Machine guns?

Didn't I see this last week on T.V.? Were they looking for a terrorist?

And just then—I admit—for a split second, it flashed that it was my...that they were looking for Luke. I know it's ridiculous. Nobody is looking for my father. Nobody cares about my father or that old war, especially over here. Besides, he was small potatoes even among potatoes. Or...*Kartoffeln*. Zip, the fingers race through the pages of the miniature pocket dictionary.

My father. Small...*kleine Kartoffeln*.

I'd be lying if I said I wasn't nervous. I had not seen Luke Anderson for six years. He used to visit the first couple of years after he left us. He seemed to want to do that, but I think it made things harder for my mother with him loping in and out of her life and all, so I think he decided not to repeat on us like cabbage.

Grenge had listed all these pointers. *Etiquette When Dealing with Strangers, i.e. Parents*, she called it. Included were:
- Don't comment on the weight problem of his new girlfriend.
- Don't ask him if he has a girlfriend; this will become apparent.
- Don't pick up and examine anything. You're just his kid; this is his stuff!
- Don't talk about your mother's lovers. He might misunderstand, and this isn't Show-and-Tell.
- Accept any and all gifts graciously, reminding him of the paternally-imposed one-suitcase limit.
- Above all, remember that he still thinks you're ten years old, so be discreet about your menstrual cramps.

We laughed a bit, but it didn't make it any easier.

"At least you have a Dad," she whispered as she hugged me at the airport.

"Good luck at *Pizza Hut*."

"We make 'em flat for you."

I couldn't see him. He was nowhere. If Grenge had been there she'd have started singing "Nowhere Man", and it would have driven me crazy, and I realized for the first time that I was glad she wasn't with me. It was like having to go to the dermatologist with a rash. You want to be alone.

"Aurora Anderson, bitte. Fräulein Aurora Teem-muh Anderson."
I spun around.
So did everyone else: me because I had just been summoned by a loud speaker in Berlin, they because they had to see the girl with the *komische Name*.
Teem-muh?

He was standing by the counter. I wouldn't have known him if ...well, I did know him. I'd have known him anywhere, but that didn't mean it looked like him. Like a relative, maybe. His face was sort of the same, but there were a few lines near the eyes.
"Aurora?" His voice.
He hadn't put on weight. Men were lucky. They just got cancer, later, and died, but they didn't have the sagging. At least Luke didn't.
The thing that really was different was his hair. It was grey. Not completely, but it was kind of a snow-slush colour, and it was short.
I guess he didn't know me either. It wasn't exactly the Classic Airport Reunion Scene.
"Yeah, it's me," I said trying to be helpful, trying to adopt an old stance or tilt my head a certain way, but I realized that, for him, even my voice had changed. And there was no disguising the chipped, black paint on my fingernails.
"It's a phase," I offered as I followed his eyes. He noticed my height, of course. And my breasts. And the rest of me. The shit-kicker boots, the nondescript pants. Torn t-shirt. Vest.
"My vest."
"What?"
"That was my vest."
I'd always thought it was my mother's. Or one of the relics left behind from the old days. His vest. "Do you mind?"
"You wear it well. Let's go," he said and swept me past the guards.

—ʍ—

Oh, it was weird at first. He was so formal. So polite. It was like inheriting a 40-year-old tour guide complete with *Angst* and garbled German. We weren't talking. What did I expect?

He kept trying to do things—buy stuff—for somebody my age. I'm seventeen. He said he thought it was a miracle that I'd finished school so soon considering I'd repeated a year in grade school.

"We settled down after that, you know." And realized I'd somehow hurt him. I hadn't seen it coming; I didn't know where he hurt.

"I skipped a couple of grades," I apologized.

He said he was proud of me. Then he took it back and struggled with some convoluted logic about having no right to be "proud" since he'd had nothing to do with it. He settled for "pleased", and I said I was pleased he was pleased.

He said he had to go out for a while. I told him I had things to do.

Living in a stranger's apartment is weird. I don't mean my father, here. The guy, whomever, he is subletting from. Who is he, anyway; who would do a neat thing like place rocks on ledges and at the same time hang up awful David Hamilton prints? John Coltrane next to the Bee Gees. Of course some of this stuff might be my father's, a thought that unnerved me.

I broke most of Grenge's rules as I walked around the room. I glanced in drawers and found nothing interesting. In Luke's bedroom I found two things: his dogtags in his night-table and a picture of his family. Funny. They are all squinting at the sun. That always looks especially strange in a black and white picture, everybody screwfaced at a grey sky. Luke is skinny. Ray is smiling.

I decided to write some postcards. The one to my mother was simple. Yes, he was there to meet me. No, I will not need any more money. I wrote to Grenge, but you really have to talk to Grenge. And this is one time I'm not sure she'd understand what it is I've been feeling since I got here. Because I found something else, too.

One of the nicer prints in the living room is a photo of a ruined building with a tree growing out of it, tall grass all around. Luke had said it was in East Berlin and we could go there if I wanted.

I held the photo and turned it over. And there we were.

Me in a blue snowsuit holding the red shovel. My mother in her old paisley jacket with the pockets. Percale Street. And the words: "My Wife. My Child. My Love. 1976".

Funny how it came at me sideways like that.

It's a hard thing to make small talk day in and day out. I don't know how my mother does it. Add to that walking your feet off all over the city, and you have two world-weary travellers cueing up for *Würstchen und Bier*.

I liked it. Sitting outside along the Ku'dam with a *Schültheiss* or a *Warsteiner* and watching all the fancy people, and the tourists, and half of Berlin going by.

He seemed happy there. I couldn't tell if there was a woman or not. I did see a pair of women's shoes in the closet, but then Luke was subletting.

So there we were, two chic European types, quaffing cool ones at a streetside *Cafe*, watching the sun set at the end of the street, the building balancing the hazy summer ball. It looked like a poster. We looked like a poster, one of those ones they give you free at the travel bureau.

He was talking now, onto his third *König Pils*. He was telling me about his research into "Cities After Wars".

"It was a long time ago, though."

I mean, before Luke was even born!

He didn't mean that, he tried to explain. I couldn't tell whether he was talking about cities, or architecture, or subway systems, or bombed-out train stations, you know, or something else, some lost soul with burned-out eyes like that Edvard Munch painting that's probably also a poster somewhere, the scream in it less scary than the empty haunting eyes.

He wanted to take me fishing, but it wasn't a good place for fishing. He was going to rent a car and some rods and take me out somewhere, God knows where. He had somehow, I guess, decided I liked fishing and was explaining all these casts in the living room and had moved the cushions onto the floor to represent rocks and had moved the owner's rock collection onto the floor to represent smaller rocks, and I was laughing about that, saying the cushions looked more authentic, and he was so damned serious about this fishing stuff that I felt I had to listen.

"See this part here...."

"Behind the floor cushions? I mean, the big rocks?"

"Right behind here, see, that's a sheltering lie."

"A *what*?"

"A sheltering lie...see...the fish are safer here, lots of shade, less of a current, and they can still feed from what's floating by."

I joked with him some more about fishing until he finally clued in that I wasn't into it.

"I like climbing," I said hopefully.

His long face lit up slowly.

"Ray...your uncle...he was a good climber," he said.

—m—

Hi, Minnesota Grandma!

I'm here! Going all over, busy busy. See if you can spot me in the street scene. Luke okay. Seems good, actually.

Has a picture of you (w. Ray, Grandpa, and Luke for a change!) Says he'll write you. Says you are 'a rock' which I think is a compliment! Bye for now, Aurora

—⁊⁊—

I didn't know what to tell him about myself. It all seemed so...so what? I told him about Grenge and the *Pizza Hut* job. How Grenge had wanted to come. How she was probably the closest thing to a hippie left walking on this earth.

He smiled, from somewhere, and asked me about my mother.

"She's okay. She...keeps busy and all. Still working for that insurance firm."

Did she still have the Klee print? How about her winter colds?

I was starting to feel uncomfortable, like my mother's Klees and Kandinskys were privileged information. I don't know much about this kind of loyalty, but it didn't seem right to let him know that she still danced around when a golden oldie came on the radio.

Was she still doing yoga in the living room?

WAS SHE STILL THE SAME?

It was getting pathetic, so I spared him the humiliation and said, "She's fine. She goes to painting class twice a week. She's taking a course in tax planning at the community college. She's sort of seeing someone...heavily."

"Do you like him?"

It must have been the way I said it. I couldn't answer him. Besides, he'd only get pathetic again.

It was very cool that evening when we walked along the *Ku'dam*. We had quite a way to go to get to *Bahnhof Zoo*, and I had this terrible urge to urinate. It's beer. And me. And candlelight and Fred Astaire. A "symbiotic sabotage" as Grenge would say.

Finally I couldn't stand it anymore, and I had to pull over this half-drunk stranger (my father) and explain the situation to him and get him to act as American Decoy while the unobtrusive Canadian peed in an arcade passageway.

No.

Don't ever do this in Berlin.

Cities After Wars, nothing! There are legions of old ladies, war survivors all, patrolling at all hours with their dogs in little carry-bags yelping and leading the way, and they're just waiting for moments like this to send the canines yapping and snapping at your heels and various other parts which sends you running, zipping and tripping, down the *Kurfürstendam,* while the old ladies scream *Anarchist! Anarchist!* in your wake; until you are the only one leaping the Wall into East Berlin.

We ran.

Luke was exploding with anger or laughter; he grabbed my hand and pulled me along. I was looking back and trying to explain to the woman in English, but he kept yelling "Forget it!" which was drowned out by the Anarchist Solo.

We ran until we couldn't hear her anymore. I started laughing, too. I looked over at Luke and he was completely white, his eyes concentrating on something up ahead.

"It's okay," I choked out. "We can stop...Luke...?"

I stopped.

And Luke kept running.

—⟋⟍—

What am I supposed to remember? What do you say about whirlwind trips to Europe? They're supposed to be incomplete. You're supposed to lose your camera, or get back somebody else's prints, or mix up all the pictures, anyway, and not be able to tell one museum from the next.

Paris was great, but everybody knows that. I bought Grenge a sweatshirt with a good graphic on it and an advertisement for an upcoming jazz concert. After I bought it I realized that, of course, she wouldn't like it. I bought my mother a great sweater which I plan to borrow. And I got the latest boyfriend a trivet shaped like the Eiffel Tower. You can put the handle of something along the tower, so you don't burn yourself.

She's probably going to marry this one. I couldn't tell Luke even if I'd wanted to. *She* may not even know it yet. But she's tired of the good fight, I think, and with the pickings slimming out Wade Hardigan looks like a sure candidate for brand New Dad.

Does she love him? Luke would have asked.

And I wouldn't be able to explain, a woman over forty.

A sheltering lie.

"Aurora," I heard my name from somewhere. I'd fallen asleep by the stereo, lying on some cushions and listening to jazz.

I opened my eyes. I felt something and looked down and saw Luke lying on the floor near the stereo. His head was on the pillow near my knee. His hair was the colour of slush, and he seemed troubled in his sleep. I watched until his head stopped stirring. When I was little he used to do this. My animals on my bed, the curtains billowing gently like sails.

What I remember best about the trip was the flight home. It wasn't just the turbulence or the same movie I'd seen on the way over (there are only so many times you should have to believe in Robert Redford). It wasn't the prospect of my mother and what's-his-name picking me up at the airport or the possibility of fitting in a concert with Grenge. And it wasn't the fact of having screwed around too long to get into university in the fall.

That was all there and had always been there. That was the stuff every traveller lugged around, slowing you down at the gate, setting off the alarms when it showed up on the X-ray.

It wasn't all that.

It was me at Tegel Airport watching Luke watching me. The guards, the guns, the woman frisking me in the booth, a big woman, stereotype from the Second World War. She passed a bar over me that looked vaguely like a dildo and pronounced me responsible with a nod of her head. I had an old woman's *Anarchist!* ringing in my ears and smiled at this casual dispensation.

I had Luke Anderson pouring his heart out to me in a taxi on the way over. Luke holding my arm as if to say, "Please, look at this!" "Will you take this in, too?" But not looking at any of it himself. Wanting me to know that "Look at this" meant "Listen to this". Wanting me to convert the flat window pictures into words I would remember.

I knew I would try to explain it to Grenge. And I knew, just as clearly, that she wouldn't understand me. Not this time. Not about this.

No. It wasn't the flight: Berlin a series of lights and patterns disappearing below, the airline hostesses all looking like every B-movie starlet who ever had something called 'gams', or Robert Redford and a *Halb-Trocken* German wine and Grenge's sweatshirt draped over my shoulders. It was Berlin, something showing up only on an X-ray, setting off alarms all through my system; the guards hoisting machine-guns; the woman guard hoisting a dildo while a man my father used to be slips out an exit into anonymity.

Leonard Cohen on a Windy Night:
Val: 1989

*W*ade picked Val up at precisely 7:15, which didn't surprise her, since he was punctual whether on the job as a management consultant or lining up for his yearly flu shots.

"What's the matter with that?"

Short bristly hair and a hint of a neck, a loud—too loud—silk tie.

What surprised her was the tie and the suit, and herself decked out in what passed for dinner clothes, all to go to a Leonard Cohen concert at the Congress Centre.

"Look at us," Val marvelled.

"Yeah. *Some* of us accessorized."

They were going to meet another couple in the lobby, Julie and Charlie. Val didn't know Julie that well, but when she had mentioned the concert at work, Julie's eyes misted over, and she confessed her long love to Val. Like a couple of kids. When, in fact, they were both edging up the ladder from forty, Julie with three children, one of whom had Downs Syndrome, Val with one child and a younger lover named Wade.

Val had vacillated over whether to invite Julie. She had even had her doubts about Wade. But in the end, she had decided that it didn't matter who else went with her as long as she got to go herself.

"What's she look like?"

Wade's nervous strutting, Jimmy Cagney in herringbone tweed, eyes shifting back and forth.

"Kind of short. Dark hair. Short, dark...."

Val spotted them, Julie and a stout man, round faced and bearded.

"Julie!" Val lifted her hand as she walked toward them.

"Jesus, he looks like a biker..." Wade followed her over.

Val hated the venue. Drinks were being sold in the upstairs lobby, shots and wine doled out in plastic wine glasses. Val didn't know why they bothered shaping the things like wine glasses. She felt ridiculous holding on to the little plastic stem.

The concert hall contained large round tables covered with white tablecloths. At least they were real.

"Oh...we're going to have to share...."

A little upsetting since other people seemed to have arrived in large noisy groups. Val and Julie both spotted one of the empty tables quite far from the stage.

"If everyone's sitting there shouldn't be any problem," Julie suggested. Val's plastic wine glass toppled over as the corpulent Charlie squeezed around the table.

"She-it," Charlie offered.

Val ignored Wade's obvious discomfort, his rapid-fire attempts to get out of the verbal hole he had dug himself into with Charlie, ignored Julie's office talk, her PMS confession and her Leonard Cohen gush. Val even ignored, or tried to ignore, the six people who joined them at the table, joyously inebriated, younger than Wade; three couples who had paid to listen to one song.

Finally, the lights dimmed. The lighting and staging created the deliberate aura of an old nightclub, hints of pre-war Germany, precisely what the majority of the audience would have expected. After all, wasn't Leonard going to sing "First We Take Manhattan, Then We Take Berlin?"

He appeared in black, elegantly understated, in the company of two female singers.

"Wish I could see better," Julie cooed.

His face was weatherworn, his build mature, but, then again, weren't they all.... Val paused looking at the young people at her table, then at Wade, then at Julie...aren't we all getting older? A tremendous feeling of isolation hit her like the wave of sound; the wine stain on the tablecloth looked like South America; the room was quickly turning into a smoky nightclub; just like the stage Leonard strolled with a woman on either arm, and it was his voice she remembered, not this middle-aged man in basic black. The voice of a man singing with someone's arm clamped round his throat. Val closed her eyes on the unfamiliar scene, and the voice continued to sing.

It was the same man, same voice, but if she opened her eyes she would find herself in a roomful of complete strangers and perhaps would not recognize even herself among them.

Eyes closed so tight they hurt.

Wade's voice barging past the barricade of skin.

"Something wrong?"

"No," she shot blindly. "I'm just listening."

And remembering someone in a green cotton shirt and a pair of cut-offs walking down a dirt road on her way to the cabin. A camp just north of Montreal and five teenaged girls, one catching fireflies.

She had initially gone along as a favour to her neighbours, the Holtzes, but this had been forgotten once she was there.

She remembered how surprised she was whenever she left the city, the discovery of how dark the night was and how bright the stars. But this was twilight, the best time. They had finished their campfire and songs. Embers and sparks and grey moth angels peeling off from the wood and floating up and up and up. One of the girls, Nora, pulled out some marijuana and proceeded to pass it around, but Val declined, watching sparks shiver whenever she flicked a branch against the log.

Then it was finished, doused and turned over. Gone, the orange outlines, only fireflies, now.

"They look like fluorescent lights," somebody says.

"Like the inside of elevators."

And then silence, and the others trudged on ahead, and the girl in green cotton felt the road close behind her.

In the dark cabin, five girls undressed by their bunks. The cabin was freezing, and there was only cold water, so there were quick jumps from the sink into sleeping bags. The usual cringe at invisible spiders.

"Can't get this marshmallow crap out of my teeth."

It is perfect black until the girl on the end, the one closest to the window, unzips her sleeping bag and pulls open the dish-towel curtains. She fumbles beside her orange-crate shelf. The portable record player hums and clicks and then the room fills with the deep lost voice.

"Susanne," it calls out, and "Sisters of Mercy."

And one girl absolutely still in a cold, musty sleeping bag understanding all at once that she was completely alone and was the only person on earth lying under that specific piece of sky, that they were all of them separate points as self-contained as fireflies, stretching their light and loneliness to the edges of their sleeping bags.

When had that understanding gone? She had felt sad then but frighteningly free, laying back against the earth, looking past the dish-towel to the sky.

Val on the top of Mount Royal with Mrs. Molloy. Both of them peering down onto the tops of trees and buildings, the water ribbon in the distance.

"Is this the top of the world?" Val asked the squinting face of Mrs. Molloy.

"It is, here, girl. It certainly is."

"Great, eh?" Julie yelled clapping her hands and nodding.

Val smiled back, scrutinizing Wade, who might be enjoying himself.

Julie leaned forward and practically screamed in Val's ear.

"I used to go to the *Seven Steps* to hear him."

Val smiled. "You're from Montreal?"

"No, I moved there in the Seventies. Kept hoping I'd run into him."

"Seventies? But...the *Seven Steps* became a jazz bar, didn't it? *The Rainbow.*"

"I know."

"But you said...."

And on stage he had begun to sing "If It Be Thy Will."

Val glanced at Julie. Enraptured. The woman had once moved to Montreal hoping she would bump into Leonard Cohen. She had gone looking for a club that no longer existed. Nobody was paying attention to time anymore.

But there wasn't much she could do about some chronology, the fact that she was eight years older than Wade. It shouldn't bother her, the years. She knew that she was supposed to relinquish anxiety over that. But it wasn't "eight years" it was *those* eight years...he remembered only vaguely what were her own tumultuous times. And how did you explain that; how did you gloss over it in conversation?

He remembered the hippies. His mother didn't want him going near them. They had lice.

He remembered Vietnam as a name that interrupted his T.V. shows. He saw Bobby Kennedy on a T.V. mini series. He knew the Stones, "but they're over the hill."

"I didn't know he sang 'Bird on a Wire', too!"

"He wrote it."

He didn't know Leonard Cohen at all.

And Aurora didn't like him, not that that was an indicator, but Aurora did say she wondered what Val could see in a man like Wade.

"He's...on time," Aurora mused, tapping her lip with her index finger.

Aurora's catalogue of Val's lovers. It had been humorous once upon a time when Aurora was younger, and it was possibly a way for Aurora to mask awkwardness over her mother's sexuality. And, as Aurora always pointed out, she did have a stake in the choices. One of them could have legitimately become her dear old Dad. She certainly hadn't been given much in that department.

Who knew where Luke was now? Who cared, Val wanted to add but couldn't. Maybe Celia had been right, and all women were being bled unconscious by debilitating lovers. Celia who now had a position with a lobby group in Toronto.

When Luke first left, Val had been so busy with her anger and her daughter that they had buffered her for some time: running around finding day care, seeing the shrink once a week, taking her insurance exams, going to her encounter group. Perhaps some people were able to fend off absence forever with such busy days. It worked fine for a spell, Val's nights with other men. But then came the one time the chronology slipped.

It was a windy evening; Val remembered that, walking briskly from the bus stop along the lighted street. She didn't remember where Aurora was, a friend's? But Val was not hurrying home for her daughter; it was dark and she wanted to get in. And she recalled thinking, at the time, that she never used to be afraid out alone at night, all those years in Montreal wandering the streets or up on the mountain.

It was like loneliness. Growing up she realized that no one else would ever come to know her, and that even if they did it would be that person's version of her. And this had struck her as neither sad nor tragic; it merely was. Then she met Luke, and when he went away she understood that she had learned loneliness. It was something learned just as companionship was something learned, and the reaching out left its counterpart—negative space somewhere under the heart, dark hollow hiding behind the ribs.

And it wasn't the trust, that overrated eternal. She had trusted and had gotten blasted to the core and had come to trust again. There seemed no end to the number of times human beings could recharge that battery. No, it was loneliness, a longing stretching out from a sleeping bag to the stars, knowing that from the stars she was a tiny gold cocoon with a leopard-print interior, and the edges of herself were merely zippered shut.

So Luke had given her both companionship and loneliness; just as the gym teacher at high school, in teaching them to jump had first taught them how to fall. And Val could never understand people staying with others who brought them only pain. But this, the thing and its negative space, this she understood.

And Mrs. Molloy and her sad life splayed open on Tuesday afternoons, her confidant a child of seven or eight, her painful past a game of "Q and A".

"But why don't you go and get little Ricky if you still want to be with him?"

The logic of innocence assaulting a woman in thick support hose, a son who might not even be a child anymore, an absence as fresh and as private as the sandwiches the woman kept in the tin box that had once held cigars.

And Mrs. Molloy's saving prayer—you don't have to like them—said over and over as an incantation against the reality of having to love. Val realized years later how Mrs. Molloy had loved, how her whole story had been an enactment of the rewards and ravages of love: her flight from Ireland, little Ricky, her grudging devotion to a child named Valerie. Years of shrugging off disappointment, dodging humiliation. Years of 'putting up with.'

"Noisy unctions," Mrs. Molloy would say.

And you didn't have to like them. You really didn't.

There was a break in the show which allowed people to go out and buy more drinks. Wade pointed at Val's plastic wine glass, or rather at the wine stain, and she nodded adding, "Maybe I can do Australia." His compact body rose and went to stand in line.

Julie and Charlie were slipping out to try to find a place to smoke a joint, so Val sat alone among the young couples who were loudly commenting on Leonard's "two good songs" and the fact that he had already sung them.

Val wondered whether she should go to the bathroom but realized that Wade would be back any minute. He had an intensity in lineups as if he knew that this wasn't just a lineup for drinks but some sort of cosmic competition that was being broadcast somewhere on closed circuit television, and he wasn't about to be made a fool of on t.v.. No, not on t.v.,anyway.

When Wade made love there was an economy to his movements, his body running the show and the whole act like some kind of training film. He did everything, and did everything competently, but Val was never quite sure he wasn't checking points off a list in his mind.

There was no pain with Wade, no private agonies of spirit. It would be inappropriate.

"Here, don't spill it."

"Just in time," Val said.

She hardly ever thought about Luke anymore, and it was maddening to have the one evening she'd looked forward to ruined by him. He drove her crazy then, and he was driving her crazy now. And she understood, like Mrs. Molloy, something past bitterness, past despair, even; a haunting, a thought that would have appealed to the woman's Irish ghosts. A haunting by someone or something she couldn't shake through the many years. A cold, echoing hollow space just in behind the rib cage captured so it couldn't escape without breaking her in two.

Mrs. Molloy had lived with her ghosts, sitting with them through all the Sundays on the streetcars of Montreal. And Val remembered at once a snatch of song Mrs. Molloy used to sing. Val had always wanted to know what it meant, the Gaelic sounding so strange in her ears. Mrs. Molloy, with one of the fierce looks softening for a moment, had translated as best she could. The image had frightened the child.

"I will lie across your grave, and you will find me there forever.... It is time for me to lie down with you; there is the cold smell of the clay on me...."

And she would go on about the lock on her heart and the melancholy beneath the hurt. Val had not understood those words for sadness: the melancholy *"as black as the sloes"*. Mrs. Molloy would revert to the Gaelic and sway slightly as she sang, leaving Val behind, and the house, and the frozen continent.

Luke and Val under blankets, under the stars; each one alone, each one believing in impenetrable boundaries, and yet all the years later Val noticing a hole behind her rib cage. And it frightened her, this contradiction, that she was filled with emptiness. That this music and Luke Anderson could fill her with such absence. Like the old Italian woman in black up on the mountain hobbling to her husband's grave, using tombstones as rest stops and crutches, so complete in her loneliness, in her perfect reclamation.

"You were certainly quiet. Didn't like it?" Wade pulled his seatbelt across his chest.

"I loved it. Really. Thanks."

"It was okay," he volunteered. "Can't sing worth a damn, but the staging was pretty good."

Wade reminded Val that tomorrow he had an all-day meeting and would only be home around seven. Home, the apartment they shared, with room for one guest if that guest wasn't Aurora. Wade let Val off in front and pulled around back to park the car. Val tugged the keys out of her little evening purse and opened the door, nudged her shoes off and went to run water for a bath.

The next morning Wade would be gone before she was even up. She'd lie in bed looking at the dark sky through the crack between curtain and window. Yes, dark. And cold. And she would wonder.

And drop feet into slippers.

Mrs. Molloy's voice admonishing her, "Move along Valerie, and where did you leave your hat, child?"

I don't know.

Somewhere in Montreal.

And her love somewhere in Ottawa.

And her daughter, she will read about in the news.

She just couldn't get the hang of it. Shirley Maclaine did and decided: I don't like this era here, or this particular time. How about that little decade over there, the one on the continent in the corner, yes?

You could throw it all back in their faces if you wanted.

You did not have to like it.

And Val knew that part of what had made the eighties so gruelling had been the attempt to deny the milestones, to forget the fact that she had a teenaged daughter. That her own life was going by. The aerobics outfit, the MTV she actually tried to watch with Aurora, the neon clothing that made her look like a misshapen popsicle or a time-warp Carnaby Street Twiggy. Even Wade. Val had tried to subvert from within. Shirley Maclaine, it seemed, had chucked the whole routine—a decade here, a century there. And saved herself the embarrassment of nostalgia.

"*Christ on a crutch*," Mrs. Molloy muttering down the road.

Wade was in what he called his "friendly" mood, and Val had wanted to ask him, to beg him, to please leave her alone. It was bad, this feeling, and dangerous. And Wade could be easily hurt when turned down. In the end it was easier just to go along with it, to let Wade check off his list and then roll over after a job well done.

Cruel.

But so was *this* cruel, unspeakably cruel, to wrench a girl off a dirt road that had fireflies, to pull her roughly from the bed of her lover and make her lie with this strange man, because it was not then anymore, it was now. Simply because it was now.

Now, a middle-aged singer mouthing miracles, a man in black who prays and curses into microphones. Now, a man who walked away from Val and captured all the fireflies. Now, Wade Hardigan reaching over to set the alarm clock, now kissing her somewhere near her mouth. And now this silence, now.

Land O' Lakes: Aurora: 1991

This was the last time. Aurora was led into the cell with the hookers. One of them limped around on six-inch heels until she was reminded that it wasn't her corner, at which point the shoes were kicked, one by one and with apparent delight, against the pockmarked wall.

Aurora never had to stay in all that long, but it still bothered her when the door slid shut. And the talk, so casual, so hourly. It wasn't just the hookers; it was everybody paging lawyers, calling pimps. Aurora had not made her call; that would already have been arranged. It was part of the media circus and she was merely the foot in the door. Or the cell.

Never again, she decided. This action had convinced her. The organization had been pissed off at her anyway, had taken her aside and reminded her that *their* lawyers were for committed activists. And she had smiled at that, coming as it did from the new action man. Aurora knew about the lawyers; they had bailed her out a few times. She had climbed the stacks and scaled bridges, and, yes, she had been taken care of by these lawyers who would get her off with a reprimand and dropped charges. Another coup.

The new coordinator had never been arrested. He had been on three actions that Aurora knew of where he might have been arrested, yet he had mysteriously disappeared, fading into the blur, barking commands by walkie-talkie. The new regime.

Aurora, on the other hand, remembered the unmistakable welcome of a shotgun pointing at her as she was called down from a smokestack, one man fiddling with her climbing ropes.

"Look out, she'll fall!"

The earth unconnected.

"No! —"

Then the jolt of the safety line, holding, the earth spinning below her, without her.

It was all the Image now. Sound bites and speak carefully; speak as if you were talking to the third grade—"they always do!"—better still, don't speak at all, we'll do the talking. You're just the action person. Got that?

Don't speak.

Yet she heard it sometimes, almost out of earshot, the pressurized crucible of voices calling. It was in nature when nature was not. It was in the station as she waited for the outbound bus. It was in the wind; dandelion tufts blowing, summer snow.

Aurora had known, even as she tied the bowline, even as she was being belayed up the stack, that this would be her last climb for the organization. Last time I pose for a picture. You got that?

Aurora had slammed her right knee against the stack and now did a couple of deep knee bends to test it. A woman in a brocade turban stood watching her. She did not look as though she belonged in a holding cell, although, Aurora admitted, no one ever did. The woman was in her fifties, easily, and had nervous hands that shot up to rearrange her hair every thirty seconds.

"I'm Aurora."

The woman was poised to take her hand, then saw the handkerchief wound around the right one and immediately rescued a few curls that had escaped her turban.

"Iris. Iris Carrington," the woman replied.

Aurora turned the name over a couple of times. Of course she remembered it, during the long years of missed classes, long winter afternoons waiting for her mother to come home. Iris Carrington. A soap-opera diva.

"*The* Iris Carrington?"

The woman nodded emphatically and began talking about "Daddy". Daddy would get her out of this horrible mess. It was all a terrible mistake. Daddy's lawyers would see to it somebody paid.

Aurora turned away.

Daddy was another soap-opera character; the actor who had played him for years and years had died suddenly sometime ago.

"Daddy?"

Iris Carrington nodded.

One thing about pimps, they got things done. The three hookers left within the first hour, and Aurora found herself alone with Iris Carrington. She remembered the T.V. Iris. Rich and domineering with everyone except old Daddy who had somehow managed to catch her heart. At one time a very beautiful woman. At all times not a graceful loser.

Aurora's hand was stinging badly now. Rope burns. Aurora T. Anderson. Description: rope burns. Everyday hazard for the veteran and novice. So what? Aurora had dangled from the stack like a bird caught in invisible tracery while the security guard below tampered with her ropes. She could have been killed. Were you supposed to get used to this?

"I can't imagine what's keeping Daddy."

Iris Carrington was asking for her meal.

It had been two hours since Aurora had talked to the guard about Iris, and it was only when Aurora displayed the blisters on her hand that the guard offered her anything in return.

"You still have your call."

"I know. The lawyer's already on it, though."

"You're one of those climbers."

Aurora said nothing.

"Call someone else," he suggested.

Like who, she thought. She could call her mother, but calls like that always disturbed Val. She could call Grenge, but she had other plans for Grenge. She looked at Iris Carrington. Iris had nobody, just like on T.V.. Rich, yet remote, and in the end alone; nobody, not even Daddy, to ease the troubled days. Aurora tried explaining it to the guard again, asking about psychiatrists, or at least a counsellor?

Iris Carrington was calling for her car.

—◊◊◊—

"Not good enough! Look at you!" Grenge shouted at the defence department analyst. "Move it!" she goaded the inhalation therapist.

"Suck city, man, that's pitiful! Get those legs up!"

At her command they lifted knees high, breathing in "wuh" and out "huh" like a single complex organism.

"Gerbils with Gumby legs, get *moving*!"

Aurora took a place at the back of the room against the wall. She liked watching Grenge work. The private fitness club had hired her to teach a simple aerobics class, but when they discovered her latent skills, and her popularity, they gave her three classes instead. These must be the masochists, although they were never addressed that way. It was Grenge's private filing system.

"Punch the sky, you wimps! Punch as if it's the boss. And if you're here with your boss, punch your boss!"

The room thudded loudly. *Shriekback? Sonic Youth?*

Everyone was striking out at invisible employers, arms flailing, buttocks quivering. A real threat, Aurora grinned, catching Grenge's eye.

"Alright, down for twenty push-ups," she nodded back.

Grenge had noted early on that this group liked to submit, so she had altered the music and the exercises and adopted the drill-sergeant abuse.

Aurora moved along the wall until she could see their faces. They were enraptured.

"Okay, okay...that's about as pitiful a scene as I can stomach. Sit down, flex your toes...good, now, back straight. Okay, a slow head roll, left, right. Hey, not all the way around—these things aren't screw-tops! Good, good, you all look like you've got "666" tattooed on your heads. Go on, get out of here, and don't let me see your ugly faces 'til next week."

At that they picked themselves up from the floor, looked for towels and pulled off sweatbands.

Aurora made her way over to Grenge.

"Nice. Genteel."

"You should see the intro." Grenge wiped her face and drew a striped towel around her neck. "Where you been?"

"A little business trip."

"You got arrested."

"It was okay."

Grenge pulled a kleenex from her sports bag and blew her nose loudly. "So, what's up?"

Aurora closed her hand around the bandage.

"Yeah, I noticed. Take the quick way down?"

"I had a little help. One of the guards played double-dutch with my ropes."

"Great. You piss me off, you know."

"Can we go somewhere and talk?"

Grenge shook her head. "One more class yet. Why don't you stay and do it? I have a spare pair of sweats in the bag. Just stay off your hands."

"Which group is it?"

"The *All Arethas*."

Forty-five minutes exercising to Aretha Franklin.

Aurora knew there would be a backlash when she decided to leave the group. Not that she was indispensable; there were always action people. But she had bothered telling them what she thought, and that had labelled her.

"They said I had an attitude."

Grenge nodded as she slid into the seat at the club. This was Grenge's headquarters, a downtown comedy club. On stage, somebody named Daisy Circus was dying.

"Well, I was wondering when you'd leave the Corporation."

It was a corporation, Grenge was right, but still it was hard to give up on it. Or watch it warp in front of you. Aurora had watched her father and her mother and the compromises, but this had been her first encounter with....

"Disgust? Sure you're disgusted! Shit, where have you *been*, Chickie!" She paused. "You must have been the last virgin. The very last one."

"Eh?"

"It's cute you're surprised by the hype and all. It just isn't very useful."

Aurora had been waiting for this.

"That's why, Grenge, I've been wondering...."

Grenge had a great car that her cousin Murgatroid had sold her. It was a '75 Exploding Pinto with no frills.

"Floorboards are frills?"

Grenge was proud of the car, had decorated it over time with fuzzy dice, then baby booties, and had settled, recently, on *faux* fur for the seats and dash.

"Feels like you're driving around on an animal."

"Yeah, think of it! All these Pintos getting recalled way back when, and this guy giving them the finger and heading up north."

Grenge's cousin Murgatroid had grown up in Cleveland.

"Well," Aurora said, "we'll need a car. It's just..." how to be delicate about Grenge's objet d'art, "it's bad enough that this car is so old without it being noticeable the way it is."

Grenge pushed the little fur-covered button and squirted cleaning fluid onto the window.

A non-descript, a completely non-descript, paint job in olive green, the Pinto stripped of its glory; two sets of clothes purchased at the Sally Ann: dark pants, flannel shirts, two pairs of cloth gardening gloves.

"Don't collect too much equipment in advance," Aurora warned, "let's take it slow. We can start with a stake-out."

"Oooooh...," Grenge responded, "can I buy the donuts?"

A stake-out with Grenge. A simple, almost simple, walk through green pastures, a walk along the city's Green Belt.

"This is it? We walk?"

"This is part of it. Get used to hiking; get used to being out here with a backpack and runners."

"No headphones?"

"Get used to keeping your mouth shut."

Learn to look legitimate and inconspicuous. Carry, maybe, a book on birds, or ferns; keep that classically ignorant expression handy.

"You're looking down the business end of a stupid face."

—⁓—

They were in the woods on what was no more than a rough dirt path. "How'd you *find* this?"

Aurora put her finger to her lips.

Grenge sighed and fell in behind Aurora.

They walked a ways, Aurora pointing out recently cleared areas, and soon they came upon their first flag. The new road cutting through the brush.

Aurora explained to Grenge that she'd known about the flags some time before but had waited until the process was further along. "To cost them more."

Picking flowers, she called it. A 'stake-out'.

Plastic tape impossibly bright amid the browns and greens. "Watch for the break in terrain," Aurora whispered pointing to the tiny ripple of water that snaked beside them.

"There it is!" Grenge croaked trying to shout quietly.

Aurora bent down and read the stake: 1325 PC. Three hundred and twenty-five feet from the start of the line.

"This is good. Get rid of the turns and they'll have to re-record the angle and direction, on top of doing a cross section. "Lotsa work."

Grenge stood lookout as Aurora got busy. Her recent weight training was helping with the more deeply embedded stakes. She pulled out her claw hammer and pried a stake out of the ground. One by one, the stakes went into the pack.

Grenge was a good lookout. As usual she had thrown herself completely into the cloak-and-dagger routine, but in Grenge's case it actually made her more careful, and she kept her movements spare and her hand signals clear.

When Aurora's pack was full, she carefully picked her way through the untouched brush to dispose of the stakes. She found a hollow beside several rotted logs, broke as many of the stakes as she could, then covered them with brush and dead leaves and finally the rotted logs.

Grenge gave her the thumbs-up sign from the road.

They repeated this until Aurora was satisfied they'd covered a complete section. Aurora knew about the proposed construction site, and the probable construction stakes, but if the road to the site disappeared completely, well....

"Shangrila-la-la," Aurora whispered pulling out her wildflower book.

"Oh, look, Grenge, a *ladyslipper*!"

This was to be the first of many hikes. Bus rides to neighbouring cities, small dollops of glue in the keyholes of construction equipment. Officially, Aurora and Grenge visiting the museum, visiting friends, developing sudden interests in botany and entomology.

Aurora's mother wasn't buying it. Val had spent one too many evenings laying low herself to swallow Aurora's nature treks.

"But Dad was a woodsman, wasn't he?"

Val gave Aurora a look.

"No. I mean he and Grandad; they were outdoorsy."

"Your father was a lot of things."

—∙∙∙—

One time when Aurora was about five her father came home with a small puffy toy. It was a coat. It went around her shoulders. It was a "life jacket."

"What's a life jacket?"

Luke punched Aurora's shoulder lightly.

"That. See? You can go in water now, and you'll stay up."

Once when Aurora had gone in the pool, her fingers slipped from the side and she drifted into the deep end and tried to stand up but there was no bottom. Ever since then she had been afraid of water.

So her father took her by the river. The girl liked the canal, the little boats, the hot dogs and ice cream. But her father took her down to the Ottawa River. There was a boat, a canoe he said, that he had borrowed. He had no life jacket, but Aurora had her reddish orange jacket tied up over her pink and blue striped t-shirt. Together they put the boat into the water.

Tippy, scary.

"Do like I said, there, slowly now, sit down. Good!"

Aurora sat on the little board, not moving at all.

"Good. Now I'm getting in."

Tippy. Aurora grasped the board looking straight ahead as she felt her father behind her in the canoe.

And then they moved. Aurora didn't remember any starting up feeling, no sudden zoom, just a pushing away from the land like the land wasn't there any more, like putting your arm out and gently pulling the water by.

Her father paddled quietly. There were just water noises and bloops and plops from frogs and fishes. Aurora held on to the seat less tightly and breathed more slowly now. She was too afraid to turn around because the land would be far away, but if she looked forward—it was funny—sometimes she could tell where the next land was, but if she squinted her eyes she couldn't always see it. Sometimes only a bunch of clouds, or a rim of small hills, sometimes only sky and water. Squint. Sky and water.

Then, in a very low gentle voice, her father started to tell her a story about Land O' Lakes. All the waters got mixed up in her head, but the Land O' Lakes had green and blue water with lots of fish, and you could look right down and see them in their homes. And sometimes they lived underwater...no...under ice in the winter. And the ice was thick but underneath was still the green and blue. The afternoon was long, and the peanut butter sandwich and orange drink were gone. Luke pulled the canoe up along the bank, and Aurora stepped into shallow water and onto rocks, then ran into the bushes to pee.

Her father was talking to his friend who would take the canoe away, and Aurora kicked over shells by the water. She felt a bit dizzy. No, it wasn't dizzy. She felt tippy like she was still tipping in the boat, like she wasn't standing on the ground. But it wasn't like that time in the pool. This time it didn't matter that she didn't feel ground.

She fell asleep making strange noises in her throat that were the way the birds sounded when they were calling far away.

TREE [trē]: see deciduous, see Christmas, see Aurora's
　　　　legs dangling beneath the leaves.

In the Nature Hike Club for Teens at the community centre they were told: "Take nothing but pictures, leave nothing but footprints." This pretty well covered it except for the chemicals used in printing, except for the plastic film cylinders scattered from coast to coast. Aurora had begun to get sick of the contradictions. Besides, as she found out, there were better things to do than take pictures. And there were better things to leave than footprints.

—m—

They would need another car. Grenge's old car wouldn't make it to the trees. They did not want to play around with a rental car under an assumed name. This left Val's. Actually Val and Wade's Toyota. Conveniently, Wade was out of town on business.

"That happens in real life?" Grenge marvelled.

"What do you want it for?" Val demanded.

Aurora needed to check out a university. "I hate those brochures. You can't tell anything from a brochure. How am I supposed to make a decision?"

Aurora having played her trump right off the top, knowing her mother and school were a match.

"I'll need it by the weekend. Wade's home."

The dark green Toyota was perfect. It looked like any of a thousand foreign cars speeding across the Canadian landscape. The little green Toyota in parking lots, on metered side streets; Aurora and Grenge hitting the stores and buying pieces of equipment. The clothing was easy: a Sally Ann toque, a green or brown windbreaker. Two pairs of *Zellers* sneakers. Convenience store for the marking pencils. *Home Hardware* for cloth gloves and the one-handed sledge-hammer which raised the eyebrow of the sales-clerk.

"My boyfriend's back and he's gonna be in trouble," Grenge sang and grinned.

On to another hardware for nails. Aurora bought some and had Grenge hit the competition for the rest.

"Never buy everything in one place."

Aurora stood holding a 6¼ inch nail.

"And what would you want these for?" the clerk asked.

"My...uh, boyfriend's building a footbridge over this little creek on our property. Would these be the right size? I don't know anything about it."

Big smile.

Grenge's basement apartment, and Grenge packing a pair of bolt cutters.

"My uncle planned to fence in his property, but my dad borrowed them before he died."

"You've had them that long?"

"It's all I have to remember him by. I guess I should give them back to Uncle Eddie."

Aurora was sewing slender green cloth bags.

"Wow, a drawstring and everything."

Grenge hummed "Don't Fence Me In" as she wiped fingerprints from the nails, inserting them carefully into the bags.

"Anything we're missing?"

Aurora surveyed the equipment.

"Safety glasses."

"Ta-da!" A pair of safety glasses appeared from Grenge's knapsack.

"Anything else?"

Aurora paused. She'd been frowning about this. "We should have a third."

"A third what?"

"Person. It's really safer with a third."

"Well, I tell you, I don't have anybody else I trust."

"Me neither."

Everything would eventually go into their knapsacks, but for the moment it was stored in the back of Grenge's closet in Luke's old army duffel bag.

"We should turn in early. We have a long drive."

"What, no pizza?"

Aurora shook her head. Then she stretched out on the couch and closed her eyes.

The first time she got arrested it was a climb. Actually, a hanging. Aurora and five other action people had hung from ropes suspended from a bridge. They were protesting pulp and paper industry discharges. The media was out to take pictures of the dangling protesters.

"You looked like those Mexican dingleballs," Grenge had observed. "You looked like unstrung yo-yos."

Aurora had believed in it. Well, it was belief, but it was also the rush, the amazing push to the tips of her nerve endings. It was the most alive feeling she'd ever experienced, as if she were charting history, stepping one foot at a time into the chronicle of events made up of "here" and "now". Bigger and bigger the rush, the river going flat, and then reflecting, and then becoming a well that she could fall into if she wanted to; just slip and fall right into the rushing current, time eddying and tumbling, thundering in her ears.

She was still intoxicated from the climb when she was belayed down into the boat, read her rights and arrested and lead into the cell. None of it bothered her; it was scarcely real. What was real was the fact that from that high up she could hear each seagull squawking below her on the rocks; she could make out every reed and every beer can. She was part of the here and now as manifested in photographs of Aurora and the others being herded up by police. Aurora's face defiant, almost smiling. No, smiling. Why?

"You looked like the tails of a kite."

Aurora had wondered, then, whether this was what her father had felt like when sliding someone through the system. Is this what her mother had meant when she said she had wanted to do something important?

And had either of them ever found the feeling suspect?

Her mother's face had scarcely been real, either. Val had appeared from somewhere as the group arrived at the police station. She must have driven....

"Mother?"

Val's contorted face made her look a lot older than she was—older and thinner.

"Mother, how did you get here?"

Of course she'd figured out what was going on from all the hints Aurora had dropped. Of course she was not to approve, hypocrite that she was; she was going to race down here and try to change her daughter's mind about taking part in a peaceful protest just as her own mother would probably have done. It was pitiful.

"You shouldn't have come."

Her mother gluing hard clear eyes on her.

—⁓—

Aurora,

How nice it was ... your letter so long! You sound busy with your hiking. Your father, both of the boys, always fussing about in nature. Have you heard from him— Luke? Don't know what I'd do without your cheery notes. Know how busy young people are. Luke is at the university; he never gets home.

Love to you and your mother,

Grandma Rose

"Weird," Aurora said, slanting the letter in her hand.

"What?"

"Letter from my grandmother. Weird."

—⁓—

The radio played something techno-bluesy as Grenge aimed the Toyota away from the city. They had not even had breakfast yet, and their moods were less than buoyant, Aurora mentally rhyming off the equipment they had packed, Grenge pulling the map out of the glove compartment and tossing it in Aurora's lap.

"Be useful."

Something her mother used to say to her.

Val worked when Aurora was a child, and Aurora would set the table and then run the vacuum when she finally figured out how to get the little light working on the front of the machine. She refused to run it without the tiny spotlight. So, about half an hour before her mother was due home, Aurora would pull the machine out of the closet, plug it in, and turn on the light. The floor beam led the way, Aurora zooming along the hall in its wake.

"Show me where to go," she commanded, and the machine sent out an arc of light.

When she was still very young, Aurora would dream that her parents would reunite. She would jerk her head every time a tall man walked by, adjusting his girth, his hair colour, his clothes. Once she even called out "Daddy?", and the man turned around. Only it wasn't her father; it was just a man.

Aurora wondered whether her mother had done it, too, cased the joints in search of Luke as if he could be found at the used furniture store, as if Luke would ever walk into a disco.

—⚏—

They began in earnest. Grenge was to be lookout, and Aurora would do the first spiking. Off came the knapsack; out came the gloves and the bolt cutters.

"Safety glasses," Grenge hissed, tossing them over to Aurora and positioning herself near the road.

It seemed unnatural. All her life Aurora had loved the trees, and now here she was with a nail and a sledge. Placed it, tapped it twice; a small piece of bark broke off. Aurora reached down and pocketed it. Next a few hefty slams with the sledgehammer, and the nail began to enter the trunk. Aurora grimaced as she hit watching the nail go deeper and deeper, imagining pain, imagining the Cattle of the Sun in her child's version of the Odyssey writhing on the spit and bellowing.

"Okay," she whispered pulling up the bolt cutters. The nail was three-quarters of the way into the tree. Aurora clamped the nail and squeezed as hard as she could. The head flew off. Two more hard smacks with the hammer and the nail had disappeared into the tree.

"Not bad..." She surveyed her work. She reached inside her pocket and pulled out the sliver of bark and wedged it carefully back into place.

"Glue," Aurora muttered.

How could she have forgotten?

"Heads up!" Grenge whispered hoarsely and tossed a small tube of glue at Aurora.

Perfect.

Perfect. Natural.

For three hours they took turns spiking the area. It was important to hit trees that had already been targeted for cutting, and the spray-painted boundary trees had defined a perimeter situated close to the road. Individual trees had been marked, and Aurora and Grenge had hit all of those as well as a random number right on the edge of the stand.

It was approaching supper hour.

"We'd better get out of here. If there is anyone in the area, they'll be coming through pretty soon."

Aurora packed tools into one pack-sack; Grenge collected a few dusty cones and nuts and pulled out her pocket *Trees of North America*.

"Ready?" she asked.

Aurora nodded.

They began the half-mile hike back to the car.

—⁓—

When Aurora quit the group, her mother had been so relieved. Val had been bartering with Aurora to go back to school.

"A degree in environmental studies or ecology and you'd be further ahead." And her face so earnest, an expression that practically held up a sign saying: LISTEN TO ME. I'VE BEEN THERE. GO TO SCHOOL.

So there could be no mention of the new activities. The stakes were much higher without the lawyers and the press. There was safety in the spotlight, Aurora remembered having been told.

Grenge found the whole thing bizarre.

"Your mom...and your dad. I mean, they used to get off on this. What happened to her?"

Aurora wanted to say "She got old" or "mid-life crisis". She shook her head and said, "she loves me."

"Yeah, but why is it people always love you more when you're doing things they want you to do?"

"I think she wants me to go to school—then meet a nice guy and get married."

"Original."

"Well, you can't blame her."

"Okay, why don't you marry my cousin Murgatroid? You'd love him."

"What's his real name, anyway?"

"Burton Müller. He's great. He's got this car-parts shop, "The Part Institute", you know, like the Heart Institute, and he delivers the parts in his van which he's made up to look like an ambulance."

"He does this in...?"

"Cleveland. Really, want to meet him?"

Grenge's mother also wanted Grenge to stay out of trouble. But she never inquired further since the time Grenge told her that her dream date was Candice Bergen.

"Not only that, but I have this thing for puppets," she said, then growled and left her mother sitting with the china patterns.

—⚬—

Aurora and Grenge in a downtown bar, holding up steins of dark beer. "Congratulations, Grenge. Good work."

"You were magnificent, Aurora."

The slightly stilted celebration was all they would allow themselves, and when it brought a question from the bartender it was dealt with squarely.

"LSAT's. Blew the fucker out of the water," Grenge boasted.

Aurora didn't know. It was one thing to cut your teeth on some group rally on Parliament Hill. It was another to destroy or damage a $30,000 tractor. She'd disabled a crane, a few bulldozers, and even if it wasn't permanent, there was intent there, and that's what they tried you on. Intent. She could personally justify the survey stakes, the trees. But where was group consensus? Where was democratic process?

"Democracy doesn't process anything but cheese," Grenge said.

It was non-violent, but it was not really peaceful any longer. The intent did not necessarily involve peace. Was this what had changed from her father's time? Luke had broken laws, but he had done so peacefully. Aurora had broken laws, and she had also destroyed property. And Aurora knew that in the system, destroying property was worse than taking the odd life. So her actions would be seen as extremely violent.

—⚬—

"I guess I have to get a job," Aurora was saying as Val unpacked her groceries. Aurora had managed to have the car cleaned and the gas tank filled prior to returning it. She was grateful that her mother hadn't inspected it or she would surely have noticed the pebble dents and the mileage on the odometer. By the time Val, or Wade, did notice, Val would take sole responsibility, and Wade would have to let it go. Aurora didn't like putting her mother in that position—especially with Wade.

"Are you looking for anything in particular?"

"Like I said, a job."

"Well, if you think you'd like office work I could ask over at the company...."

"Mother."

"Just to see if they're hiring. It's a family firm, after all. They might not be averse to a little nepotism."

"I'm not into that kinky stuff."

"Will Grenge be doing anything this year?"

It had an edge to it and was meant to.

Aurora knew that Val had never approved of Grenge, thinking, mistakenly, that Grenge was the bad influence on her. After all, it was Grenge who had decided university was a waste of time. At least Aurora had tried it for a term. Grenge was content to drift from job to job; what did that girl do with her spare time?

"She's still teaching, you know. She has three aerobics classes and one weight-training session."

"And that pays the bills?"

Grenge, who never had a break in her life, who paid her bills and Aurora's, too, half the time.

"So, you didn't say, Aurora. What kind of job?"

—⁓—

They had to use Grenge's car.

"You think I'd know something about plants by now."

"Lichen. We're looking for lichen, remember?"

It was overcast, dark cannons of clouds positioning overhead. An uneasy wind that started and then stopped.

"We're gonna get caught in it. Maybe we should turn back."

Aurora shook her head. "This road's nearly in, and once it is the whole project starts up. It has to be today. Besides, the dirt's softer. Should make the job easier."

Aurora retreated to the green duffel bag in the bushes and, in an instant, realized that they should not have used Luke's army bag for this. She pulled out the foot-long road spikes.

"The better to eat you with, my dear."

The spikes would be effective, but they would not do for heavy equipment. Still, the heavy equipment would come later. This was for the survey crews and inspectors.

Aurora took the first shift with Grenge as lookout. Grenge had purchased a pair of binoculars and was sitting in the crotch of an oak tree.

The cloud bank shifted a little as Aurora set to work.

Aurora placed the cap over the head of the spike, covered the cap with a rag and began hammering. The spike easily entered the ground, leaving a few inches exposed. She removed the cap and checked the spike, testing it with her foot. Good. Not really sharp enough to threaten a shoe sole...but drive a car over it....

Aurora bounced her foot against it again. Simple idea. Based on the Vietnamese "punji stake".

A hawk screeched overhead, and Aurora shot Grenge a look.

—⠀⠀—

A thunderstorm enveloped them as they headed back to the car. Afterward, driving, Grenge broke the silence with her announcement.

"Listen, Chickie..." Grenge darts her a glance. "You're not gonna like this."

"What?"

Grenge allows herself a sickly grin. "I...uh...think I left something behind."

It could have been the implanting tool, crudely made, covered with fingerprints probably. Or the hammer, also probably covered with prints despite the gloves they were careful to wear. Would the rain wash off the prints? Stupid, stupid. It didn't matter anyway. What Grenge had lost was her book on lichens.

"Old book, generic," Aurora tentatively comforted.

"Yeah...." Grenge drew the sound out. "Old book, all right...with my name and address in it."

Aurora stared. "You're kidding. Grenge, you're kidding!"

"I wish...."

"Jesus! The one thing you never do is carry things that point *right at you*! Shit!"

Perhaps it was merely paranoia, but Grenge would have to take a holiday.

"Go see Reddick or Murgatroid. Go see Sandy Loray."

Grenge's Pinto took a trip to her mother's boyfriend's country place. Grenge took a bus down to Cleveland. Aurora decided to lay low herself and perhaps use the time to earn a little money.

It was pure paranoia. Who was going to worry over a few lost hours of work, a few flat tires here and there. Who was going to add two and two and the lichen and Katie Grenge and come up with Aurora and Grenge and tie them to fifteen other adventures? These things didn't get reported—there was no media watching. And the company would keep things quiet until they came up with some answers. Like names and addresses, fingerprints. Like a stupid book with an arrow pointing right at Katie Grenge.

—m—

"Something's wrong," Val said when Aurora showed up at the door.

Aurora shrugged and pulled her wet knapsack inside.

"What is it, Aurora!"

Her mother had that look, again, which forced Aurora to make light of everything.

"What?" A voice and then shuffling down the hall and Wade's face appearing around the corner.

"Oh."

"Hi, Wade."

There was a truce between Aurora and Wade Hardigan that she hoped still held. Their mutual dislike was obvious, but still, Aurora didn't want to sabotage her mother's marriage. Val in a pale green skirt that pinched at the zipper, a linen jacket, a corsage of tight faded flowers. Wade in one of the several dark suits that made him look like a well-dressed bouncer. The ceremony so civil; Aurora taking the only picture and buying lunch at the Italian place near the courthouse.

"Aurora's come by, and I've invited her to stay over...in the guest room," Val added unnecessarily.

"Swell," Wade replied and forced an insincere smile which allowed Aurora to notice a broken tooth on the upper right side of his jaw.

They had purchased the townhouse only a month before, and this was Aurora's first visit. Val tried to make Aurora comfortable. She gave her the tour, asked her if she was hungry, and made "ignore him" signals with her hands which Aurora accepted as the simple gestures they were.

"I just need a place to stay for a couple of days. Grenge is out of town, and I'll be taking over her aerobics classes, and you just live so much closer to the club."

Not to mention Aurora had been staying at Grenge's since she'd been evicted from her own apartment. Not to mention she was avoiding Grenge's apartment because of the address in the book.

"Not to mention, we haven't seen you for a while," her mother inadvertently added smiling for the first time since Aurora had arrived. "I have some roast beef in the fridge."

Now Aurora smiled. Things sure had changed from the days when Aurora would open the fridge and find a seaweed salad, some hommus, a vegetarian paté. She had longed, then, for *Kraft* dinner, or *Spaghettios*, or all-dressed hot dogs, but Val and Luke would listen to the whining and then dole out the rice.

And Val was trying to build something. Her new home crackled with faith. A forest of trees was growing in the living room, one or two trees taller than Aurora.

"This is nice..." Aurora spread her arms and slowly circled the room.

"Are your socks wet, Aurora? Listen, you're going to catch a cold! Here, let me get you a pair of slippers."

This was nice.

This was almost a home, and Aurora felt suddenly protective of her mother's new dish rack. She fingered the leaves of a plant carefully.

"I like something green," Val said simply.

Aurora nodded. "So do I."

Could she tell her? It would be easier, but not for Val. And Val needed this intricate paisley carpet and those wrought iron fireplace tools. Val needed to hear Wade grunting on the rowing machine down the hall. She needed the plants and the matte-finished walls, and Aurora knew that this was how her mother was going to remain alive.

"It's really nice."

"Oh, it's not finished yet." Val's arm swoops around to take in invisible projects in other parts of the house.

"You look tired," Aurora says.

"Thank you."

"You know what I mean."

"You...sure I can't get you anything?"

Her hands hover near Aurora. If they were different people, they would probably embrace.

"No...if it's okay with you, I'll just sit up awhile. I kind of like your grove, here."

Val nods and looks down the hall toward her bedroom.

"Mom?"

The word stops Val cold and sends a tingle through Aurora.

"Thanks...for putting me up."

Val says "forget it" with her hands which Aurora clasps, briefly, between hers.

She could hear them, for a while, talking in the bedroom. Wade saying it was idiotic to support this kind of behaviour. Wade reminding Val that by Aurora's age he had owned land.

Val saying nothing, then gently pointing out that there was a time when doing what Aurora did was seen as a proper response to the world.

That one, Aurora knew, going right over Wade's bristled head.

Wade reminding Val of the curling tournament, all of the happy obligations.

A loud silence. And Aurora sitting up at the sound of Val's suddenly intense voice.

"She's my daughter! She's...don't you understand?"

Wade Hardigan, eight years younger than Val, never previously married, never a father. And Val's voice understandably faltering in the face of it all. So much to lose in the middle of a life.

"Careful, mother, don't bet the bankroll," Aurora whispered stretching out beneath the *Ficus benjamina*.

It was okay as indoor trees went. It had become accustomed to the lack of light. It was not supposed to grow here, so it was primped and snipped and put in a window and still it tried to be alive. It would wither outside, or curl up in the cold.

The trees that made it here shot huge roots deep and spread limbs wide or bulleted from the ground in one shot to reach the sun. And they did it now with spikes crosswise through their trunks, the twentieth century deep within their rings.

The old stands. Aurora marvelled—"old", "stands". The old world. To be a guardian of the old world. This was what she had wanted from the organization, and it had failed her. Or she it. It really didn't matter.

She would have to leave here too, of course. Wait until dawn and then clear out. It was a mistake to have come here. Her mother would do anything for her, and that was a most heartlifting sadness. Val was trying hard to weld all the little pieces like the wrought iron light fixture in the hall, an odd curlicue, a lump of iron that was Luke, a pane of bevelled glass that shimmered like blue ice.

She would do anything for Aurora.

And that made it hard to leave; for Aurora knew she would spend the rest of her life looking for that kind of commitment.

She shook the branch overhead, and the Ficus rustled its meagre leaves. It was remarkably threadbare if you lay under it and looked straight up. Like the tree Luke had brought home that year to the apartment on Percale Street, a stick of a tree that they tarted up with popcorn, cranberries and tinsel.

She had sat beside it with her father, squeezing the needles until her fingers almost hurt, mightily amazed at a tree inside a house. And Luke had put his arm around her shoulder.

"Land O' Lakes. Let me tell you about Land O' Lakes," he said. She looked over at him. He closed his eyes and began to speak.

"In that country the people celebrated the cold, cold winters by breaking holes in the frozen lake and swimming underwater races. Blue skin. Blue night skies big out over the lake. Cold half-asleep fish nosing you under the ice. Moon shining down, silver swirls on the surface. Look at it, Aurora! You're the fish, breathing the only true air in the winter sky of Land O' Lakes. See the icicles splintering from your tail as you break the surface? Can you feel the rush as you flash through the water?"

And in Aurora's own life there had been a boat that plied the lakes, navigating the moving waters. And Aurora and others had taken samples of the waters, posing, holding jars of opaque fluid for the cameras. And the boat docked one day at a reservation, and ancient people stood on the shore and watched. Blinked. And had seen this all before. Dandelion tufts were everywhere; they blew around the boat; they landed on people and cameras and equipment; they caught in the vents of the portable hair dryer, and someone said, "It's snowing...."

Aurora smiled. And her father's own tumbled entry into the North of North America. Her father's stories were beginning to spill into hers.

The talk had stopped. The light down the hall was out. There was only moonlight, now, from the window. The sound of car tires and the central heating system. She should go to the guest room, she supposed. But there was something about sitting up as a night went by. Something, not wistful, but haunting as it went. The spirits of late-night revellers tripping their way along the street out front. The spirit of the radiator, tapping its message in trusting repetition. The spirit of her mother, somewhere in the dark, who would face a dark and empty bed if Aurora asked her to, who would otherwise curve herself around this man she would spend her life with.

Spend it, a life, cold hands along the rope, the protective gear too stiff, rope too cold to manipulate. Hang from a monument, like an ornament on a dying tree, a tree with a spike ladder growing inside; Emily Carr's trees bursting from your skull, your home, your home, your home and native land. Climb the smokestack and look at the view. Take it all in from this height.

"The castles in the Land O' Lakes were few. There was no need for them where the trees were so tall, no need to dig tunnels where the lakes were so deep. And once there was a bird that flew right out of a painting...."

Aurora listened to the trapped ticking of the radiator. Tomorrow she would be off. She tried to recall a poem her father used to quote, but it had been too many years. She folded her sweater beneath her head and bedded down in the Land O' Lakes in the moonlight under a stand of trees.

ICE AGE: ROSE: 1992

The sun angles long rays through the corridor as they walk along, the attendant nodding and jotting things down in a pocket-sized notepad.

"And this is Rose. She's pretty good. Aren't you, Rose? She's not too much trouble. Fusses a bit when she needs to be changed or when she's frightened, but she's not like Mrs. Mortenson over there, are you, Rose? By the way, we have to get her dressed. Her sister's coming by to take her out for the day."

"What's in the box?"

"Oh. I'd be careful how I took that from her. There was a time she carried it everywhere, even to the bathroom."

"Does she still do it?"

"Well," the nurse smiled, "she doesn't use the bathroom anymore."

They continued down the hallway, commenting on the softener in the patients' laundry, and the lovely gold colour of the autumn trees.

—∭—

Once she remembered this: waiting for Eric to come home from work so they could go dancing at the Nite Hawk. She had put on her beige linen dress with the ivory insert trim and wondered whether it wasn't too prim, too sophisticated, perhaps, for the setting. The Nite Hawk was quite a swinging place; she was always listening to Eric talk about the bands that had played there: Clarence Meyers, Tony's Swingsters, Nate Lee and, further back, Husk O'Hare.

She felt a slight tenseness, the same nervousness she used to feel when she had first met Eric, when it was all new to her. Red-faced Eric remembering to stop for flowers, picking them himself, pricking his finger as he tied them with twine, Rose holding the flowers tight, twisting the blood-stained cord around her own finger.

Her hips are swaying and it is hot, hot, hot when you are dancing. She is per-spiring right through her dress and should be mortified at the visible circles under her arms. She keeps telling Eric that they should sit the next one out, but he has promised her both music and dancing tonight, and he leads her to the floor for another spin.

And when she is dancing it doesn't really matter. Eric has his sleeves rolled up, his broad chest bolstering his shirt, his tie, his comical tie, askew. He is flushed, his face even redder than usual, and she knows that look in his eyes. It means that when they get home, he will take her up to bed and then, without the lights off, he will put her to bed. And this makes her blush and breathe out slow proper breaths in the mid-dle of the dance floor, the Nite Hawk under a hunter's moon.

—☈—

Breathe.

Once: lying prone listening to the strange sounds around her as she strained to hear the murmurs of her newly-born child. The pain and the cruel long cramps done—numbness, now, and dull discomfort.

There was a curtain to the right of her, and behind the curtain a child was stir-ring. Moonlight caught the outline, cast it against the milky fabric, and suddenly there was a wonderful unfolding. There, tiny arms reached and roiled stirring up the air. From where she lay she saw a plant, tendrils unwrapping, fingering up toward moon-light for a trellis, a hold. From where she lay the algae and seaweed swayed behind a liquid curtain graceful in the underwater current. From where she lay she heard the first language of her child, a squeak or a gurgle, a small animal reaching for a hold.

It is all of it alive, she thought. All of it was alive.

—☈—

Breathe.

"Stop it, you Wrigglestiltskin!" she laughs grappling her baby back onto her lap. One of the other women joins her in a laugh, holding on to her crawling boy by his sus-penders. And Rose marvels that it is so real to examine these folds and wrinkles, to smell the whole day on her child's skin. These ladies, who always seemed so busy before, now talk to her and share a joke or a tip for getting stains off the arms of the sofa.

The radio plays in the late afternoon as the boys are taking naps upstairs. In her own way, she has mastered how to sterilize bottles and make up formula while setting down supper and hanging up clothes. In her own way, she knows that this is more real than anything else, more truly her than her most private thought, and she can call this up and it will always be here, and hers, the diapers like Christmas doves on the line.

—☈—

Breathe.

A charivari *for Nels Nelson and Tina Erickson. Young couples, arm-in-arm, arriving at the house. The beer is poured, is poured, is drunk and poured again. Eric is holding forth about last winter's fishing hole as Nels swats away remarks about which fly he tied to land Tina Erickson. Rose is passing around her rolled sandwiches which someone, from a distance, has mistaken for pickled herring. Outside the wind blows icy from the lake; the trees are bare, their leaves shored up against the fence posts and battered shed doors.*

Fire crackles and hisses as Rose basks beside the hearth. She is thinking that this is how they must have come up with the name "firecracker", and the observation makes her smile as she watches her husband embroiled in a debate with Wilt Jackson.

How is it that one can be so happy with this glass of beer in one's hand? Beer! Her sisters would be horrified; Rose Ellis Anderson perched on the edge of the hearth like a cricket, like a sparrow. And her sisters would not understand what it meant to be sitting by the hearth with some of Nels Nelson's beer glowing in your glass, the tingling just starting at the edges of your senses as full as a faggot of kindling, ready to spark.

—〜—

They groan like old men, her boys do, in their sleep. Perhaps they are having dreams.

—〜—

Breathe.

Minnesota snow. The boys are out in it shovelling against the sky. One on either side of the drift, a shovelful up, then the other. Brutally beautiful the way the two dark spots attempt to merge, throw up jagged chunks of white against the charcoal sky.

—〜—

Remember: a movie house in Minneapolis. Rose, Veronica and Amanda with bags of mints and caramel chocolates waiting for the picture to start. They have all been looking forward to "You Can't Take It With You". Veronica and Amanda are in love with Jimmy Stewart, but she, secretly, has a great fondness for Lionel Barrymore. She would not dare tell her sisters this. They already think she is odd to continue seeing that Anderson fellow. He should have left town long ago and would have if it hadn't been for her. The sisters already refer to him as "Rose's leading man". No, it would not do any good at all to be mentioning Lionel Barrymore.

The lights dim. She sees her blue wool coat disappear.

Then everything becomes black and white and flat.

She blinks.

—∞—

Dark. Sheet sounds at her ear. Wake up. Where is she? Big square in a pink-ish room, shimmery square with dull shiny spots. A small shape on the night stand. People. A man and a woman. She stares hard. A room. Her room. Her house.

—∞—

The nurse helps Veronica Ellis wrap a blanket around Rose's legs.

"So, where's she going this lovely fall morning?"

The sister sighs.

"To a funeral, I'm afraid."

This causes the nurse to pause.   She knows better than to inquire for details.

"Mind she doesn't chill, now," she says to Rose's sister.

—∞—

She is in school. The desk tops are polished; like tiny skating rinks. She opens her desk and pulls out her brown paper copybook; it feels rough against her fingers. On the front, thick pencil has stroked her name: Rose Ellis.

White blouse, dark tunic.

Rose Ellis.

Tag through the snow, snowballs spinning outside the leaded glass panes. Felt boots by the heat; mittens against the grate. Three called to the board to draw a Christmas scene for the party. Virginia Madsen. Myrna Hyatt.

She squeezes her pencil and holds her breath.

Rose Ellis.

And hears her name.

—∞—

Breathe.

Big house. Everybody here. Mama, Papa, 'Ronica, Baby, and Rose. Mama is singing in the room. Smoke, smoke from papa's pipe.

—⁓—

The next shift has come on duty. There is the usual banter as charts are signed and lunches are stored in the staff room. The attendant, vigilant, makes one final round noticing the stuffy air and the sudden smell of urine.

"Rose. Rosie? You had an accident, honey? Here, let me take that box from you so I can see if you had.... Come on.... Let me put that away for you. What's in here, anyway?"

She manoeuvres herself to the other side of the patient and catches her unawares.

"Oh! Pictures...all these pictures! Let's see, it says: "Ray and Luke." This one is "Rose: 1960." You were kind of cute, weren't you, Rose? Here, let me take these."

The hand resists, fingernails slipping along the cardboard box; and then they let it go.

—⁓—

A river of milk winding through oatmeal. The world smells like bacon, sounds like her mother's voice.

Sparkling, sparkling, icicles out the window.

She could reach out and touch one if Mama would let.

FLOATING ISLAND: AURORA: 1992

*W*e are collecting stones against the wind. Perfectly round, like miniature bowling balls, fit right in the hand. You can throw them like an Olympian, or you can drop them into buckets to tamp your structures down against the wind. We were warned about this island, and this harbour, and what happens to boats in the fall.

James the carpenter would have stayed in Jackfish, building on the ruins there. He's aware of the time before the cold and snow set in. But some of us wanted to push on, and so we made the ten mile passage across from the mainland.

It is hard to see by firelight, and even by the fire my fingers are cramped from the cold. I will have to start making better use of the sun. I volunteered to "take the minutes"—Eta Carina laughed—to take the minutes of our time here on the island.

Grenge won't be able to join us, not now, not 'til spring. By then she may have decided whether to bring her latest conquest along. A legless man would not have made it across to the island in those waters. We barely balanced—and cursed—our way through as it was.

The claim stakes are still here from the days of the miners. Futile that was, and so the companies left just like they always do, just like in Jackfish and Central Patricia, just like in Pickle Crow. They were fools to have come here anyway. This is the Island of Sleeping Giants, the Island of the Gods.

Jean-Marc showed us around the ruins. The old building with the sign "A Place For Everything And Everything In Its Place". We laughed, ragged against the grey sky, and scavenged for pieces of boat, old shingles, in the brush. The shipwrecks are still out there; you can see the hulls when the mist clears.

At night we look to the lighthouse, its single cyclops beam. It is not far, over on the next island, but sometimes the mist is too heavy and it seems to disappear, and then it is dark and cold and endless through the night.

In the morning it feels like you're walking along the edge of the world when the sun hits the water and your nostrils burn. The rocks are beautiful, magical streaked agates, just like the legend says, and you feel like you are here, wherever here is, because the outlines are so precise, and the stone so wet in your hand.

—m—

Loretta joked about where the tree would go. Loretta was an interior designer in an earlier life; she brings her skills to bear on warped timber and scarred oilcloth. She will find a place for the Christmas tree. She is late of James, but they travel well together and have a most sane friendship based on compassion. "Passion is so foolish," Loretta says. "Compassion—well, there you're dealing aces."

Loretta has a child lost in the labyrinth of the Children's Aid Society. She won the distinction of 'unfit mother' the same year she got her design degree.

Jean-Marc doesn't mind doing the cooking when it's game. He misses his *aromates*, yet he does a good job coaxing the wildness from the meat which makes it bearable to me and delicious to the others. All except Eta Carina who has sworn off game and meat. I worry about her with the cold coming on, but she just says, "Don't give me steak knives for Christmas."

How we all come to be here makes for strange stories around the fire, details swallowed up in the perfume of game hoisted over the flames, as the shadows recede, and circle, and as the shadows close in.

—m—

We all come from somewhere else mouthing our own adventures. Most desire anonymity, and I have promised them as much. In fact, the desire to record at all is an anomaly coming as it does on the heels of a life spent destroying evidence, coming as it does in the Company of the Invisible. I believe it has something to do with my own recent adventure, still circling above the fire.

—m—

My mother's face was almost bruised when she answered the door. At the time I immediately thought of Wade, but I know that for all of his other problems that isn't one of them. She had sounded so urgent; it's a voice I hadn't heard in years. It brought back the old nights in the kitchen when I was a kid.

You don't need much. You really don't need much to understand another human being. She fixed me with one glance, and I saw every expression of anger and pain and sadness I'd ever remembered on her face.

And again I thought: Wade. Bristle-top. The Porcupine Mousse.

She pointed—literally—pointed me inside the house like a spectre doing show-and-tell. I had been called, or rather "found", lying low at a friend's place. Three different calls, it took, to three different numbers, and she found me at Eta Carina's on that particular Friday night.

We sat in the living room. Wade was nowhere in sight. She uncorked a bottle of red wine and poured two glasses carefully. Again, it was the intensity that got me. I was handed a glass of wine I hadn't asked for, and my mother held hers out and said: *Your father.*

That was all she said.

And my mind did the usual Rolodex thing—what—is this an anniversary, some kind of special occasion?

My father.

It is strange. Even now I think it is strange. They found him with his dog tags between his teeth. He was armed with a knife. The papers speculated that he was probably an escaped convict or another crazed Vietnam vet. Which makes no sense to me.

"But what was he doing there? What was he *doing* down there?"

My father was found along the banks of the Rainy River. Cause of death, they said, was exposure although the animals had gotten to him as well.

My mother was crazy as she was telling me this because, somehow, Luke had had her most recent address in with his papers. She kept repeating that. I don't know what bothered her more, the fact that he was dead or the idea that, somehow, he was still carrying her around with him.

"Does Wade know?"

"I called him. He's in Winnipeg this week. I...don't know what to do."

I hate seeing her cry. Luke was always able to make her cry. This is a funny way to find out about love. I remember, as a kid, I was always afraid they might stop loving each other. I was always watching to see what they were doing, how they were being with each other. I thought that if he loved her he wouldn't go away. I thought he didn't love her when he went.

—៣—

Michipicoten Island. The natives used to say it wasn't attached, that it floated this way and that in the wind. A Floating Island with toxic vapours; you could die from the air, or from verdigris, or the huge gods standing sentinel among the pines.

We keep these stories close; we talk of them around the fire.

—⁀m⁀—

I decided to go to the funeral. Grenge said she'd better come with me.

"Can't have you going through family shit alone. And your ma's not biting."

My mother is not biting. I never saw her make a harder decision. Part of her desperately needed to go; she begged me to help her make up her mind, but I couldn't tell her what to do, not about this.

It was kind of sick, really. It was almost as if she was asking me whether I wanted them to get back together again. There was this schoolgirl thing happening, like a first date or first- time sex. I had to remind her that he was dead.

I don't know how she finally decided, but one minute we were going together and the next minute I was on my own with an envelope of money and her old tiger-eye ring.

"He gave me this, you know."

It was never a great ring.

"Listen...," I said, "why aren't you coming?"

My mother caught this cry in her throat and held her lips closed until it passed.

"My mother loved him," I told Grenge as she adjusted her seatbelt and settled into the cabin.

"She gave you the money."

"No...really. Big Time Love, the kind you and I are always looking for."

"Does this little button call the flight attendant?"

I don't know why I should have been annoyed with Grenge. She didn't have to come with me. She'd just as soon have been doing something else, and her money had been earmarked for a trip to Hay River. I bunched my jacket against the small of my back and settled into my seat.

—⁀m⁀—

It's strange how places come and go. I'd seen some of that when I was doing actions. You'd go in to protest the destruction of some region—pick a cause—and you'd find a kid's rusted tricycle half-buried along main street. When we were at Jackfish we were always reminded of the ghosts. We walked along the dock and could imagine the coal yards heaped high, and the boxes of fish waiting to be loaded and sent to the market in Montreal. The water tower, the net sheds, the fishing boats. The Hotel. Jean-Marc told us about The Lakeview Hotel, a wild place in its day. This was when the Civilized Southerners would visit, spend a few days out Looking at Nature, a few nights in the taproom of the Lakeview listening to tales of the old-time outlaws. The painters of The Group of Seven were among these visitors. And, later, the northern wilderness took one as payment for the privilege.

The *Lakeview* is gone. The people are gone except for the summertime curious. And people like us. We could have stayed there, but it was still too close. The day Eta heard a radio out along the path, we realized we would have to move again.

And so we came to the floating island which disappeared twice in the mist as we approached it.

—∿—

The wolves have been around. There are animals here. Ironically, it is a sanctuary of sorts despite the past and present intrusions.

The animals got to my father. His upper body was spared, so the mortician dressed him for viewing. The top of the casket was open. I kept thinking of his body, what was missing, the way his brother's body had come back. And it bothered me that I was viewing his body like it was a painting or a video on *MTV*.

The animals and the world.

You can walk away from the world, but the animals always find you.

—∿—

As we approached the village of Warroad, Grenge said something about the strange cloud patterns. It always bothers me when she notices these things while she's driving. One time last year she announced "raspberries at 10 o'clock", and the bushes were quite a ways in, mind you, and she was pointing and slowing down, and neither of us was watching the road. We wound up in the ditch, and all Grenge said was there'd be time to pick the berries before the tow-truck came.

"So, this is where your *paterfamilias* came from."

She pulled over to let me take in the scene, the rental tag swaying on the rearview mirror. The wavy clouds and the green green trees.

"Feel strange?"

I shook my head.

"Then why do you still have your seatbelt on?"

We stepped out into the town.

Once upon a time in the Land o' Lakes....

I had heard these names before: Lake Street, Wabash Street, *Christian Brothers. Marvins. Marvins* was where Luke's brother worked before the war.

We wander up and down, over past the railroad depot. Over to the *Memorial Arena* which looked like an army barracks. I think it is only when I get down to the lake that I know I'm walking forward into a memory, some dreamy Alice pushing her hand through the looking-glass, just a slight quiver as the molecules pass through her body.

And even in grey light the lake is flashing.

"Wow," Grenge says a couple of steps behind me now.

It is a lake.

I think this is supposed to be magical, and I am supposed to swoon. But it is just strange, this lake, these people beside the campsite. I smell lighter fluid and a barbecue—no meat, just charcoal smell from somewhere.

Grenge is pointing at the seaplane coming in skimming the water like it was landing on ice.

—m—

Michipicotan.

Loretta and James have been exploring the island. She has a good pair of boots, better than mine, but my parka is warmer than hers. We will all be sharing this winter. We laugh at the condom supply Jean-Marc has brought— enough to last for several years. He disagrees. We laugh some more.

I am accustomed to being alone. Grenge used to say I was a spore addict. Sporadically needing human closeness. Sporadic and indiscriminate (she disapproved of some of my liaisons). We always set the highest standards for one another's behaviour, and then we sit back and wait for all the heads to roll.

It seems to get colder, here, by the day. Eta Carina says it is going to be a long winter. This sounds so banal but it didn't when she said it. When she said it, it was as if it was the first time anyone had truly heard it. Or the first time anyone had made sense of the words.

—⁓—

As Grenge and I stood in the middle of the Land o' Lakes, I was thinking how odd it was that they had found my mother. It wasn't Luke's mother who had contacted her. It was somebody named Olson whom my mother didn't know.

And I was thinking how one of the lakeside houses in the distance must have been my father's home. But which house? And was my grandmother still there?

"What's she like?"

"Never met her. We used to write each other all the time. I haven't written in a while, though. I meant to."

Grenge shrugged and pulled at a tall weed growing out of the water. We both walked along in silence.

I knew that he would look older than when I last saw him. It had been about five years and he'd be getting up in his forties. I could never imagine Luke making fifty. I can see myself, an old fossil, sitting on a beach—and even my mother, a well-preserved eighty-five giving in to a cane. But I never could envision Luke far off into the future.

Grenge pulls up to the building and parks, and I do not want to go in.

"Listen, he's not going anywhere. You want to drive around?"

Grenge had a father once, but that was long ago.

I shake my head, so she unstraps my seatbelt for me. She gets out of the car and comes around and opens my door.

And I am on my own.

He is there in the corner. The room is empty except for him. Like a Taoist tea ceremony. The candles I can do without.

His face is thinner. Hair almost completely grey. An unhealthy waxy expression. Was this how he looked when they found him? He must have been spotted right away, before the body had time to.... Just time enough for this blank acceptance to spread across his face.

I had heard about the colour grey, how you can't really disguise it no matter what makeup you use. And his hands. They even put makeup on his hands.

I never went to church much. I never got taken to church. Once in a while, when I was little, one or the other of them would take me. One time they both did, and it was near Christmas, and there were carols and lessons, and I remember I didn't like the lessons much but fell in love with the carols. There were candles then, and they were very beautiful. And even my parents started singing.

My father's hand on one side, my mother's on the other. My father's hand was always cool and still, my mother's hand would fidget. Like me, like mine, we'd fidget out our energies, the lightning passing through us until it grounded in Luke's hand. And I looked up at him that day, and if he wasn't my father, I would have sworn he was crying, just a few quick tears, not even tears just blurry eyes.

And I tried to blur my eyes, and, sure enough, it made the candles flicker and made halos around the other lights. Right then and there I wanted to lose just a little of my sight.

—⁓—

Just like here on the island where every day I lose the sound of something from before.

I no longer hear the sound of trucks rumbling empty over rocky roads.

I no longer hear the buzz saws in my dreams or the television volleys of the soft-drink wars.

I walk along the island, and I hear the wind and hear water smacking up against land. And I hear loud silence. It removes everything else.

—⁓—

"Excuse me, dear...."

I remember pulling my eyes away from the face of my father to follow the voice, and there was a tiny woman in a veil. She was sitting on the edge of a chair in the corner. Had she been there all along?

I left the casket and walked over since she didn't seem to be making any effort to get up.

"My legs—rheumatism. Would you pull up a chair beside me?"

I have seen two pictures of my grandmother, and I was sure this wasn't her. I reached for a folding chair and set it down beside her.

"Are you a friend of the family?" I asked which seemed pitiful in the context of the empty room.

"My dear...oh, my dear, I think I just about *am* the family," she sighed in a slightly exaggerated fashion as though she had said this out loud before.

"I'm Veronica Ellis. I am this boy's aunt."

Ellis.

"But that...you're related to Luke's mother."

"My sister Rose.... And you are? I'm sorry, I'm not from town. I've just come to take care of things. Are you one of Rose's nurses?"

"I'm...."

Grenge walked in then. It was all so strange.

"Did you know my nephew?"

Looking back to the casket. Looking to the casket.

"He was my father."

Grenge later told me how dazed I looked when I said it. The old lady, my great aunt, was shocked as well. She'd heard of me, of course, but, since I'd never met the family or gone to Warroad in my entire life, she hardly expected to see me there.

I wanted to know about my grandmother. The woman had implied she was alive. Was she okay?

"Oh...."

We were invited back to the house. Veronica Ellis insisted.

"It was your father's home," she said simply.

My grandmother didn't live there anymore, and they were hoping to sell the place.

"Too big?"

My grandmother Rose was in the nursing home. Although she was younger than Veronica, she had Alzheimer's disease and needed constant care.

"It was so tragic. After Eric—your grandfather—she seemed to lose her spark. She was such a peppy girl when we were young. But, nevertheless, she was determined to stay up here; nothing I could say or do would talk her out of it. We visited more often, though. She would come to Minneapolis and stay a week or two, and I even made the trip up, especially after our sister Amanda passed on."

Another great-aunt. A family tree appearing limb by limb, and the storm picking off the all branches.

"Rose always hoped...she never truly gave up hoping that he...would come home," she nodded in the direction of the casket. "And that you, her only grandchild...oh...excuse me, I don't usually get like this."

Grenge appeared out of the shadows with a polka-dot handkerchief.

"Maybe he was coming home," Grenge volunteered.

—m—

We keep trying to understand things.

—⁓—

I can now chop wood as well as Jean-Marc can. I split decades with my axe, and hear the rumble of the sleeping giants, and see the spirit of the tree slide down along the blade. This thing which is so holy, or which is pulp and paper...my hand pressed to a page, I'm both damned and sanctified. My axe scuffs along bark, yet elsewhere trees have hidden spikes. I throw the wood into the pile of split warmth.

I will do this again.

—⁓—

What I don't remember does not exist.

What I remember does not exist.

What I don't remember does exist, here, with Grenge following Veronica's directions, the car turning off the road and down a long driveway.

A simple house. A drawing of a house squared-off but with shrubs and bushes growing out of control. The kind of place where you expect to see cotton-ball smoke curling from the chimney.

"You realize, of course, the place hasn't been lived in for a while. A good neighbour comes by from time to time, but it is, frankly, in terrible shape."

"How long has she been gone?"

"It's about a year now. Almost a year. Here, take my keys and you can open up."

It is not as I expected, except for the front room and the fireplace. They appeared in Luke's stories. Grenge is walking around touching things, trying out the overstuffed armchair.

And there they are lined up on the mantel like they're in a shooting gallery, my...family. I've never seen these. My Uncle Ray. Grandmother. Grandfather. I look. Look again. A picture of my mother and my father and me walking beside a river. I don't remember this. But it is my outline between them.

Grenge mutters something about "your 19th nervous breakdown", and my great aunt joins us in the room.

"Open that window, would you, dear? Let some air in this place."

I peer out. The trees are still good here. It is the animals and fish that are taken.

—⁓—

I went through the house slowly looking for...clues? To what I cannot remember. I do not know which details are important.

Once upon a time in the Land o' Lakes.

Her preserves? The margins of the lake?

Grenge was good, staying out of the way, talking with Veronica and volunteering to make supper.

"Toss me the keys, Aurora. Gonna pick up some grub."

Which left me with this old lady who was my father's Aunt Veronica.

Her hand grasped at the tea cup, all of her fingers in a single crook.

"We never saw them enough, you know. They lived so far away. Rose was adamant about life in the north, she said it would be good for the boys. And Eric.... Well, rest his soul, I won't go into that.... Eric had his own ideas, which kept some of us at bay."

I wanted to hear about my father.

"Actually, I knew Ray a little better. He was older and he was quite a gregarious child. One summer, he insisted on a visit to his Auntie's place, and his mother was forced to comply. He showed up on my doorstep with a suitcase full of comic books."

She chuckled, then, or coughed.

"We were all heartbroken when he was taken."

I listened. "And my father?"

"Luke...your... well, really, he was a quiet one. I never did see him enough."

I looked away. Me neither.

And that was it.

—⁓—

I used to think that anybody carrying a decent camera was someone after the truth.

—⁓—

There was still the final viewing to go through before the funeral, set for the following morning. Grenge said she would stay at the house, so I headed back to the funeral parlour with Veronica. I asked her if she was expecting anyone else, and she pursed her lips and said she doubted it. I had been avoiding the obvious all afternoon but felt I couldn't any longer.

"I want to see...will my grandmother be there?"

"Oh, no...she wouldn't know him. It would only upset her. She'll go to the funeral. You can help me take her. But this other...she really wouldn't understand it, and it might only upset her."

I don't remember the last evening with my father. There were a few people from the town who identified themselves to Veronica, one or two who came over to me. A man, somebody Olson of the same Olsons who had contacted my mother, came over and spoke to me about Luke. He said he and Luke had been friends when they were young.

"Ah, he was a good kid. Such a dreamer. They were quite a team, Ray and Luke. I remember one summer Luke decided he had to protect the birds' nests he kept finding out on the trails. He figured if he could find them, other people and animals could, so he kept guard out there for hours. Ray would bring him lemonade from the house. They were pretty good friends."

I had to approach the casket one more time. We would both be glad when this was over, Luke and me.

I remember how he always told me stories when I was lying down, and he would always look away as he told them. He wouldn't want me staring at him now.

The mask of my father.

Like the art project in school. I made mine with an egg carton, the huge symmetrical bumps all over my face.

I am looking at his hands, the nails tucked under, still a little stained. His hands were always grass-stained, the nails in the corners a translucent green from the mowing and landscaping. And, now, from the trip along Rainy River. Makeup along the fingers, patted over the back of the hands. Made-up hands holding little green claws tight.

I pulled the ring off my index finger. Dull, taupe and golden tiger-eye.

I don't like touching the dead. It's a problem, I realize, but I don't like touching dead people, so it is difficult to wedge the ring behind the folded hands.

Now the hands cup it. Something is completed.

He twirled me around in the grass.

Daddy.

Ah, Luke, I wish there was more than this.

—⁓—

That night at the house I bundled up and sat out on the porch. The sky was dark; everything was still. The lake was just an absence, a black linen space. The moon kept going behind the clouds.

—⁓—

We made a small but impressive group, the people who came to Luke Anderson's funeral. Grenge was there in a navy-blue anorak and a pair of army fatigues. My great-aunt Veronica wore traditional black and needed help to negotiate her way to the pew. There were a few people from town who knew the family—the Olson brothers, a lady who said she was a friend of Rose's.

And there was Rose, my grandmother, who'd been dressed in a royal blue pantsuit and a bright yellow woollen hat that Veronica kept threatening to remove.

My grandmother.

They wheeled her in. She could, apparently, walk a little, but they weren't taking any chances, so they had her in the wheelchair. She did not look like the pictures. Her expression was different, but I knew the shape of the head.

It is like my father's. And it is like mine.

Veronica and I were to sit with her through the ceremony. Poor Rose didn't know what was going on. Veronica kept hold of her right hand while her left drifted in space in the aisle. She looked over at me, but there was nothing, just a blank expression. That's when it hit me. It was the same expression Luke was wearing in the coffin.

And somehow this was worse.

The ceremony was over. I rode with Grenge while Veronica went along with Rose and an attendant. At the cemetery, I looked at the graves of my grandfather and my Uncle Ray. Raymond Anderson 1945-1970. And now my father would be there, too. Luke Anderson 1947-1992.

She was so pitifully sweet in the wheelchair, a small clump of baby's breath and roses in her lap. Veronica was weeping softly. I believe she was doing it for Rose, instead of Rose, and there was frustration in her voice when she whispered, "Give me the flowers, Rose. Please!"

The minister kept looking over at me.

"He wants you to say something," Grenge elbowed me.

The minister, the townspeople, the teary eyes of Aunt Veronica, the blank eyes of my Grandmother Rose.

I stepped over to the casket.

"Uh, look.... My father was a man of few words. He was careful about them, so I guess I should be the same. He loved Lake of the Woods. He used to tell me about it when I was a kid. I'm just kind of glad he got the chance to come back."

One of the Olson men was nodding.

We all threw clumps of earth.

My grandmother threw her flowers down the hole instead of placing them on top of the casket.

And we buried him.

The silence was empty as we went back to the house.

Grenge and I didn't hang around much longer. Aunt Veronica wanted me to stay a while especially since they were trying to sell the house. And when I looked at her struggling to walk beside Rose's wheelchair, I was almost persuaded to remain.

The lake was deeper than in all the stories, and I could imagine him sitting on the porch dreaming his kid's dreams while my grandmother puttered behind his head in the kitchen, all the rivers and lakes connected, the continent itself flowing through his mind.

—◊—

I don't know why we went to the Memorial. It was way back in DC, and neither Grenge nor I was rolling in cash. But it seemed inevitable, somehow. We flew into JFK and got a car into Washington.

Government towns. I'd grown up in a government town, so it didn't faze me as much as it might have. But DC was so much bigger, bigger in every way.

We found the Vietnam Memorial.

And we were not alone.

I was given materials to make a rubbing and moved along the black granite wall. It's like a mirror; you can almost fall into it; you see yourself in the other world just beyond the surface, like the bottom of the lake, another mirror, another Alice testing.

And I found him. My Uncle Ray.

There are always volunteers more than willing to assist. One tall, crazed-looking man in a special forces beret offered to help. I let him take the rubbing for me.

I didn't know what I was going to do with it. Thought I might send it to old Aunt Veronica.

The former soldier was most solicitous. He wanted to know about Ray, but I had no information to give him.

"Damn shame," he kept saying. "Nobody knows who they were. Damn fucking shame."

I talked with him for a while, learned about the Veterans' Programs and was brought up to date on a few of the Agent Orange cases.

By the time I caught up with Grenge, she was in intense conversation with a vet in a wheelchair. He was, I'll admit, a fine figure of a man except for the missing legs. That is, he seemed fit and bright and extremely personable. I don't know why that should have surprised me.

I can be pretty slow especially when I'm preoccupied. So it took me a while to realize that there was a Big Time Connection happening between them. It was only when Grenge pulled me aside and tossed me the keys that I realized she wasn't coming back with me.

"But we're going up to Jackfish!"

"I'll meet you there."

"But it's getting too late to make the trip. I thought you...."

"Me and the Duke will be along."

That was it. I left her there with the Duke and drove back to the airport. I haven't seen Grenge since, although I'm hoping that come spring, if all is well here, we might be able to bring them across.

—⁄w⁄—

My great aunt Veronica had offered me a share of the settlement once they sold the property. She even wondered if I might want to own the place myself.

I glanced over at Grenge.

We'd never owned much of anything in our lives.

It didn't seem like a good time to be starting.

—⁄w⁄—

Michipicotan Island. I don't know how long we'll stay. So far we have avoided anything that borders on the political. Game plans. Strategies. It all seems so distant from tins of bread in the embers, the wild grapes that blue our fingers as we drop them into the cast-iron cauldron.

Michipicotan Island; floating; unattached to the rest of the world. Optical illusion? A result of the mists? Silent stones rubbed round by the fingers of gods, plashes of colour that made the painters cry.

It isn't rooted, but its rootlessness is ancient, old and true and maybe even holy. I find beautiful agates, but I leave them where they are, like the gods who have so far left us alone here.

If something was ever forbidden, maybe it was this the gods forbade, this keeping company with rootless things, this borderless shifting of continents.

It is enough to be here, wherever here is, to feel the solid land and the liquid earth beneath it. We will try to stay here until the millennium clicks over. We will do our best to confuse Columbus.

Everlasting Sky: Luke: 1992

*H*e had drifted. It was not the same as having changed, moved on, hit the trail. It was not as formerly current now currently quaint, as having kept on truckin', having kept on keeping on. He had drifted—Ottawa, Saskatoon, that time in Alberta, lobster traps on the east coast, Gabi in Duisburg, Petra in Berlin, years of tired meetings in community centres and church halls, three, four people against a company. He had grown thinner, more skeletal. He felt his bones, pushed them out to the surface and let the UV rays beat hard upon them and then stared sideways, amazed, at the stick-figure he made.

In the old days it was the marionette, sad clip-clop of wood along the pavement. Now it was the skeleton free of entanglements, free of flesh, boarding a bus and finding a window seat, a bag of peanuts and an apple in a pocket, for later.

He had drifted, but as the bus engine turned over and hummed, he felt a sudden sense of direction. He was going home.

—⁓—

When he was a boy it was a simple thing to lose a day. It began with the songbirds, perhaps a yellow finch, or the wind waving the tops of pine trees. Dirt road or rut road, paths along the river. The perfect stillness of the overturned canoe. And he would be de Noyon again, crazy voyager from Trois Rivières, who had travelled down the Rainy River until he saw, for the first time, the Lake of the Woods. Young Luke had thought the man ancient, as ancient as the old Medicine Man whom he saw, sometimes, in the brush trails along the shore. But de Noyon was twenty years old, an adventurer, a voyager in a...North canoe? The boy hadn't known, had known only that it was the water that connected things, Jacques de Noyon on the river with

Assiniboine guides, before the United States, before such a place as Canada, who knew it wasn't land, it was the rivers that took you places, the rivers that kept you from them. It all began with water.

—〰—

Luke had been camping these last weeks, and it was getting cold at night. He refused to give in and pick up a tent, using instead the same old tarp that had travelled with him all the years. He would have to purchase a small frying pan, though; he was tired of eggs sticking to tin foil.

"Where's your spirit of adventure, boy?" his father would likely have said improvising with the lid from one of the tin supply canisters.

His father. A vision that stretched only as far as the lake, no farther, and yet his father had taught him to survive.

"That's the wilderness out there. You got to be on your toes."

Like Ray was when he stepped on the punji stake?

"You got to expect nature to put up a fight."

His father. The same man who painted crude green arrows pointing the way to the cabins could sit on the porch at night for hours amazed at a storm over the lake. Luke had not allowed himself to notice that because it didn't fit in with the rest of the theory. It was too hard to imagine.

"You wouldn't want to imagine, would you?"

His father was a good one for the last word.

But he had imagined, sometimes, sitting in windows in rented apartments, imagined himself retracing the route of the retreating glacier, Val beside him, the child on his back, ice-axing his way over an outcropping, his crampons holding tight. It was not that he thought of Val or Aurora often it was just that when he did, it was always with the three of them on the glacier or in some other extreme situation in which, against horrendous odds, they would survive together.

One time, about three years ago, he had thought of contacting Val. Her old number was no good; he learned later she was living with someone. He found an A. T. Anderson listed in the Ottawa phone book and gave his daughter a call. He twisted the receiver cord until the skin on his fingers went white. Nobody was home.

He was amazed at how easily the bus passed through Customs and borders almost as if they didn't exist. A bus at a crossing, a declaration of intent,

RITA DONOVAN

a bunch of tourists, a bunch of shoppers, a Canadian's right to visit the continent. His landed immigrant papers like leaves, like birds flying south as if there were only waterways beneath him and his eyes were fixed on the next bend in the river.

"Anybody sitting here?"

A not-so-young woman with green eyes pulled off her jacket and dropped her woven bag on the seat next to Luke.

"Sally. Sally Ride. Actually, it's Sally Armstead but I got the nickname doing this," she motioned the length of the bus with her hand, "whenever I can. Yours?"

"Luke." He held out his hand.

She would be about his own age; mid-forties he guessed. She was pretty in that old way he remembered, the eyes looking off into middle-distance, hands that gestured when she spoke. She was on the road having quit her job as a uniformed, unarmed security guard. She was on her way to Disneyland.

"With stops along the way. *Gummi-Bear*?" she flashed a small sticky package.

She was an unmarried aunt, she told him, legitimizing this role. She was going to pick up her sister's son and take him west to Disneyland. The boy was dying of a brain tumour.

"Ever notice how it's always people with brain tumours who want to go to Disneyland?"

She liberated another green *Gummi-Bear* from the plastic. "He had wanted Disney *World*, but I told him Disney*land*, seeing as they live in Wyoming. Besides, what's the difference? World, land, a *papier mâché* head is a *papier mâché* head, I always say."

She put her feet up on her bag and sighed.

The miles went by. The bus stopped for gas and a twenty- minute break, and Luke bought his companion a coffee. She was wearing rope sandals, and it was not that warm out. Luke commented in passing on her clothes and the season.

"You know, I used to wear animal skins on my feet. Then there were those sandals, you know the ones, made out of rubber tires? I liked those a lot, but then I started feeling, I don't know, radial, or something, like I had to go, go, go. I couldn't take the pressure."

"And these?"

"Hemp. Rope, whatever. They don't last too long, but I can sleep at night."

Back on the bus Luke smiled.

"Nice. Nearly herniated yourself, there, but nice smile."

She had a tiny tattoo of a bird inside her cleavage. Luke could see it when she leaned down to slip off her sandals.

Sally fell asleep, and soon her head was against Luke's shoulder, her blonde, slightly frizzy hair brushing his neck. She had given up her job to go and take her nephew on his last trip. She had moved back home with her mother when "the old doll" became incapacitated and had helped care for the woman until her death. She had had her share of romances. "God, romance is the best! I just don't understand those twenty or thirty years they tack on the end of it". And she had voted three presidential elections in a row for her grade-ten civics teacher, "the only guy I ever trusted to do what he said he'd do."

It was easy for Luke to feel the old longings. She was beside him, her head softly on his shoulder, her shirt open just enough for the bird to snag in his imagination. He had not slept with a woman for longer than he dared remember. And she talked as though time didn't matter, that she wasn't forty-one or forty-four and still travelling the length of the country by bus. That she wasn't getting those crows-feet that almost disappeared when she closed her eyes. That she'd have all the time she needed to show her nephew "the time of his life."

And he could see them at the entrance to Disneyland, the boy's bloated body in a wheelchair, his mouse-ears tipped dapperly to one side of his swollen head, a small boy swimming in a sea of chemicals, and he looks up at his Aunt Sally and receives a smile of absolute benediction.

Tiger was his name, or had been since the cancer. Tiger, or Robbie, and Sally Ride at the Gates of the Magic Kingdom greeted by a mouse, a cow in country-and-western gear, and a dog named for a faraway planet.

Luke slipped his hand around Sally's as she slept, her breathing quiet and whinnying.

—⚟—

It was a few years ago now. He had been in the public library in Edmonton the day he saw the article. Some newspaper, it didn't matter which, and the small article with the dateline International Falls.

They were giving away land in the northern US, Luke read. If a person would only come to the deserted northern homesteads, someone who could commit to a ten year stay without any government assistance, then that person could claim a plot of land. It was starting all over again.

Luke had sat there listening to the rain against the window, looking past the blurred outline of the Woodwards store, and felt a pull so strong it nearly yanked him from his seat.

International Falls!

And Warroad only a short way off.

—⁓—

Warroad is a dream in the back of a fisherman's head, in the rushed, clipped speech of a Wall Street stockbroker. Warroad came so far and then turned into water, the Warroad River, the Lake of the Woods, huge and simple myths with childlike names, but so overwhelming that the names do not adhere to the green moss...look, they are sliding off the rocks: Rainy Lake, Lake of the Woods, Red Lake, Rainy River. War Road.

Chippewa War Road.

Sioux War Road.

La Rue de Guerre.

Simple names.

Ancient *anishinabe* in the woodland mouthing *ka bek a nung*, the end of the trail, memories, battle dark and bloody. Warroad: dark and bloody end of the trail.

Someone was giving away land.

The absurdity of the gesture.

Woody Allen holding up a clump of sod and talking about land.

Scarlett O'Hara streaming dust from her fingers and talking about land.

How many countless westerns: cattleman with his hand on his boy's shoulder proclaiming, "Someday, son, this will all be yours."

Handing over a valley like it was a piece of fruit.

He had told Sally Ride he was going to see about some land.

When had it happened?

All the years of dreams, the first ones of escape, of canoeing the river route of de Noyon or hanging onto a retreating glacier as it skidded and scraped its way north through Canada—except it wasn't Canada yet—all the way up to Hudson's Bay—except it wasn't Hudson's Bay.

When had the direction shifted, the dreams of home begun? The sweating dreams of *punji* stakes ringing the Land of the Free, and Luke with a packsack filled with pieces of his friends dancing between the poison-sticks. Luke facing off against the brilliant angel, glittering sword between its hands, and Luke with his brother's taped-up hockey stick.

Sally shifted and took her head from Luke's shoulder as they drove through a town past houses with lights that glowed behind pale curtains. Luke could almost smell the simmering beef stew, burn his tongue on the cherry pie.

Sally Ride got off along the way having promised to visit a friend "from back then". She gave Luke two joints which he later discarded in the washroom, and then she kissed him with a familiarity that excited and dismayed him.

"Maybe we'll run into each other again. I'll tell you all about Daffy Duck, and you can tell me all about...."

"Home," Luke smiled and held her, feeling her bones.

—w—

Whenever he thought of home, he thought of his mother hovering near the house. He never pictured her down at church with the ladies or doing errands at the stores along Lake Street. He never saw her with her sisters in Minneapolis going out to dinner downtown. She was invariably in the kitchen, or on the porch, or out pulling up weeds in the border flower bed.

He could show her a thing or two about landscaping, he smiled. Design a V-shaped flowerbed that would highlight the corner of the property; fill it with seasonals and perennials of varying hue and duration, flowers that would involve minimal care. He could, well, he could cut the grass, at least.

I am the Mower Damon, known...

He should have written. Or called. It was too many years.

He had sat up top in another country while the icons and touchstones fell: Huey Newton, Abbie Hoffman, Ralph Abernathy. Huey gunned down just like in all the old days; Abbie pulling the covers over himself along the Hudson, a smile starting on his strangely silent lips.

He had sat on top of a country watching the desperation building below while in the north the nation blustered through another long cold winter.

"My son, surely...."

One of her letters had begun that way, so plaintive and yet so removed. My son, surely. It spoke of a right, a mother's right that had been denied. Because he had been so sure of who he was and of what words meant. Caught in the fishhook of rhetoric, gasping in that way that sounded almost alive, not seeing the same words on the Roman walls, Latin graffiti through the centuries and Luke's voice, the same voice, the voice of change against a pissed-on wall.

He had given it all up for talk.

In the Olson family the men never talked. The father never spoke directly to his sons. If he needed two or three of them to work a specific field he simply pointed, or grunted, and the three of them would go. He trained them so they could be counted and counted upon. Sometimes Luke would see them in the hardware, Christy or Willie standing by while the old man scooped up wood screws. The boy would wait, like a clumsy manservant, an Igor with stoop-shoulders and an attitude.

An Igor. Ray had stood by while their father shot the shit with Ruddy, or Eddie, and never said a word.

"The Men," he'd proclaim to Luke which would sometimes get them laughing. Especially on the porch at night if the others were in the kitchen.

"Another dead soldier," their father calls out except it comes out "shoulder", and Ray grasps his own shoulder and turns into an Igor and slurps the words, "The Men."

Luke had been determined not to stand by and take it and so had grown into someone who could fire back fusillades of...phrases, word balloons like the large tomatoes the Blue Meanies carried in *Yellow Submarine*, word balloons that still stuffed the *Doonesbury* frames, but came now from an invisible president, a blank with a voice.

Or an Igor with no voice?

Luke had started off so quietly, and he had understood the quiet. He should never have opened his mouth. His brother had died in silence, holding onto screams of agony, biting down hard on his dog tag, his teeth moulded into the metal.

"Hey, big brother."
"Sssshhh...."
"What if we take off and leave the old man out here?"
"Ah, he doesn't care. He's got *his gear and his beer.*"
"Mom would miss him."
"Maybe."
"Maybe we could...."
"Sssshhh...."

History had set them all on the road, ruffled the skins draped over Palaeolithic road people, set them off across the Bering Strait, nomads roaming North America. Adventurers, voyageurs, conquistadors, jailbirds, stepping gingerly onto the rock or spongy sod.

"Hello? Is there anybody home?"

History kept them all moving across a continent on which they were all immigrants. Tired—and no rest-stops along the interstate.

LANDED

His last letter to his mother was years ago before he left for Europe, a page and a half to let her know that he was still alive. She had written back immediately curious about Alberta, words brimming with hope for her son and his life in the west. But careful.

My son, surely.

And he had sensed it then, a small loss of control. His mother had always had trouble with time. It was one of her endearing traits. She paid more attention to it than most people did in the area of celebrations and anniversaries. But she either refused to, or simply could not, respect its hold over lives, its logic that made some people here and some people gone. Luke had thought that his mother was, in her own way, a subtle anarchist.

There. Another definition. He had laboured to be so precise, to name the thing, and not to name what he did not know.

Val wiping her eyes on her sleeve, trying to keep her voice down, the two of them whispering finalities in the living room while their daughter slept in the tiny room down the hall.

"Just say it, Luke. Fucking say you don't care!"

Which, of course, he could not do.

"Oh, what, you're gonna tell me you love me? That this hell we're living is love?"

Silence.

He knew silence then. He could use it then. And he used it with his mother.

Yet he was good for throwing words and sweat into ideas, into causes. He gave them all his words, and there was nothing left for Val or his mother. Nothing at all left for his daughter.

Luke got off in Duluth. He put his hands at the base of his spine and stretched taking a couple of deep breaths. Then he claimed his knapsack and tied-on tarp from the belly of the bus, and put it on his shoulder.

"Another dead shoulder," Ray lunged at him.

Luke waved at a couple of fellow passengers and then strode through the station.

—〰—

He was back.

He would have to rent a canoe someplace.

He would have to find out about some land.

He would have....

He was watching it, the glacier in the far field, blue ice shuddering, chipping apart like scree, like the sherbet his mother made on hot afternoons, not quite solid, a shimmering substance suspended, almost, in the cut-glass bowls as the flies buzzed against the screen and his father went on about wisdom teeth.

A vehicle. Luke stood in front of the desk as the man studied his licence.

"Alberta boy. We got quite a few come down here from Alberta, Manitoba. Not so many from Saskatchewan. They don't believe in water up in Saskatchewan, do they?"

"What do you mean?"

"Well, it just looks like a flat piece of cake or like a tooth, there, don't you think? Like one big buck tooth."

"Well...."

"It's kind of hard to respect something that looks like a buck tooth, now, don't you think? You want air-conditioning?"

The car had taken a hefty chunk of his available cash.

"Can I get racks?" he'd asked.

The man nodded at the stranger from Canada.

Luke found a place to rent a canoe. The northern US really was a sportsman's paradise just like the brochure said. They made it so easy: here's your car, here's your canoe, you sure you don't want a two-man tent? Luke had his cooking utensils and tarp; he carried a knife.

"Sure you don't want a shotgun?"

Of course, in America, this could be anywhere.

He had carried the knife for several years now on the pretext that he liked to live in the bush. Most of the time this excuse would not have stood; he carried a concealed weapon and did so in the city.

This canoeing was somehow part of it. You canoed before you spotted the promised land. The Voyageur National Park, The Boundary Canoe Area. You canoed and then you discovered countries or other peoples' countries. Or that you were lost.

Bells somewhere. Church bells. Luke listened to them echo off hills. Once, this was how America sounded, and before that the sound of crackling fire and chants.

He liked the bells. They pealed, forged promises, and everything was peaceful and possible: clean linen on a Sunday afternoon, starch smell gone since Saturday, just the clear crispness left, three or four roses in a vase. The sound faded, and Luke finished strapping the canoe to the top of the *Skylark*.

He would canoe the border lakes and breathe with the ribs of his canoe. He would train his eyes to look for the diamond willow, rough bark like old skin tattooed with diamonds. His father used to tell him about the old days when it got so cold that the trees would make snapping sounds. As a boy, Luke had listened for it, but it had to be on the days of deep deep cold and usually what he heard instead was, "Get in here, you fool, you want to freeze your tonsils off?"

The old days harvesting ice from the lake, sawing the cakes and stacking them in ice houses. His father remembered those days when he went to the fridge for a cold one.

The border lakes.

Even the waterways had been defined. But this had been wrong. Tip the rim of the canoe into water and even this boundary disappeared, and the water was all there was, and if it divided anything at all, it divided right there—smack—on the interface. It divided water from air, surface from depth. These were the only boundaries that mattered.

He had put in partway across the Boundary Waters Canoe Area and would proceed through Voyageur Park, through Smokey Bear State Forest, Pine Island State Forest, and past the Red Lake Reservation. The Rainy River would take him home to the Lake of the Woods.

"Check out the Snake and the worm."

Two brothers trudging along Lake Street.

"Hey, your old man's telling a whopper over at the Dollar."

Ray and Luke heading home in the twilight.

"Ginny's got some people over. You guys wanna come?"

Ray's steps hesitating, measuring Luke's.

"No, hey, thanks," comes the voice. "We're walking for a while."

And he falls back into pace beside his brother.

He was canoeing light and wouldn't have minded a body in the bow. He had canoed stern most of his life, his father or a vacationer in the middle, his brother feathering up front.

Luke stepped off and pushed away from land. In the bush the deer and moose would be rutting; he would hear the loud clack of their racks. He would have to hunt small and in silence. A knife was all he needed. A knife, or a pointed stick, or a copy of *The Captain and Tenille*. Petra had found it once in her apartment left behind by one of the fleeing lovers. She had never heard of them, understandably, as she was almost exclusively into the electronic statements of *Kraftwerk* at the time. She listened, stunned, and turned to Luke and pronounced that the Americans had found the ultimate weapon.

Petra tasted of spiced butter and sunshowers, as if she had rubbed small leaves and petals against her skin. He almost could have stayed with her.

"Lass mich im Ruhe, Scheißkopf, Ami!"
American Shithead, reporting for duty.

He almost chuckled aloud at the ludicrous lyrics, Tenille belting out her assuring belief that love will keep us together. That all it took was a honky-tonk beat and a few rhyming bleats. That you didn't pass your heart through a wringer-washer two, three times a day. He thought about the women he knew, how they were willing to flatten their breasts in a machine that would tell them, perhaps, that they would live. It was so chancy. It was so brave to love.

He was unused to canoeing long hours and felt it the first day out. His leg muscles and shoulders were stiff as he gathered kindling and laid out his tarp. As he brushed the twigs from it with a pine bough, he paused. He had done all this before. He boiled some water and opened a package of dried vegetables. Freeze-dried. Reconstituted. He would like to be reconstituted. Whatever it meant. And he sat back on his heels taking in the familiar cracking sounds: the smell of cedar scraps, the rustle of dead leaves all around him.

He was pushing himself this day, the weather threatening overhead and a vague uneasiness, like ducks, settling on the water around him. He knew what he was capable of daily, and he had no intention of overdoing it, but he felt the desire to press on whenever he thought of Warroad. Had his problem always been the same—the desire to be wherever he was not? Would the same thing happen when he reached the Lake of the Woods?

The first raindrops hit his back, the size of quarters on his arms. They were cold. The day had gradually been cooling down, but he had exerted himself to the point that the change in temperature was refreshing. Now he felt the wind come up as the rain spattered the water. Now the wind shifted, and he was canoeing into it. The water was turning into cubist chunks; it chopped sideways against the craft and rocked the small boat wildly.

Steady. Steady. Luke balanced with the paddle.

He had to get out of this. Luke scrambled to secure his supplies.

Steady, boy.

His father's easy command, no expert himself but solid in a situation. Steady and don't start squirming.

This is it, Luke. This is the world.
Ray's easy knowledge, his feet up on the banister.
You're the one, Luke. Pointing a gun-finger at him.

The rain drummed down; Luke could barely keep his eyes open. His hat was useless, and then it was gone, the wind whipping it from his head.

Ice water. The glacier.

Water hissing so loud he wanted to put his hands to his ears, but he held on to the paddle as the canoe drifted blindly.

When he heard the sound, it was a groan, a wrenching. He thought he'd dislocated something, but then he felt a cold gush and knew. Luke grabbed at his supplies but there was no time, and he threw himself over the side just as the canoe tipped under.

Cold. Concentrate. Cold.

Luke pushed up for air.

Quick.

He was weighed down, and yet he felt weightless. Tired and numb. He swam by instinct not able to see the shore. His left arm, his right, a roar somewhere over his head. The water tasted malty. Like a giant vat of beer.

"Right, Dad?"

Quit fooling around! Get over here!

Their father yells at them as they splash one another in the rubber swimming pool. Ray is sitting on the metal seat and kicking as fast as he can, the water arcing and catching Luke across the chest, and Luke bending down and slapping back water with a cupped hand.

Get over here!

One more handful of water.

And back.

"Quit it! Dad said!"

And one more.

And then they are running—grains of dirt, blades of grass sticking to their legs—over to the shed where their father expects them to tie flies. Ray pushes Luke who falls face first into the earth pile, which stuns him. He pulls himself up slowly. His hand is bleeding.

Luke lifted his hand out and felt the reeds and then the clumps of outcropping and clawed at them for a hold. He half-crawled, half-pulled himself up onto the bank, and looked up through the driving rain. Then he saw it. There it was—the apex of the glacier. It was right in front of him wavering like a mirage. Luke reached out his hand to touch it, and collapsed.

He found himself lying on a marshy bank. The rain had stopped. He checked himself over: bruises, or what would become bruises, forming on his legs, a welt on his right arm, scrapes; otherwise he seemed all right. He stood up and immediately became dizzy, so he sat on a fallen log and put his head down. At least nothing was broken. He was lucky.

As his strength returned, Luke surveyed the situation. The canoe was gone and with it the supplies: his gear, his tarp, his rations. All he had on him was the knife strapped to his belt and his identification papers which he had placed, from years of habit, in a small watertight pouch inside his jeans.

Luke searched the area for shelter. It was wooded enough; he could put something together. But he had no matches, and the wood was wet, and he didn't know where he was. For all he knew, he was a half a mile from a collection of cabins just like his father's, and men were nearby eating beans and listening to the racket of nature.

He didn't know how far he'd come, and now the maps were gone. There was nothing to do now but follow the river. He would run into someone eventually. Luke took off his sopping jacket and slapped it over his shoulder. He would have to keep moving.

There was breakthrough sun in the late afternoon, and it actually felt warm. Luke pulled off his clothes and splayed them across rocks and stood naked in the clearing. The bruises were colouring; the welt on his arm was raised which would make it hard for him to lift or carry anything.

"See? You're *lucky* you don't have anything!"

Thank you, Snake.

He was hungry. He had found some edible weeds and had tried eating, but he guessed he wasn't hungry enough that time. Still, there were always squirrels.

He started along concentrating on skeletal movement, trying to remember Thoreau's thoughts on walking. Sally Ride had had her own theories on footwear, at least. She was probably drinking wine with an old friend by now, phoning her nephew to keep him primed for their trip. It was *The Canterbury Tales* all over again or *1,001 Nights* or *Marco Polo*. Tell us your adventures, stranger. Tell us what you saw.

Late asters, almost freeze-dried, reconstituted in the sun.

Brush grass green and brush grass grey.

A hawk in the tip of a damaged jackpine.

He remembered the lone pine that had stood so many years in Warroad, the tree almost legend, part of everybody's past. His father remembered it as a boy and said his own father had as well.

Luke's daughter would remember...a rusty set of swings at the park? The chlorine stench of the community pool? And, amazingly, she would love these memories.

He wished he had given her more.

He and Val had been so sure, so selfish, and he by far the worse. For hadn't Val sat through winters at the kitchen table watching Aurora press her letters into her smudged copybook? Hadn't it been Val who made their daughter's Halloween costumes, staying up nights to sew ears and tails onto sheets?

And where was he? Where had he gone that was so important? Another meeting? Another trip? His feet put him on the road, and he looked back and there was his little girl at the window.

Tell us your adventures, stranger.

Words and walking.

That's all he had done. The wrong words at the wrong time to the wrong people. And walking because it was more subtle than running, because Thoreau and the gang made it all seem okay. Palaeolithic man walking across the Bering Strait, and Luke, thirty-five years ago, waiting in line, shifting from foot to foot, until he muscled up to the counter and walked away with a malted, down the street in the August sun toward the blistering glare of the lake.

Rainy River, Rainy River.

Flowing across the continent. The ways of water are different than the ways of soil no matter what the eskers tell you.

Funny, he had been thrown back onto land.

Hunger was strange. It was like conscience gnawing at you for a while and then, if you ignored it, going away. Luke had felt severe pangs the first couple of days, now it was a lightheadedness, a lightness, that he felt. He would have liked to have explained it to someone, but there was no one to talk to.

He smiled.

His father used to talk of evenings like that, whole evenings spent down at the Dollar with "not one soul worth talking to" which hadn't kept him from closing the place. His father had, ultimately, been a very private man. And Luke realized with some amazement that they were much alike.

Stubborn.

Hopeless.

Opinionated.

Scheißkopf.

But Luke had not found his Rose, a woman willing to live with such a man. He congratulated Val on her good sense before reminding himself that it was he who had left her.

Luke managed to start a fire using his Boy Scouts of America training, thinking, oh, this is perfect, Disneyland and Boy Scouts of America. If he blinked, it would be like nothing had changed, like no time had passed and no sins in between. The Lone Ranger and Tonto on the T.V. while old KaKaGeeSick tramped the woods outside his door. Ray farting and Luke hitting him with a pillow. Hi-Ho Silver and a bag of pretzels.

If he could just blink the way his mother had, her uncertain eyes uncertain, is it her son or her husband as a boy?

Luke leaned up against a tree and closed his eyes to stop the dizziness. An image flashed, startling him. It was very strong, vivid: Val pregnant in a flowing muslin dress; the baby's face pressing against the fabric; the infant's eyes staring at Luke; Val and Aurora staring at Luke; Val's hand moving up and pointing while muslin flowed like a veil all around her. Luke felt his skeleton pulling toward her, the bones in his rib cage heaving as if they were crying, as if they could cry.

His useless skin was being etched from behind. Luke pushed off from the tree and turned. His fingers traced the rough bark. It was the diamond willow.

His legs dragged him forward, and he cut through tall reeds with his knife. Now and then something looked up at him from the ground unafraid. His feet were constantly wet. He pulled his collar up which did little against the seeping cold, and hacked up phlegm from his lungs.

He had stopped wanting. The desire for food was going, and the cold was numbing his responses. It was okay. It was quite lovely, the way peace could replace need and anger, Bobby Sands disappearing in a cell in Northern Ireland.

When desire leaves, there is peace. Only then does the heart beat for its sake alone. Luke could hear the sound of a heartbeat in his ears, but far away, like hearing the ocean in a sea shell. A tempest in a teapot. A tempest in a sea shell, an ocean in a...?

Fill it with some good Lake of the Woods water, boy.

His father's tempest.

Four hearts beating in a house on the edge of the Lake of the Woods.

Three hearts breaking in an apartment in Ottawa.

If only the heart had done its job and pumped and filtered instead of blasting through the chest like a seismic drill. The heart demanded. It needed. It desired.

The sump pump in the basement and his father's holy curses.

The Desires of the Pump.

His mother stirring the tea bag in the pot.

He would surprise her that was sure. Rose Anderson's heart had been strangely silent for a long time. No careful, hopeful letters to her long-lost son.

She would bake him pies and cut asters for the table and spoon whipped cream onto bowls of hot apple crisp.

One more stab. Not from the stomach. The mind remembering food and sabotaging the stomach. Luke bent double until the cramp went away. His face was pressed to the ground. He could smell the snow and coming ice.

Luke, come down from there! I don't want you up on that all alone!
He looks over and she is there, beside the pale clothesline pole. Now she has clothespins in her mouth, and they look funny and he laughs at her toothy smile. She is putting them all out on the line. Dadda's brown and blue shirt with the little squares, and his own green pants, and now Ray's blue pants, Mama's flowery blouse poofing and filling, his little shirt arms spread wide and flat against the sky. They're dancing in the air wiggling back and forth as she tugs on the line, jiggle, jiggle, jiggle.
Birds on the lake. Far away, though.
"Mama, the water...."
You heard me, dear. Come down here!
Round on top, like the top of the world.
He looks over at her smile, at her hands waving red socks at him, and then he climbs down from the big high rock.

He is on his back. He feels rain or dew on his face, something wet running into his ears. His dog tags lying cold against his clavicle. The earth is beneath him now; he rests his spine along it.
It is so beautiful here.
Trees nearly bare, swaths of orange and yellow over there, like a Canadian landscape painting, the bowl of margarine when his mother squeezed the pouch of colouring in, valleys and ridges cut with brilliant orange, transforming, transformed. The sun the pale yellow of *Land O' Lakes* butter.

When his brother arrives it is only a little behind his father. Luke has been leaning up on one elbow watching the large, red-faced man who is surprisingly reticent, his strong arms stiff at his sides. The man's canvas jacket is harpooned with fishhooks. They are silently taking the measure of one another yet without the rancour of two men squaring off in a clearing.
In the distance, far enough back that Luke has to pull himself up yet further and shade his eyes with a hand, the outline appears. Solid, opaque, not skeletal. Luke recognizes immediately the stance of his brother. Luke's father turns and a smile starts on his lips and Luke thinks: *This is my beloved son.* And it is okay to know this as the figure starts towards them walking with a casual birthright through the weeds.
His expression is impossible to read, neither serious nor comical. He is wearing a short-sleeved summer shirt striped like the canvas on the old deck

chairs, those faded blues and yellows, the thin line of red. His brother looks to be in his mid-twenties.

He is young.

He is so young. He could be my son.

The figure pulls a hand out of his pocket and slaps at a mosquito as he approaches.

And that is somehow perfect.

There is a father, old, white.

There is a man of middle years who hears fish smacking the surface of the river.

There is a young man with an earnest face, a sunburn on the bridge of his nose.

No one speaks.

The father and the young man embrace. It is simple.

It seems like this goes on forever.

They are standing on either side of him now. He cannot sit up, but it doesn't matter for they frame him like bookends, and they are so bright, the blue is almost blinding in the corners of his eyes. Luke raises his hands to his face to act as blinkers and sees straight ahead to the river. Old *oshki anishin-abe, kagige gijig,* is getting into a canoe. It is Luke's canoe; it streams water, but somehow it holds the ancient man. He is wearing the blue suit they dressed him in when he was laid out in the Warroad School Gym. The tattoos on his forehead are blue.

kagige gijig, after the *anishinabe midewiwin* ceremony, after the organ strains of the Christian farewell, an old man getting into a canoe.

KaKaGeeSick. Luke blinks.

His name means Everlasting Sky. Luke's mother's voice soothing the calm evening air.

Luke sees the old man's face reflected in the glacier, the river mirrored in the shining blue.

It is so beautiful here.

The old man appears to nod then disappears down the river in the cold bright air.

Aurora: 1994

*W*hat I don't remember does not exist.

What I remember does not exist.

What I remember, catching like burrs on boots and jackets, stippled with the bubbled spit of plants. What I remember clinging to crosshatches and crows-feet, my mother's slight shadow across the crabgrass, my father gesturing the rain.

I have been here three months now in the house down by the bay. She is with me, although she is not. What I don't remember does not....

Grenge thought I was crazy to take her out of the Home. What would I do with her; what would I do with my time? I have smiled at that pronouncement from afar. It recurs often as I change her bed, pin single sheets out on the line. Rose finds comfort here; I am sure of it. She sits in her chair in the kitchen listening to the radio. She looks out the window, or at it, or at nothing in particular. Hey, I think, I do that, too.

Grenge is busy with her family. The twins are a year last week. A year. It is tough for her. The Duke does what he can but the children are walking now. I was surprised, though, at how little there was to say in the end. We wished each other well. We wished each other well in our lives.

I was glad to leave the island. It was like I had heard all their explanations. And that was okay, but the island was crowded with their presence, and there was no trail left that wasn't claimed by anecdote.

I am tired of explanations.

My mother was amazing. She understood perfectly the absence of words, the shrugs, the gesture I am making to my grandmother. She surprised me. I think I had explained her away, too. And I was wrong. It feels so good to be wrong.

I talk to my grandmother about this. She sits with her head slightly tilted. Almost in thought, we sit. We talk about linen tablecloths. About death.

"What will it be like?" I ask her. "As huge and grappling as life? As perfect, in its way, as the light along the roof of the shed?"

What stories will you tell me? Lips moving because your mouth is dry. I dip the sponge stick into water, and we skate the dry cracked ice of your lips, you and I, and you press your lips into the sponge in what is maybe a kiss.

Without the useless waste of words, you are eloquent telling me stories as the sun moves down the refrigerator. Are you already with Luke, with Ray and Grandfather, scudding the edge of another planet's atmosphere?

Don't explain now; just tell me a story.

—m—

We can't sit here forever.

"I'm making supper," I announce. The soup the ladies from the club have sent over. They want me to go out; they say they'll come and sit with Rose. But I have nowhere I have to be. I can be anywhere. And for now I have the time.